TRAVIS TOLD HIMSELF
TO WALK AWAY

He told himself to leave her.

But found he wasn't too good at listening to his own advice. What was it about Brooke that made him burn . . . made him want to touch her . . . made him want to taste her? He could usually get any woman out of his system, but this one was different. Maybe if he kissed her, it would frighten her enough to leave and also satisfy his curiosity.

Unable to resist her poignant sweetness any longer, Travis lowered his mouth to Brooke's. Her eyelids fluttered shut, and her arms wound inside his jacket and around his back. She yielded with a sigh of surrender as he moved his mouth over hers and devoured its softness.

D0048490

BOOK YOUR PLACE ON OUR WEBSITE AND MAKE THE READING CONNECTION!

We've created a customized website just for our very special readers, where you can get the inside scoop on everything that's going on with Zebra, Pinnacle and Kensington books.

When you come online, you'll have the exciting opportunity to:

- View covers of upcoming books

- Read sample chapters

- Learn about our future publishing schedule (listed by publication month *and author*)

- Find out when your favorite authors will be visiting a city near you

- Search for and order backlist books from our online catalog

- Check out author bios and background information

- Send e-mail to your favorite authors

- Meet the Kensington staff online

- Join us in weekly chats with authors, readers and other guests

- Get writing guidelines

- AND MUCH MORE!

Visit our website at
http://www.kensingtonbooks.com

SOUTHERN SEDUCTION

Alexandria Scott

ZEBRA BOOKS
Kensington Publishing Corp.
www.kensingtonbooks.com

ZEBRA BOOKS are published by

Kensington Publishing Corp.
850 Third Avenue
New York, NY 10022

All Kensington titles, imprints, and distributed lines are available at special quantity discounts for bulk purchases for sales promotion, premiums, fund-raising, educational, or institutional use.

Special book excerpts or customized printings can also be created to fit specific needs. For details, write or phone the office of the Kensington Special Sales Manager: Attn.: Special Sales Department. Kensington Publishing Corp., 850 Third Avenue, New York, NY 10022. Phone: 1-800-221-2647.

Zebra and the Z logo Reg. U.S. Pat. & TM Off.

ISBN-13: 978-0-8217-7824-1
ISBN-10: 0-8217-7824-2

First Printing: December 2007
10 9 8 7 6 5 4 3 2

Printed in the United States of America

*This book is dedicated to Kate Duffy
for all her hard work in the industry.*

*For all the raw talent she's taken and molded into authors,
we thank you for
caring and holding our hands along the journey . . .
especially me.
You are the BEST.*

Prologue

Courtesans rose from various backgrounds to positions of great power, independence, and wealth. Some became the toast of London. They controlled their lives and the lives of others.

Most embraced the life they lived and wanted nothing more. And then there were women such as Brooke Hammond, who wanted none of it.

She didn't start out to become a whore, but life was a game of survival, and that was exactly what Brooke had been doing . . . surviving and hoping a better life would come along.

At long last, she had her chance. . . .

Chapter 1

Brooke Hammond, Shannon McKinley, and Jocelyn Rutland were all survivors in one way or another.

The women stood on the rolling deck of the
Flying Lady, watching the American shoreline grow
bigger, wondering what adventures awaited them.

A warm, gentle breeze blew strands of hair across
Brooke's nose. She reached up and removed her
hat, then tucked the wayward curls behind her ear,
not that it helped much as long as she remained
positioned at the ship's rail.

Brooke glanced at her friends standing on either
side of her. They were much too quiet. She imagined that they were afraid to say anything for fear
they would wake up from this wonderful dream of
a new life and a new beginning.

Brooke wouldn't let anything stop them now. She
and her friends were no longer the naive women
they'd once been, waiting hopefully for a man to
change their lives.

Well, maybe Shannon still believed that there was
someone out there just for her, but she was Scottish,

so that explained her far fetched, romantic notions. And what man wouldn't want Shannon, with her soft white skin and beautiful auburn hair?

But Brooke didn't believe in love. From what she'd seen, men and women used each other to get what they wanted. And if you didn't have money, you had to depend on others. She could remember what it was like to be in the streets of London with no home . . . no money. The thought still made her shiver. She had experienced being poor, and she wanted nothing to do with that ever again. Nor did she want to depend on someone else for what she needed. She was going to make something of her life, and there wasn't a man alive she'd let stand in her way.

As a young girl, she'd had visions of true love dancing in her head, but they were soon dashed in the harsh light of reality. Sometimes life doesn't turn out like you'd hoped. But it would now, for her. This was her chance at a new start. Brooke sighed as a group of seagulls cried raucously, bringing her attention back to the present.

"I wish you were both going with me to New Orleans," Brooke murmured wistfully to her friends. They had been together over the last few years, and understood each other well. It would be sad not to have them nearby to talk to every day.

Shannon shoved thick red hair over her shoulders, then tied the long locks back to keep them out of her face. "I'd love tae see the plantation, but we agreed when we started out that we'd be wantin' tae find our own ways," she said in her Scottish brogue. "'Twas nice of Mr. Jeffries tae find me a position on a ranch, though."

"That's right, we did agree," Jocelyn chimed in. "At least you both know where you're going and what you're going to do." She pointed to her chest. "I, on the other hand, don't have the vaguest notion of what I want to do. Hopefully, there is a respectable job for a woman somewhere in that city," she said, nodding toward New York. "Mr. Jeffries gave me the name of an acquaintance of his who might be helpful, but I'll take no handouts. I intend to support myself and be independent."

Brooke smiled. She'd known Jocelyn the longest. They met at boarding school and had liked each other from the start. Jocelyn definitely didn't believe in love anymore. Of the three of them, she had tasted love, and what had it gotten her? A broken heart and tossed out of her father's house. So she'd turned to her uncle, Jackson Montgomery, and he had taken her into his home where she and Brooke were reunited.

After Jackson Montgomery, Duke of Devonshire, entered Brooke's life, everything had changed. He understood that she wasn't living the life she wanted. Who ever started out wanting to be a courtesan?

It was true that he'd kept her in a town house he'd bought just for her, but Jackson wasn't like the other men she'd known. He had been her friend, never so much as hinting at sexual relations. It seemed as though, in some strange way, he saw the good in Brooke and wanted to protect her. When he'd taken in his nieces, Jocelyn and Shannon, who were very close to Brooke's age, they had become a family, as the girls bonded with each other.

Jackson had promised that he'd leave Brooke and

the girls well taken care of. When he'd died, he'd left Brooke his American plantation and enough money for the young women to leave England and make a fresh start in America. He also left them the incomparable Mr. Jeffries, the solicitor in charge of his affairs, to help the women travel and get settled.

Brooke had been astonished that Jackson had done as he said he would. It had been her experience that people didn't usually follow through with promises, so she'd had no real expectations. She'd heard too many empty promises in her lifetime.

Shannon shook Brooke's arm, bringing her back to the present. "Where is Mr. Jeffries?" Shannon paused, then added, "Ye seem tae be daydreamin' a lot lately."

Brooke gave her a faint smile. "I was remembering the duke. He was such a special and extraordinary man."

"And a good uncle," Jocelyn added. "I can't say the same about my aunt, though. I was young when she went away, so I don't remember her well."

Brooke frowned. "I thought she was dead."

Jocelyn glanced at Shannon. "Do you remember her?"

"Nae. I just remember that no one ever spoke o' Aunt Barbara again, sae she must huv died," Shannon said then went on, "but our uncle seemed tae be a happier mon without her."

Jocelyn nodded in agreement.

"As for Jeffries," Brooke said, "I've not seen him since breakfast. He told me that he had to make preparations **for our travel to New Orleans.**"

"Wasn't it grand of Mr. Jeffries to accompany us

from England?" Jocelyn turned and propped her arms on the rail. "I'm not sure any of us would have known what to do. We would probably still be standing on the docks in London, watching the ship sail away without us."

"Now, now," Brooke countered. "Somehow, we would have found the correct ship. However, it was Jackson's instructions that Mr. Jeffries would accompany us, so he had no choice. Jeffries told me that I had inherited a plantation, and we were provided enough money for travel. And, of course, each of you were left a thousand pounds to help get started. I believe Jackson was hoping that we'd all go to Moss Grove. Evidently, he didn't know just how independent his nieces are." Brooke smiled. "For some strange reason, Jeffries was instructed not to read the entire will until we reached Moss Grove Plantation."

"'Tis a bit odd," Shannon said.

"I thought so, too," Brooke agreed. "The only reason I can come up with is that it will be easier for me if Jeffries introduces me to the household staff, and to be truthful, I'm glad we have him along.

"America is a strange country I've only read about. I'd be completely lost without him. However," Brooke said with a saucy smile, "I *have* studied books on the planting of cotton so that I'll know something about living on a plantation."

"I agree." Shannon nodded. "The mon has been verra helpful wi' makin' arrangements fer my trip." Her face lit up with a smile. "Just think, I'm goin' tae be a governess fer two bairns. From their descriptions, they sound adorable."

Brooke looked at Shannon with amused wonder. "Besides being a child yourself, what do you know about children?"

"Verra little," Shannon admitted as a flash of humor crossed her face. "But I ken if I can handle men and their childish ways, then the bairns wull only be smaller, therefore easier tae handle."

Everyone laughed, enjoying each other's company as they usually did. Yet each felt a twinge of sadness, knowing that their time together was slipping away.

"If you ask me, it sounds as if you're going out into the wilderness," Jocelyn said.

"Aye, the Texas Territory wull be verra different, but different is what I want," she said with a slight smile. "I want adventure and tae see all those cowboys close up."

A loud thump made all three women flinch and grab for the rail as the ship bumped, then settled next to the wooden platform. They peered over the railing, witnessing the dock spring to life with crewmen racing along the platform, grabbing the ropes to tie off the ship, and shouting instructions to their mates.

The streets leading up to the pier were filled with wooden pier drays, wagons, and fruit stalls, each vendor hawking their wares. Wagons lined up, waiting for the ship's cargo to be off-loaded. And there seemed to be a multitude of carriages waiting for disembarking passengers.

"Do you have your trunks packed?" Brooke asked. Both women nodded.

"In that case I better go and get my reticule,"

Brooke said, turning away from the rail. "I'll meet both of you on the dock."

As Brooke made her way to the cabin they shared, she wouldn't have admitted to anyone that she wasn't as confident as she tried to appear. Truth be told, she was both excited and scared, if that made any sense. It certainly didn't to her.

She would miss her friends. They were the only ones who understood her, who actually knew what she'd been through, and had experienced some of the loneliness she had. But they had a right to their own lives, and she wanted them to be happy.

Brooke raised her chin, stubbornly forcing herself to be brave. She wouldn't allow herself to be sad today. Today she had a bright new future ahead of her. Reaching her cabin she pulled open the door, strode to the bed, and grabbed her reticule.

Back on deck, Brooke noticed that some of the passengers had made their way to the dock. She left the ship and shoved her way through the crowd to where her friends stood with Mr. Jeffries.

Mr. Jeffries had rented two carriages, one for Brooke and another for her friends. He was overseeing the loading of their trunks on top of the carriage. Jeffries wasn't a tall man, but he was a couple of inches taller than Brooke. His hair, or what there was of it, was gray. He had a bald spot on the very top and bushy hair around the sides. As always, he was dressed in his gray vest and white shirt.

He turned when Brooke reached them. "Miss Shannon and Miss Jocelyn, I have secured hotel rooms for you at the Block House and have established accounts for both of you at the First National Bank in New York, so funds will be available for you to draw upon."

"How did the money get there?" Brooke asked.

"His Grace had me come to America before his death and make arrangements. I believe he overheard your conversations of wanting to come to America.

"Now, I'll leave you to your good-byes. Do remember that I'll be in this country for a good six months, so if you need me just send a wire to Moss Grove and Brooke will know how to get in touch with me."

Shannon and Jocelyn smiled their thanks, then each of them gave him a hug.

"Here, here, we'll have none of that," Jeffries blustered. "It's my job, after all."

Brooke glanced at her friends, wanting to memorize the slightest details of how they looked. She was so afraid that they would forget each other.

Shannon was the smallest of the three, but she was feisty, her redheaded temper making up for her lack of size. Her radiant hair made her stand out in any crowd. Jackson had once told Brooke that Shannon's father had often beaten her when he got drunk. It was probably one the reasons she was a real spitfire.

And then there was Jocelyn. What could Brooke say about Jocelyn other than the woman just seemed to sparkle from some inner strength? Her burnished mahogany tresses framed a delicately sculpted face. There was an elegance about her that Brooke had always wished she, too, possessed.

"I guess this is good-bye," Brooke finally said, hearing her voice crack as she spoke. She held her arms wide.

The women wrapped their arms around Brooke, and she hugged them back, fiercely holding them to her heart. They were her family and, for that matter, the only family she knew. She'd miss them a great deal.

"'Tis only good-bye for a wee bit," Shannon whispered. She managed a choked and desperate laugh, tears sliding down her cheeks. "Dinna make me cry. Let's promise that we'll meet in one year at Moss Grove."

"That's an excellent idea," Jocelyn agreed as she brushed the hot, salty tears from her cheeks.

Brooke attempted to give them a brave smile, but her teary eyes betrayed her. "Do you both promise to come? No excuses?"

"We promise."

"Good," Brooke said, nodding with finality. "And you must write often so I'll know how both of you are doing. I promise I'll do the same."

After they nodded their agreement, Brooke gave them a final hug and stepped back, making a big pretense of straightening her skirt, fighting against the tears she refused to let fall. "Now, all I have to do is figure out how to run a plantation," she said. "So you'll have someplace to come."

Shannon tossed her auburn curls over her shoulder, and her face creased into a sudden smile. "We ken ye can do it. Ye've always been the smartest and bravest amon' us."

"I agree," Jocelyn said with a firm nod. "You can do anything you want to. Don't let anyone tell you differently."

Brooke shifted, squaring her shoulders and lifting her chin. "Well with that vote of confidence, I'll do my best. But," she added, "I want you both to remember—it doesn't matter where you've been. What matters is where you're going and how you get there."

"Och, she's beginnin' tae sound like a mother," Shannon protested, then she laughed and nudged Jocelyn in the side.

Jocelyn nodded. "Then it's time for us to go."

Since there was nothing left to say, the two women climbed into the carriage, and Brooke watched the driver close the door. "You're going to miss my nagging," she called to them, her voice cracking slightly.

Gnawing on her lip to keep from weeping, Brooke waved good-bye. *If only they knew how much I wanted them to stay with me,* she thought. *But I'm on my own, and by God I will survive, one way or the other.*

Chapter 2

Her journey had finally reached its end.

Brooke Hammond's spirits rose as she and Mr. Jeffries neared New Orleans. Though she'd only caught glimpses of the city as they traveled via the main thoroughfares and straight out of town, she liked what she saw and looked forward to returning to town once she'd settled on the plantation.

Brooke settled back to enjoy the remainder of the ride. It had been a long trip, and she had grown weary of traveling and living out of a trunk, but she tried not to complain. It wouldn't be much longer now.

The country was lovely with the lush trees and fields that Mr. Jeffries had described as sugarcane and cotton.

Brooke pressed her dainty, white handkerchief to her forehead. She noticed a vast difference between the air in New Orleans and New York. There was always a hint of moisture in the air here. That, in combination with the extreme heat, made her skin feel clammy.

Finally the carriage began to slow, and through the carriage window Brooke caught her first glimpse of a sign announcing that they were about to enter Moss Grove Plantation. Her breath caught in her throat. She couldn't seem to utter a single word as a hundred thoughts rushed into her head all at once.

At last she'd have her very own home, a home that was hers permanently, not just for a little while. Most importantly, she would be the mistress. She'd never have to depend on anyone else's decision ever again. A home meant much more to Brooke than money. It was something that she had never had. Her years growing up in a boarding school were the closest thing to home she could imagine.

All her dreams were about to come true.

The mansion wasn't yet visible when the carriage swung between the octagonal, brick *pigeonniers* positioned on either side of the drive, so seeing her new home was once again delayed. However, the red dirt driveway was smooth and unrutted, demonstrating that a great deal of care had gone into the preparation of the plantation. She could just imagine what the house must look like.

So far, Brooke had to admit that she liked what she'd seen of America compared to England's damp cool days.

Today the sky was beautiful and clear, though the heat would take some getting used to with her thick British blood. Perhaps with fall approaching, the days would become pleasant. "The trees here are a bit unusual and very wide, don't you think?" Brooke asked across the carriage to Mr. Jeffries.

He slid back the leather flap on the window. "I believe they are called live oaks. They grow very large and wide," he explained. "And I see a few pecan trees mixed in the group."

Huge live oaks, of which Brooke had already counted twenty, lined the long drive on either side. As the carriage traveled down the lane, the limbs were laced overhead like fingers, dripping with a queer, gray-beard growth that Brooke had never seen before.

She pointed out the window. "What is the greenish gray substance?"

Jeffries again peered out the window, and this time smiled. "It is Spanish moss. Quite common in this part of the country, I believe." He leaned back in his seat. "The moss actually lives on the tree limbs and will spread from tree to tree. It resembles a gray-beard and can absorb water ten times its weight. Quite lovely, I think."

"Yes, it is. Perhaps it's where the name of the plantation came from," Brooke murmured. The moss was indeed beautiful, yet it also gave her an eerie feeling. She hoped it wasn't a warning sign that something sinister lurked ahead. A slight chill shuddered through her as she shook the qualms from her mind. Surely the staff would welcome a new mistress.

When she thought she could bear the suspense of waiting no longer, a magnificent plantation house came into view. A two-story, white house with one-story wing pavilions on each side sat gracefully at the end of the sweeping circular carriageway, and it was hers . . . all hers.

Ten white columns stood at attention like soldiers across the front, adding to the feeling of grandeur.

There was a full second-floor balcony, making for a lovely veranda supported by the columns and bordered with wrought iron. Two curved staircases in the shapes of half moons led up to the second floor. Brooke could only gape, awestruck at the opulence she saw before her.

"I see you're impressed," Mr. Jeffries commented quietly.

"This is not like anything I've ever seen before," Brooke whispered, afraid that someone would pinch her and wake her from this wonderful dream. How could she be so lucky? "I'm surprised that Jackson stayed in England when he had such a magnificent home and this beautiful sunny weather."

"I believe he had other ideas for Moss Grove."

The carriage pulled to a stop before the wide steps at the front of the house. The driver swung down, opened the door, and let down the step for them.

Brooke gathered her skirts so she didn't trip, then accepted the driver's hand. She had just stepped down from the carriage when a man came galloping up on a magnificent white stallion, clouds of dust swirling around the horse's hooves. For a moment, Brooke recalled her girlhood dream of being swept away by a handsome prince on a white horse. Of course, the silly child's dream had faded as she'd grown, and she hadn't thought about her prince in a long time.

Until now.

The man riding toward her made an awesome picture as he sat tall in the saddle. He reined in his horse a few feet from them, but said nothing, allowing Brooke another moment to look at him. He was dressed in riding clothes, but he wore no jacket as most gentlemen did, just a white billowing shirt and black riding breeches. His blue eyes flashed, then narrowed as he leaned forward in the saddle and looked down as if she and Mr. Jeffries were insects to be trod upon.

The sun played on his sun-streaked hair, wind-tossed and rather long, Brooke noticed as he examined them. In spite of his superior attitude, his bronzed skin gave him a rakish air that Brooke found quite appealing.

She really shouldn't be ogling him, but she couldn't help herself. He was truly breathtaking.

Back in England, the gentlemen she had known had always been pasty white dandies, most of whom had been old enough to be her father.

But not this one.

He was handsome, recklessly so, and he simply took her breath away. She wondered who he was.

The overseer, perhaps? *Entertainment?*

She could only hope.

"Jeffries," the man muttered curtly, finally acknowledging them. He dismounted and tossed the reins to a young stable boy who had come trotting up while Brooke had been looking at the man. "I had word that you were coming, but I wasn't expecting your wife."

Brooke noted that the stranger had a deep, commanding voice, but she almost laughed out loud at the notion that he thought she was Mr. Jeffries's wife.

"Travis," Jeffries said as he extended his hand. "It has been a long time since I last saw you. You look well."

"As do you," Travis commented, then glanced at Brooke. "Will you introduce me to your lovely companion?"

"Certainly. But she isn't my wife." Mr. Jeffries motioned toward Brooke. "May I introduce you to Brooke Hammond?"

Travis lifted her hand to his lips then kissed the back ever so lightly, just enough to make chills sweep through Brooke's body. For some odd reason her pulse raced when he murmured, "My pleasure, Miss Hammond." He turned back to Jeffries. "I presume then, that she is your fiancée?"

"Certainly not," Jeffries answered. "She is a friend of your father's."

Travis's gaze was riveted on her, moving over her body slowly. He stopped abruptly as he glanced back to the solicitor, Travis's brows drew together. "My father? I'm afraid I don't understand."

Brooke had a hard time tearing her eyes from Travis's compelling gaze, but she, too, turned and looked at Mr. Jeffries. "His father?" Brooke repeated. "Pray tell, who is his father?"

Jeffries's face turned a bit red before he answered, "May I present Travis Montgomery, Jackson's son."

Brooke couldn't hide her startled look as she said, "Jackson never said anything to me about a son." What she didn't add was, "And if he had a son why did he leave the plantation to me?"

"Madam, that does not surprise me one bit," Travis snapped, his eyes turning cold. Evidently, Travis Montgomery wasn't any happier than she was about this turn of events. The interest she'd noted only a moment ago had disappeared as his next words were directed to Mr. Jeffries. "What is she doing here?"

Brooke hated to tell him, but he really wasn't going to like the answer.

The next hour passed slowly as Jeffries tried to calm Brooke and Travis down to where they were not shouting at each other. Neither had taken the news well.

It seemed that Brooke's plantation had come with a few conditions attached to it, and one of those conditions was now glaring at her across the library table. She'd been rushed inside so quickly that she hadn't had a chance to observe the interior of the house. They had been ushered straight into the library, which acted as Travis's study. It was dark, just like the owner.

Since Travis had turned to whisper something to Mr. Jeffries, Brooke took the moment of silence to glance around the room, trying to get a feel for her adversary. The room was well appointed and very spacious. One wall held nothing but books. Evidently, Travis liked to read, or at least he wanted to give the impression that he did. A marble fireplace was on another wall, and above the mantel hung a large oil painting of a stern-looking gentleman Brooke didn't recognize.

The only bright spot in the room was the French doors located behind his desk.

Her gaze shifted back to her immediate problem, Travis Montgomery, as Mr. Jeffries tried to explain to him that Brooke had inherited half of Moss

Grove, and they would be able to work everything out if he'd just listen.

"Over my dead body!" Travis shouted at Jeffries. Travis's eyes were cold, his expression a mask of stone as his gaze settled on her face.

"That can be arranged!" Brooke shot back at the arrogant cad she was beginning to wish she'd never laid eyes on. Who did he think he was, shouting at her? And why hadn't Jackson ever mentioned that he had a son? To think that she'd found him handsome, reminiscent of her prince—this man might be a devil instead. His profile was strong and rigid, and she had a strong feeling that he never gave an inch in any argument.

"Get out of my house," Travis said through clenched teeth, his voice strained as if he were barely controlling his temper.

Brooke sensed there was more to Travis's rage than just her sudden appearance, but she wasn't going to cower. Instead, she lifted her chin. "Your house?" she challenged. This man . . . this . . . this adversary didn't know her very well—that was stupid, he didn't know her at all—but if he thought his shouting was going to get her to leave, he needed to rethink his strategy. Brooke wasn't about to be intimidated by him, or any man for that matter.

"Perhaps," she said in her perfect British accent, "you were not listening. The plantation belongs to both of us, so you had better get used to reality," she informed him, pleased that Mr. Montgomery didn't have an immediate retort for her. He didn't appear to be a man who liked to lose at anything.

Well, neither did she.

Instead, he glared at her for a long moment before turning his gaze back to Mr. Jeffries, who sat, looking completely exasperated, at the end of the table, his hands folded over the paperwork in front of him.

"I knew my father hated me . . ." Travis paused, a strange look flashing across his face. "Apparently, I didn't know how much," he said more or less to himself as he lowered his tall, incredibly formed body back into his chair.

The solicitor cleared his throat before saying, "If you are both finished with your shouting match, I shall continue with the reading of Jackson's will." Jeffries peered over his spectacles at both of them and waited patiently for them to acquiesce.

Finally, they each gave a quick nod.

Travis shoved away from the table. "Before you continue," he said, "I need a drink. Do you care for anything?" His question was directed toward Jeffries.

The solicitor shrugged and nodded, then turned back to his papers.

Travis started for the liquor cabinet located next to the wall when Brooke spoke, "It's quite apparent that your father never taught you any manners either."

Travis stopped. Slowly, he turned around, his gaze leveling on her, anger in his eyes. "My father didn't bother to teach me anything at all," he retorted bitterly. He waited a moment, his brow raised a fraction, almost daring her to comment. "Would you care for something, Miss Hammond?"

Brooke smiled, only because she knew it would irritate him further, then she said politely, "Yes,

thank you very much. I would like sherry, please."
She saw the fire flash in his blue eyes just before
he turned away, and she wondered what it would be
like to smother that fire out and, perhaps, tame the
beast.

Travis Montgomery wasn't something she'd
planned on when she'd embarked on this adventure. Not only his very existence, but the way he
made her feel. He fired her blood in more ways
than one. However, if he thought he was going to
intimidate her, then he had better think again.

The Duke had never mentioned he had children, and quite frankly, Brooke couldn't blame
Travis for being angry, not only with his father, but
at her. She knew what it was like to be shunned by
a parent, but that didn't mean Travis's disappoint-
ment would make her give up her one great chance
at happiness.

She watched him from beneath her lashes as he
poured the drinks. His white linen shirt pulled
across his back when he reached for the crystal decanter. A tall man . . . taller than most, he was
rough, arrogant, brash, as nearly all Americans
were, but so intriguing that he held her attention,
which was something Brooke couldn't say about
most men.

His sun-streaked hair emphasized the darkness
of his bronzed skin, and his strong features seem to
draw her to him without his ever opening his
mouth. *And it was not a good thing*. She didn't want
any part of Travis Montgomery. She was finished
with men, especially those trying to control her.

Travis handed her a glass of sherry then took his seat.

This is more what I'd had in mind, Brooke mused as she accepted the glass. *Someone to do my fetching.*

Mr. Jeffries drank his Scotch. He looked like he needed it more than anyone. He sighed, then once again gathered up the papers in front of him and began to read. "I, Jackson Montgomery, being of sound mind, do hereby bequeath my New Orleans plantation to Brooke Hammond and to my son, Travis Montgomery, equally, in hopes that, together, they can run the plantation successfully. If, after one year, they have not married, and one of them wishes to leave the plantation, then one may buy the other out.

"It is my hope that the Montgomery name will be carried on by my heirs. Therefore, my other estates will be held in a trust for the birth of my first grandson. That's correct, Travis. I can see your frown now. Even though I spent little time with you, I did give you my last name, and when you were grown, I provided a place for you and your mother to live. I will have you do two things: first you are to throw a party within two weeks of the reading of my will to announce Brooke Hammond to her neighbors. I wish I could give you my title, but since I was not married to your mother that is impossible. However, knowing you, I'm sure you couldn't care less about a title.

"Secondly, I want you to do the proper thing by marrying and having children so that the name Montgomery will continue forward. Brooke will make you a perfect wife and bring the estates to you just that much faster, along with money. Be nice to her." Jeffries finished, took a deep breath, then added, "There is one exception."

Brooke's head jerked around. "What?" she snapped at Jeffries. "I have no desire to marry this man or any other man. It's simply out of the question."

"I don't recall asking you to marry me," Travis snapped, his words uncoiling like a whip. "It sounds more like you had my father hoodwinked," Travis snapped. He jerked his gaze away from her back to the solicitor. "What was the exception that you mentioned?"

Jeffries took a drink. He looked pale. "If my son chooses to marry someone else and has a son, or his wife is expecting before or by the end of the working arrangement, then Travis doesn't have to buy Brooke out. The plantation will be his alone and a small sum will be provided for Brooke to travel to where she chooses to live. If there is no baby then the original buyout stands."

"Of all the sneaky underhanded deals"—Travis shoved away from the table—"he knew damn well that Moss Grove cannot survive without income from his other estates. Now he wants to dictate my life to the point of when I have to produce an heir. I'm surprised that he didn't live long enough that he could actually be in the bedroom to witness the consummation."

"It is my opinion that Jackson hoped you'd both see things differently," Mr. Jeffries said before Brooke could respond. "Perhaps, with a little time . . ." He paused when he received a withering glare from

Travis, but he proceeded anyway. "After all, the two of you have only just met."

"This isn't at all what I had in mind," Brooke said awkwardly. "I've traveled a long way to find that I might not have a home." She cleared her throat. "I doubt that time will help anything."

"Exactly what did you have in mind, Miss Hammond?" Travis inquired, his brow raised. He didn't wait for her to answer. "I'm so sorry for the inconvenience, your highness," he continued. "How do you think I feel? It's been my sweat that has gone into pulling this plantation out of ruin."

Travis stood, his hands braced on the polished cherrywood table. He glared at her. "But I will tell you one thing, Miss Hammond. I do not intend to have you interfering with the operation of this plantation. Since my father has so conveniently tied up his money, there is nothing to fall back on. If *we* don't make this harvest of sugarcane a success, then I—we will lose Moss Grove, and you'll be part owner of nothing. Do I make myself clear?"

It was as if he'd thrown ice water in her face, snapping her out of her stupor. Brooke shoved her chair back so quickly it teetered on two legs. She shot him a cold look. "Perfectly!" she spat. "Now, let me tell you something. You might not like this any more than I do, but I intend to make the best of this untenable situation by making this harvest a success."

He sneered. "And what do you know about sugarcane?"

"Not much, but I can learn," Brooke admitted, though she really wanted to say, *"That it's a hell of a lot sweeter than you!"*

"Then you had better learn fast, Miss Hammond, because harvest time is upon us."

"It's Mrs. Hammond," Brooke informed him, the lie rolling off her tongue with ease.

He lifted a brow in surprise. "And where is Mr. Hammond? Or do I still have more surprises to come?"

"Dead, I'm afraid," Brooke answered quickly, her eyes cutting to Mr. Jeffries to see if he'd dispute what he knew wasn't true. Back on the ship, Brooke had decided the minute she sailed from the English shores that she'd pose as a widow, so she wouldn't have to explain why she was no longer a virgin, if and when the time came.

Brooke noticed that Travis didn't bother to express his condolences, but she was quickly learning that the exasperating man was nothing like the Englishmen she'd known. It appeared as if he wasn't going to say anything at all. Apparently, he was waiting for her to speak first. Fine. She'd make an attempt at being pleasant.

"Since we are partners, Travis, why don't you call me by my given name, Brooke." He was beginning to make "Miss Hammond" sound like a swear word.

"That would mean we were friends, Mrs. Hammond," Travis said, then dismissed her completely by turning his attention to Mr. Jeffries. "My father didn't know, but I'm engaged to be married. My fiancée and my mother have traveled north to buy Hesione's trousseau."

"So that's where all the plantation money went," Brooke concluded accusingly.

Travis glared at her as if he couldn't believe that

she'd dared to interrupt him. Was his fiancée a meek little mouse who jumped at the chance to please him? "Not that it's any of your concern, but Hesione comes from a very wealthy Creole family and is therefore very wealthy on her own part. However, what money I have isn't enough to pull the plantation through another bad year."

He swung back to Jeffries. "As I was saying, we can be married upon her return, and I'm sure an heir will be forthcoming."

Over my dead body! Brooke wanted to shout, but she held her tongue instead. She had been startled by Travis's marriage announcement. She was hoping for some kind of working relationship with the ill-tempered man. It seemed that there were obstacles to surmount everywhere she turned.

However, this fiancée made matters even more urgent. As soon as what's-her-name returned, Brooke had no doubt that Travis would move quickly to marry the woman. She wondered if he really loved this person, or just her money. Brooke couldn't imagine him in love with anyone. He seemed too cold, almost dead on the inside.

Of course, Brooke had sworn to herself that she would never marry, but if marriage meant keeping the home she'd just been given, then she would have to reconsider the situation because she had nowhere to go. And she certainly didn't wish to take up the profession she'd left so far behind her. This plantation was her hope, her salvation, and her future.

Brooke wasn't sure how she was going to accomplish the task, but somehow she had to seduce

Travis into marrying her before his intended returned. Of course, she had skills and knowledge in the ways of seducing men, but if Travis was truly committed to Hesione, she would have a difficult task of it.

Perhaps, as so many men did, he could be persuaded to stray if he were away from home. With the harvest approaching, she figured she'd never get him to leave the plantation.

Still, she had to think of something.

It would have to be a marriage of convenience . . . her convenience.

She watched as Travis shook Mr. Jeffries's hand. So many possibilities ran through her mind, frustration among them. She had thought all her struggles were behind her, but it seemed that nothing had changed. Her future still depended on the will of a man.

Brooke had promised herself that the moment she'd left the ship everything in the past would stay there and she'd start anew. She had been determined to make her life happy and satisfying. Now there was one thing standing in her way.

Travis Montgomery.

Brooke sighed. The seduction of Travis Montgomery could prove a real challenge. Her subject didn't look as if he would cooperate in the least. Where men were usually fumbling all over her, telling her how beautiful she was—words she'd learned to ignore—Travis had barely given her a second glance. His scowl when he did bother to look at her was hot enough to burn. Now all she had to do was turn those fires of anger into embers of desire.

A slow smile touched Brooke's lips. Since when wasn't she up for a good challenge? Her entire life had been a challenge. Any sensible woman with common sense would pick up her skirts and run away.

The problem was, Brooke wasn't sensible.

When she was through with Travis Montgomery, he wouldn't know what hit him.

Travis headed for the door, but Brooke wasn't finished with him. "Are you going to show us to our rooms, or do I get to chose whichever room I prefer? The master suite, perhaps?" She knew she was being catty, but for some odd reason Travis brought out her need to provoke him. Perchance, she just wanted to see some unguarded emotion in him other than the frosty facade he had thus far presented.

Travis didn't answer her. Instead, he jerked the door open and shouted, "Mammy!"

That's how he called his mother? How rude. No, wait, hadn't he just said his mother was elsewhere?

A moment passed, and a heavyset black woman appeared at the door. "*Oui*, Mr. Travis. What you bellowin' about so early in de day?"

All right, so Mammy was the housekeeper. With the odd name, Brooke wondered if this was the woman who had helped to rear Travis.

Poor woman.

"Please show our guests to their rooms." Travis paused, then added, "And Mrs. Hammond will be staying permanently. Make certain that her room is at the opposite end of the hall from mine."

Well, the line has been drawn, Brooke thought with strange satisfaction.

Travis was making it utterly clear that he wanted no part of her. He deigned to glance her way one final time, and his expression was just as distant as it had been all day.

Brooke arched a delicate brow to acknowledge him, but remained silent. She knew too well that words could be used against her. It was best to remain silent and make him wonder. She knew that Travis would do everything in his power to drive her off the plantation, but Brooke Hammond had no intention of leaving.

She tilted her chin stubbornly upward and smiled to herself as she watched him leave.

Well, Travis Montgomery . . . I'd like to see you try.

Chapter 3

Mammy leaned around Travis, one eyebrow raised as she peered at Brooke. Once again, Brooke felt like an insect. The expression on the servant's face was one of surprise, and not particularly pleasant surprise at that, but Mammy didn't ask any questions before Travis left them.

"Yo' folks follow me, you hear," Mammy said as she motioned for Brooke and Mr. Jeffries to come with her.

Mammy had a strange accent that Brooke couldn't place. It wasn't quite French, but it was similar. The woman had skin the color of cocoa, much lighter than some of the slaves Brooke had seen thus far on her trip to Louisiana. Mammy was a large woman dressed in gray with a white, bibbed apron tied around her waist. Her black hair was pulled away from her face and contained in a white turban. She also had a white scarf tied around her neck, forming a sort of collar in the front.

"Excuse me," Mr. Jeffries said once they'd reached

the staircase, "I need another word with Travis. I'll find my room later."

Brooke lowered her head in a slight nod then followed the servant, whose ample hips swayed as she climbed the stairs. Brooke was learning quickly that there would be many things that she'd have to get accustomed to here at Moss Grove, and it appeared that Mammy, who apparently ran the house, might be one of them.

"How many rooms does the house have?" Brooke asked.

"'Bout sixty-four."

Brooke thought Mammy didn't sound overly happy to have her as a houseguest—correction, owner. But perhaps she was just imagining things due to the reception she'd gotten from Travis. And she was tired after her long trip, so her perceptions were not likely to be good.

When they reached the second-floor landing, Brooke glanced over the rail and discovered that Travis had been watching her from the front door. She'd dearly love to know what he was thinking.

From their short encounter, she'd learned Travis was excellent at hiding what he was thinking, but she doubted very seriously that he was capable of compassion in any form. On second thought, she might not want to know what his thoughts were at this moment. They were not likely to be very kind. No matter how surly Travis was, Brooke was determined not to cower before him.

She held his gaze, sensing the barely controlled anger coiled within him. Handling Travis was going to be a problem, and another of those things she'd have to get used to. Brooke shrugged. However, he was a man, so she wasn't overly worried. After all, handling men had been her profession. From her observations, they were all alike.

But still, she wondered just what was he thinking.

Travis studied the fetching woman, now his unwanted and unneeded partner. He wondered if he was really having a nightmare and somebody would soon wake him up. Right away would be preferred.

In his dreams was where bewitching women normally lived, not in his front parlor. And Brooke Hammond was definitely bewitching. Her complexion was flawless, and her eyes expressive and eloquent. He noticed she didn't glance coyly away as most women did. Instead, she met his gaze, almost in a challenge.

Interesting, he thought. *So the woman has spirit.* He almost liked that, and he had to admit, not only was she beautiful, but she was also taller than most of the women he knew. How long had it been since he'd heard the crisp, British accent that always reminded him of his father and the few times they had actually spent time together?

He raised his head and met her defiant gaze with somber curiosity. Mrs. Hammond reminded him of a lioness with her mane of golden hair and those rare gold eyes. Something told him she'd fight like a lioness if provoked. Just from their first meeting, she'd left a burning impression on him. He chuckled, not caring whether Mrs. Hammond saw it. He had every intention of provoking her and then driving her away.

No matter how pretty the package, Brooke Hammond could ruin everything for which he had planned and worked so hard. His so-called father had some gall to think that he could choose a wife for him after never giving him a moment's time, much less any counseling on life matters. Jackson had, more or less, thrown the running of the plantation at Travis and told him to make it profitable.

Travis turned, yanked the front door open, and strode purposefully outside. He didn't know how, but he had to get the Hammond woman away from Moss Grove before his mother and Hesione, the "perfect wife" his mother had found for him, returned. He had courted Hesione, whose Creole father was a prominent attorney, because she would make a perfect hostess for Moss Grove. She would firmly establish his status in the community and, hopefully, mend the fence between his grandfather and mother.

He would be accepted here, Travis vowed. Not that he gave a damn, but his mother did. For her, he could put up with Hesione's pampered and spoiled ways. Besides, there was always the option of engaging a mistress to keep him happily satisfied. Hesione really didn't care much about the goings on of a plantation, but she was perfectly trained in the ways of society. That suited him just fine, as long as she stayed out of his way.

Travis strode down the porch steps, took a deep breath of cool air, and tried to calm himself as he gazed out over the front lawns and the ripening cane fields beyond.

The coming harvest of sugarcane would finally

free Moss Grove, and by extension himself, from the strangling debts under which he'd found the plantation upon his arrival.

When his father had banished him and his mother to Moss Grove, Travis had sworn then that he would make the plantation a success. He had meant to show his father that he was man enough to do the job, but Jackson Montgomery had died before Travis had gotten the chance. Damn him. And to make things worse, the old codger continued to torture him from the grave by giving half the plantation to a perfect stranger.

She has no right to anything.

Just what was this woman to his father? His mistress? Surely Mrs. Hammond was a bit young for even the old man's taste. He guessed Brooke's age to be somewhere around twenty, and the thought of her with his father turned his stomach.

Not having the answer at hand, but swearing he'd find out, Travis headed across the yard toward the stables. He was determined to forget about the perplexing Mrs. Hammond and get some work done, but he reluctantly had to admit the woman intrigued him. One more reason to get her off the plantation and out of his sight as quickly as possible.

"Hold up there."

Travis whirled around to find Mr. Jeffries scurrying after him, huffing and out of breath as he struggled to catch up. Impatiently, Travis stopped and waited for the elderly man to join him. He wondered what other wonderful news his solicitor had forgotten to tell him.

When Jeffries reached him, he blew out his breath

in a long, jagged puff, jerked a handkerchief from his pocket and dabbed his damp brow. That's when Travis realized he was taking out his frustrations on the messenger when he really wanted to rant and rave at his father. The poor old sod couldn't help what Jackson had assigned him to do. Travis set his mind to try to tolerate the old man.

"I—I want you to know that I'm truly sorry about your father," Jeffries said, folding his handkerchief and stuffing it back in his pocket. "I sent word of what happened immediately after His Grace passed away. I hope you received the message," he said.

"Actually, I didn't. I learned of my father's demise from someone else." Travis noticed the man's surprise, so he continued, "Let me explain what happened."

Travis still remembered how he'd found out about his father. He'd gone to see his banker . . .

"Should I remind you that the final mortgage on Moss Grove is past due?" Harvey Midway had said from behind his desk. "I must admit that you've taken a failing plantation and turned it into a profitable one. However, that land is valuable and could be sold for a hefty profit. I've tried contacting His Grace—"

"I do not want any help from my father," Travis snapped.

Harvey held up his hand. "If you'll let me finish," he paused, looking a little ill at ease. "I received a letter yesterday from your father's solicitor, a Mr. Jeffries."

Travis nodded. "I know of the man."

"It says that your father has passed away." Harvey reached for the letter and glanced at it. "The letter was dated two months ago." The man faltered, then went on.

"I take it from the look on your face that you didn't know. I'm sorry."

Travis remembered vividly. Harvey's flushed face, his embarrassment.

Travis recalled he hadn't responded. At the time, he hadn't been certain how he felt. He'd just been told that the man who was his father had died. Travis knew he should have felt something—yet he felt nothing. The man had never shown him any kind of love or affection, so how could he have expected any feelings in return? Of course, some fathers never even acknowledge their bastard children, so maybe Travis should have been grateful, but he wasn't.

His father might have educated him, but only because there was no one left but Travis to carry on the Montgomery name. Then he'd shipped him off to America to rejoin his mother where he'd be out of the way—away from Jackson's wife.

When Travis realized that he hadn't said anything to Mr. Jeffries, he finished explaining. "Sorry, I was remembering the conversation where I learned the news from Harvey, my banker." Travis lifted his shoulders in an angry shrug. "I can truly say it wasn't a pleasant day."

"I'm terribly sorry, sir," Mr. Jeffries said, shaking his head. "My assistant must have confused the address. You were to receive your letter in advance of your father's business associates."

Travis understood that it was not an intentional slight, but still it hurt. And he wasn't really sure why. "The only thing I know is the old codger never did anything without having a reason. The education came only after he realized that I was the only one to carry on the family name. Only then did he give me his last name and acknowledge my birth. And now this insult—that woman." Travis motioned toward the house. "The woman owns half the blasted plantation—just what is—or was—my father about?"

"I cannot comment on the subject, sir," Mr. Jeffries said, his brows drawing together in an agonized expression. "But I can say that your father seemed to think a great deal of Miss Brooke."

"Evidently so," Travis grated out. "He left her half the damned plantation." He turned on his heel and strode toward the barn. "I'm going to check the cane," he called back over his shoulder. "If you want to see what Moss Grove is about, I'll have a horse saddled for you, and you can ride with me."

"Thank you," Mr. Jeffries said, huffing as he struggled to catch up with Travis. "I can understand your being upset over the situation . . ." Jeffries's words trailed off as Travis gave him a warning look, but then Jeffries continued. "I traveled with Mrs. Hammond and her friends, and they are all quite lovely ladies. Perhaps you'll change—"

Travis stopped suddenly, cutting Jeffries off, "What ladies?"

"I believe they are friends but think of themselves as sisters, sir. Quite close, I do believe. Actually the other two women were your father's nieces and your first cousins. They lived with your father for awhile."

As casually as he could manage, Travis stated, "Don't tell me I'm going to have two more women dropping in on me. As if I don't have enough aggravation." He raked a hand through his hair. "Thank God my mother isn't here. She'd be having the vapors or carrying on so that I would never have any peace."

"Oh, no sir. The ladies parted company in New York, each going her separate way."

"Good," Travis snapped, then motioned for the stableman to saddle another horse. When the horses were brought around, Travis mounted, but couldn't resist speaking his thoughts. "It's a damned shame that Mrs. Hammond didn't go with them."

Mr. Jeffries mounted. "I hope that you'll feel differently once you become better acquainted with Mrs. Hammond. She's really quite a lovely woman."

Travis gave a half laugh before he said, "Don't wager your life on it."

Mammy led the way down a long hall. The clicking of their heels on the hard, parquet floor was the only sound.

Apparently, Mammy didn't feel the need to fill the silence with chatter. When they reached the end of the hall, Mammy opened the door and announced, "Dis is your room. I t'ink you'll enjoy dis room, yes."

Everything smelled clean and of fresh lemon wax. It was a refreshing change from the dampness of the ship and the musty odor of the taverns and coaches they'd used on their trip.

Brooke glanced around the spacious room. The furniture was all dark mahogany. A large bed with a white lace canopy sat in the middle of the room, and a sofa and two rose-colored chairs faced the fireplace on the other side.

The room had been decorated for a woman— possibly the fiancée. Just how close was Travis to his fiancée? Did he love what's-her-name? He didn't look like a man in love. Love softened a man. At least, the ones Brooke had made acquaintance with and those were few. There definitely wasn't anything soft about Travis Montgomery. Cold was the first word that came to Brooke's mind. Was there, perhaps, another motivation for the pending marriage?

"Jus' you set you'se'f dere, and I'll have your trunks sent up, Miz Ha—"

Brooke touched Mammy's arm. "I prefer that you call me Miss Brooke." Brooke thought the woman might at least give her a small smile at the friendly overture, but she was wrong. All she received was a curt nod. However, she had no intention of giving up. "And what should I call you?" Brooke inquired.

"Mig't as well call me Mammy, yes. Ever'bod' else does," the plump woman said as she smoothed the coverlet on the bed with her dark, worn hand. "Will your lady's maid be joinin' you shortly, Miz Brooke?" The disapproval was clear in her voice.

Brooke thought a moment before she answered. She realized that she was the intruder and she didn't want to quarrel with everyone in this household. It would make life easier if she made friends with the one woman who could be an ally. "I'm afraid I didn't bring my maid with me. She was young and did not wish to leave her family."

Mammy straightened and looked at her with wide eyes. "You traveled by you'se'f, unchaperoned, yes?"

"Not exactly. I had Mr. Jeffries and two of my friends with me, but we parted ways in New York."

"Well now," Mammy said, hands on her ample hips. "If you don' want people to talk in Nawlins den you shouldn't go out alone, you hear. Jus' ain't proper," she grumbled.

Brooke nodded. "I'll keep that in mind, thank you. Have you worked at Moss Grove long?"

"Well now—dat's a question. His Grace didn't come here often, but de house has always been staffed, and I've always been in charge. Den Miz Margaret and Mr. Travis came, and once again, de house was lived in. We made some changes. Got rid o' de sorry no accounts, yes," Mammy said shaking her head. "We have good folks now."

"I see," Brooke said, placing her reticule on the bed. She'd hoped that Mammy had helped raised Travis so the woman could tell her something about his personality. "Then I should think that you'd be a great help in choosing a lady's maid for me. I'm certain you must have excellent taste."

Mammy actually smiled this time, showing her white teeth. Her brown eyes searched Brooke's face, for what, Brooke wasn't sure. "Jus' leave it to Mammy. I'll choose someone fo' you while you here," she said finally.

"I expect to be here a long time, Mammy." Brooke smiled. "You see, I have inherited half of Moss Grove from His Grace."

"Oh, Lordy," Mammy said, touching the sides of her face with her palms. "Lordy, Lordy." Then she realized she'd let her thoughts show, and her face once again became a shuttered mask.

"Don't worry," Brooke said. She reached out and touched the housekeeper's arm. "You can always speak your mind around me. I promise I shall do the same. I know that you don't trust me yet, and that's understandable. But I'm hoping that some-day you will. I don't intend to make any changes in the household staff." She looked around, apprais-ing the spotless room. "I can see everything is run-ning smoothly already."

Mammy's brow furrowed. "What will Miz Margaret and Miz Hesione have to say?" Mammy blurted out, then caught herself. She shook her head quickly. "Ain't none o' my business," she seemed to be re-minding herself. "I spoke too soon, yes."

"I hope I shall not be the strict taskmaster you expect, Mammy," Brooke told her as she unpinned her hat and placed it on the small dressing table. "I wasn't pampered and spoiled. I appreciate hard work and faithful service. Please, feel free to speak your mind when you're with me." Brooke looked Mammy directly in her dark, kind eyes. "Everything here is strange and unfamiliar to me, nothing like my home in England. I shall need all the assistance you can provide. I do hope you'll help me," Brooke paused then pressed on, hoping to find out what she needed to know from the woman. "Who are these people that you spoke of?"

Mammy hesitated again. "Mebbe I shouldn't be talkin'."

Brooke sat down on one of the two rose-colored chairs and motioned for Mammy to sit in the other.

"Since I asked you a direct question," Brooke

gently prodded, "I would think it's your duty to answer. I doubt that would be considered gossiping."

Mammy smiled, her eyes twinkling as she nodded. "Well now, Miz Margaret is Master Montgomery's mama, as you mus' already know."

"I didn't know her name," Brooke said.

"I see." Mammy nodded. Well, Miz Hesione, she is his fiancée. Dey is up north shoppin', to be sure. Spendin' lots o' money, I guarantee."

"I see," Brooke said, nodding. She wanted to ask what the women were like, but realized Mammy didn't trust her enough yet to offer that kind of information. "Are they expected back soon?"

Mammy rose from the chair. "Be back come November 'cause Miz Margaret wants a Christmas weddin', and she usually gets what she wants," Mammy said as she started for the door. "Get you'se'f settled in, you hear. I'll send a girl up fo' your maid, to help you unpack.

"Dinner be rig't at eight, yes. Prosper, de cook, now he don' tolerate no one bein' late fo' his table, you hear." She paused when she reached the door, then turned and gave Brooke a final smile. "Welcome to Nawlins."

Brooke stared at the closed door as she sank down into the chair, realizing just how tired she was. It had been a very long and tiring day. The intelligent thing to do would be to surrender, since she was so vastly outnumbered, but then she was tired and couldn't trust herself to think intelligently. The trip, plus the confrontation with Travis, had been more wearing than she'd expected.

He wasn't like anyone she'd ever known.

Perhaps she'd just rest for a short while. She needed to have her wits about her on her next encounter with Travis Montgomery.

And what kind of a cook made the rules anyway, she wondered vaguely as she slumped against the chair. She supposed she'd find out soon enough.

This was, indeed, a strange household. The housekeeper spoke with an unusual French accent, and the cook made the rules for when to eat. And she wouldn't be at all surprised if a ghost popped out of the wall. He probably wouldn't want her here either, she thought with a shudder.

Would she ever fit in here?

Mammy had offered one interesting tidbit. Travis's mother and the fiancée wouldn't be back until November. That was, indeed, good news. At least that gave Brooke a little time to work her wiles on Travis and establish herself as the mistress here before the other two women arrived.

She and Travis only had to be married for a year and then they could go their separate ways. Then if he still wanted Miss Hesione, he would be welcome to her. Brooke would give him up freely. Or maybe it was more like, if Hesione wanted him. That thought made Brooke smile.

At least for now it was one-on-one, but she would have to work fast. When Travis's mother and his intended returned, the odds would change to three against one.

And Brooke didn't like those odds at all.

Chapter 4

Brooke slowly came awake as the sun's first rays crept in through the window. Morning seemed to have come much too soon and she wasn't ready to face the day. Slowly, she opened her eyes, blinked several times, and attempted to wake up. Snuggling under the covers, she tried to organize her thoughts before beginning the day.

The first week had gone by quickly. She'd tried to settle into her new home, but that had proven to be a difficult task since she was considered an outsider in running the affairs of the plantation. Brooke had to remind herself several times to be patient. It would take time to win over not only the staff, but Travis.

Finally, yesterday she had begun to feel as though she was starting to win over the household staff. Several of the servants had stopped to consult with her instead of pretending that she didn't exist. Brooke considered that a big step forward.

She thought it might have helped when she'd volunteered to accompany several of the children to gather nuts from the pecan grove located behind

the big house. It was something she'd never thought
she would do since she had never been particularly
fond of children, but she decided she needed to
do something useful. So she assembled four boys,
three girls, several wicker baskets, and headed out.

Much to her surprise, Brooke found she enjoyed
spending the afternoon with the children. Having
thought that she didn't have anything in common
with them, Brooke was amazed they seemed to take
to her. It was delightful to listen to their laughter
and giggling.

George, who looked to be about nine, announced that he was the shaker. Of course, Brooke
had to ask what a shaker did.

He informed her proudly, his little chest swelling
with pride. "It's the mos' important person 'cause I
gets the nuts out the tree."

"So how are you going to get the pecans?"
Brooke asked. "That tree is very tall."

George grinned widely, his white teeth gleam-
ing against his dark skin. "Here, you hold dis, Miz
Brooke." He handed her a cane pole. "'Cause I'm
goin' to climb that there tree."

"It's pretty tall," she'd warned him.

"Don't matter none," George answered with
supreme confidence. He marched over to the huge
tree where two of the other boys formed a step with
their linked hands and gave him a lift up. After
he'd successfully reached the second branch, he
called for Brooke to hand him the pole.

"You must be careful."

"Oh, Miz Brooke, I done this a thousand times
before."

She was sure he hadn't climbed this tree a thousand times, but she'd give him credit, he was an expert climber, navigating the lofty branches as nimbly as a squirrel. Once he'd reached the uppermost branches, he began thrashing the limbs with the cane pole, and the pecans showered over everyone below like raindrops falling from the sky.

Brooke set down the basket she was carrying. "Let's see who can gather the most nuts. There will be a special treat for the winner." All the children's eyes grew wide at the prospect of a contest. "On your mark, get set, go," she said, and the children took off in all directions.

She laughed at the children scampering around and making a big game out of the drudgery of gathering nuts. She couldn't remember when she'd enjoyed something so trivial so much.

She and her rowdy crew returned to the kitchen with several big baskets filled to the brim with nuts. Brooke asked Katie, one of the girls in the kitchen, to give all the children cookies and milk for their efforts, declaring that they were all winners.

Everyone in the kitchen had smiled at Brooke, making her wonder if kindness was something they weren't accustomed to seeing from the mistress of the house.

She supposed that the servants were slowly coming to the conclusion that she wasn't such a bad person after all. It had felt wonderful to be doing something useful and productive.

Thank goodness Mammy ran the house and Prosper ran the kitchen. So far Brooke hadn't met the mysterious cook. He'd traveled to one of his relative's homes, but would be back soon, so she'd been told. Mammy seemed to be a little of everything to everyone, and that was fine with Brooke, who was still trying to win the housekeeper over. So far she'd had a little success, but not much.

She could imagine the woman's resentment. Brooke just needed time. She had to earn the staff's respect and trust. It would have been one thing if she had come to them as Travis's wife, but that wasn't the case.

Brooke remembered yesterday with a smile as she stretched, not yet wanting to give up the warmth of her covers. Even with all the problems she'd encountered since her arrival, Brooke was glad she'd traveled to America. Back in London, she had been readily welcomed at parties and had even set some of the latest fashion trends, but she'd never been completely accepted. There were always a few that whispered about her. Now she had a chance at living a normal life, even if she still had to work through a few problems here.

But Brooke Hammond was nothing if not a survivor. She would figure out the solutions to her problems.

As she slowly came awake, she looked around her room. She really couldn't complain about her accommodations. They were at the far end of the hall, so it was very quiet. At night, the only sounds she heard were the cries of night birds calling in the wind.

The walls were painted a warm rose color. The four-poster mahogany bed was big and soft with a feather comforter and quilts of pink- and cream-colored silk. All in all, the room was quite lovely.

A crackling sound caught Brooke's attention, and she pushed herself up on her elbows to see. Apparently, one of the upstairs maids had crept in while she'd been sleeping and built a small fire in the marble fireplace. Good, Brooke thought, the nights had turned surprisingly cool, considering the balmy days, and the idea of the cold, wooden planks under her feet was not appealing at the moment.

She yawned and dared to stick one foot out from the warmth of the bed. The air in the room was tolerably warm now that the fire was going. She couldn't solve her problems by lounging, so she tossed back the covers and slid out of bed.

Today, Mr. Jeffries was leaving to attend to few matters before he returned to England. Last night, he'd explained that he had business with other clients that would require his attention for a couple of months in St. Louis. Then he had to make sure that Jocelyn was settled comfortably in her New York home.

Mr. Jeffries pointed out that his departure would give Brooke and Travis time alone together, so they could get to know each other. Brooke had her doubts that even ten years alone with Travis would help.

He seemed to have little desire to know her at all. Since she'd arrived, he'd made himself scarce, so getting to know him had proven difficult. However, he had managed to grace them with his presence at dinner every night so far. Although the conversation continued to be strained, Brooke kept trying.

Travis was proving to be a very stubborn man, and Brooke was slowly learning patience, not an easy task for someone who had none.

If she didn't find a way to get Travis talking to her soon, she'd never be able to win him over.

Brooke splashed cool water on her face, remembering the scathing looks that Travis sent her more than once every night at dinner. She often wondered what the exasperating man was thinking as he seemed to be studying her. Whatever it was, he hid his thoughts very well.

Damned man.

She sighed. Travis Montgomery was an ever-changing mystery. Brooke wasn't sure how she was going to break through Travis's frosty outer shell. She suspected that he was trying to drive her away by being rude, but that wasn't going to work.

She was nothing if not persistent.

Brooke had to do something to make herself indispensable, and today was the day to get started, she decided as she peered into her wardrobe. She needed the perfect outfit, she thought, hoping she remembered how to flirt and seduce a man after being out of practice for so long.

Perhaps it was like riding a horse, and one never forgot. She smiled, then sobered. It had been two years since she'd lived the other life. From the moment Jackson had taken her in, she'd not had to work her wiles to get what she needed. At the moment, she felt like a brand-new virgin—well, maybe a well-experienced virgin. She chuckled to herself.

Her maid, Millie Anne, swung into the room, a bright smile on her face. "Good mornin', misses," she said cheerfully. "I come to help you get dressed. I sees you are already thinkin' on what to wear," she said, standing behind Brooke. "Yo' got so many pretty things to choose from. I reckon you turned every man's head back home."

Brooke chuckled. "Perhaps a few," she said modestly. She tapped her chin thoughtfully as she looked over her selection of garments. "I believe I shall go riding today," she said over her shoulder. "It's about time that I inspected the rest of the plantation."

"Fresh air will do you good."

Brooke was glad to have Millie Anne. The young woman seemed to be the only cheerful person in the entire household. She was pert and sassy, perhaps sixteen, and usually wore a bright smile, her dazzling black eyes snapping with intelligence and humor. It seemed Millie Anne was one of Mammy's nieces and like Mammy, she was a free black woman. Brooke learned that many of the workers on the plantation had been freed and now earned wages for working.

"Is it cold outside?" Brooke asked.

"Oh, yes ma'am. Or rather cool. Fall is in the air, and it's only de end o' September. Sometimes, October can be mighty warm, and dat's good for sugarcane. If'n we get an early frost dat won't be good. I heard the foreman say we's goin' to start cuttin' de cane today."

Brooke had gotten used to the fact that once Millie Anne started talking, she would likely rattle on and on about whatever she was talking about. But Brooke also realized that she learned quite a lot of useful information from Millie's ramblings.

"What does the weather have to do with the sugarcane?" Brooke asked as she selected one of her several riding habits.

Millie Anne moved over to the bed and began straightening the covers. "Dat dere cane is sensitive to cold. If'n we have a freeze, Master Travis will lose de crop. Somethin' about the sugar won't be sugar. Don't know whats dey mean 'bout that, only dat it ain't good. Three years ago we had us a hard freeze, and Master Travis, he was in a real bad mood for a right long spell."

Brooke laughed. "You mean his present demeanor is an improvement?"

"D—demeanor?" Millie Anne's intelligent eyes narrowed with puzzlement.

"Mood," Brooke explained. "Do you mean that Travis is in a good mood now?" Brooke asked.

"Yes'um." Millie Anne smiled. "I even seen him smile a couple o' times. But not much," she added, fluffing the bed pillows. "He jus' seems"—she paused, searching for the right words—"kind o' like he's tryin' to prove somethin'."

"Well, let me know the next time you do see him smile. I would really love to see that for myself," Brooke said with a laugh as she brushed a bit of lint from the green, princess-style riding habit.

Millie Anne giggled. "Yo' sure do make me laugh, Miz Brooke. I'm sure you'll make him laugh, too."

Brooke arched a brow. "Believe me, Millie Anne, that hasn't been the case thus far." Brooke shook out the habit, trying to eliminate the wrinkles, then handed it to her. "I think I'll wear this today."

The girl held up the garment so Brooke could step into it. "I used to work in de cane, you know. It be hard work. I sure like workin' in de house much better." Millie Anne tugged the ends of the riding jacket together. "Dis here was sure made fo' you. It fits like your very own skin."

"I had it made that way." Brooked tugged on the sleeves to adjust them. She inspected her reflection in the mirror. "I don't like to wear anything bulky when I ride."

"Come sit and let me do your hair," Millie Anne said and gestured to the stool in front of the small dressing table. "I don' want nothin' to do with those horses. They're too big fo' me," she said, shuddering.

Brooke watched in the mirror as the girl dressed her hair, pulling her heavy gold tresses up to the crown of her head, then fastening the curls with gold combs. Once she had secured the hair, Millie pinned a dark green hat to the front.

"That's perfect," Brooke said, and Millie glowed at the compliment. "Considering the way you dress my hair, I would have thought that you had always been a lady's maid." She reached up and patted the hand that rested on her shoulder. "And I'm really glad that you're my lady's maid."

"Thank you, ma'am."

Millie Anne beamed all over. Evidently, she didn't receive many compliments. Brooke couldn't help thinking that at least one good thing had come out of her trip to Moss Grove—it had gotten the girl out of the cane fields.

"Tell me something," Brooke said, pausing as she stood up. "Were you going to be Hesione's maid?"

Millie Anne shook her head. "No, ma'am. She has her own maid," the girl said, placing the hairbrush and combs back on the dressing table. "'Sides, Mammy wouldn't want me to."

"Why?"

"Well—I," Millie Anne hesitated.

"I won't say anything."

"Mammy don't like Miz Hesione. And she'd thrash me good if she knew I was talkin' about her. But . . ." Millie Anne grinned. "Mammy said Miz Hesione is lazy, spoiled, and not good enough for Master Travis."

Brooke wanted to know more, but she didn't want to let on that Millie Anne had given her some valuable information. Instead, she said, "I think Mammy is probably a good judge of character. Tell me, why does everyone call her Mammy?"

"When she was much younger, she had a child, but he died with the fever when he was one. After that, she never had no more young'uns, so she started motherin' ever'bod' else and we done called her Mammy ever since. She seems to understand everythin' no matter what the problem we has."

"I haven't known her long, but there is something comforting about Mammy," Brooke said. "What's her real name?"

"Esther," Millie Anne said. "Is dere anythin' else that you be might needin'?"

"Is Mr. Jeffries in his room?"

"Yes'um, he's packin'. I can show you. I'm headin' dat way now."

Brooke followed the maid out of the room and down to Mr. Jeffries's room. Brooke saw that the door was open, but she rapped on the door jamb just the same. Jeffries stood by the bed. A trunk was open nearby and clothes were strewn all over the bed. Millie Anne knocked louder than Brooke had, and

Mr. Jeffries glanced their way. Smiling, he motioned for them to enter.

Brooke stepped into the room, staying close to the door since it wasn't proper for a lady to be in a gentleman's room. He was supervising the folding of the last of his clothes as his temporary valet placed them in the trunk.

"I'm going to miss you," Brooke told him.

He gave her a smile as yet another garment was added to the contents of the trunk.

"I'll finish that fo' you," Millie Anne said to Ulysses, taking the shirt from the servant.

"I'll be back in a few months to check on you, then I shall have to return to England," Mr. Jeffries said.

"I see it as you leaving me with the enemy," Brooke said, cheerfully pouting as she stood just inside the door.

He chuckled. "I don't believe Jackson Montgomery would have put you in this situation if he didn't expect that you could handle yourself."

Brooke didn't know how to respond.

When she didn't reply, Jeffries arched an eyebrow. "You don't strike me as one to give up easily. After all, it's only a year and then you can both go your separate ways, providing he doesn't go through with his impending marriage."

"Oh, I shan't give anything up," Brooke assured him. "It's just that I didn't expect this . . . this formidable a man." She gestured expansively.

"He is a rather remarkable opponent," Jeffries agreed. "But now that he's become a man, I can see a lot of his father in him. It is unfortunate that

Travis could not inherit his father's title, although, in this country titles mean little."

"I'll admit Travis is a handsome man, but his disposition is in vast need of improving."

"Perhaps he's never had a reason to change his ways. You might be the person to do just that," Jeffries said as the last item went into the trunk. Then, dismissing Millie Anne, he pulled the trunk lid down and fastened the hasp. "Shall we go down to breakfast?"

Once downstairs, they went straight to the dining room where they found Travis, much to Brooke's surprise. Travis was usually long gone before she had breakfast. It appeared that he had just finished eating and was leaning back, enjoying a last cup of coffee before he started his day.

When they entered the room, Travis rose and greeted them with a casual yet polite nod. "Good morning, Jeffries, Mrs. Hammond. Please, sit down." He held a chair out until Brooke was seated. Then he slipped back into his seat. "I hope you're hungry," he said, picking up and ringing a small brass bell. Instantly, one of the kitchen maids appeared with fresh coffee and began to pour.

"Please serve our *guests*."

Brooke frowned, wondering what had caused Travis to be in such a seemingly good mood. Usually he appeared determined to keep her at arm's length. Now he was treating her like a welcome guest. She bristled, but she didn't quite know how to react to Travis's change in attitude. She wasn't a guest, she wanted to remind him. Whether he wanted a partner or not, he had one.

Come to think of it, Brooke thought, she wasn't sure she'd ever met a man who didn't want her. Before Travis Montgomery, that was. Hmmmm, she thought, she must be slipping. Of course, Travis's attitude just gave her one more challenge to meet.

"I have ordered the coach for your departure," Travis informed them as he placed his coffee cup on the saucer. "The driver will take you wherever you want to go."

"Thank you, sir," Jeffries said with a nod. "I'll return by the end of November, if not sooner. Provided that you meet the conditions your father set forth, you will have estates to manage both here and in England. That reminds me, have you planned your ball to introduce Mrs. Hammond to local society?"

The furrows between Travis's eyes deepened. "I don't have time for entertaining," he snapped. "But in keeping with my father's demands," he added, tempering his tone. "I will speak to Mammy and have a few invitations sent out."

"Good." Jeffries nodded. "Perhaps, Miss Brooke can help you with the necessary arrangements."

Brooke laid her fork down and looked at Travis. "It would be lovely if you let me know of your plans. I'll be happy to assist you."

"I'm not in the habit of discussing what I do with you or anyone else, Mrs. Hammond."

Brooke recognized his condescending tone, and the urge to throw something at him was so great she had to hold her hands in her lap to keep from acting. "That is certainly most apparent," she retorted. "Considering your father's wishes, however, perhaps you should start including me. I do expect to be the hostess at the party."

Travis gave her a sidelong glance of utter disbelief. The furious expression on his face told volumes. She evidently had hit her target.

After a moment of strained silence, Jeffries spoke up, "I believe your father wants you both to be happy," he said tactfully.

"Well, I can take care of my own happiness without interference from my late father," Travis snapped. "I do hope that you'll return to Moss Grove in time for my wedding to Hesione. That should take care of my father's wishes."

Mr. Jeffries wiped his mouth with the linen cloth and placed it beside his plate. "I shall do my best, sir."

Brooke noted that Travis didn't look much like a man in love. As a matter of fact, he was frowning as was his usual habit, and a muscle flicked angrily in his jaw before he continued. "My arrangement with Hesione will provide a perfect match," he said.

He sounded like he was trying to convince himself as well as the rest of the people in the room, Brooke thought. Perhaps there was hope that Jackson's plan would succeed yet.

Travis shoved his chair back from the table and then stood up. "Now, if you'll excuse me, Mrs. Hammond, Jeffries, the cane harvest starts today."

"Then it will be the perfect time for you to show me *our* plantation," Brooke said firmly. She folded her hands on her lap and waited to see how Travis would respond.

He stiffened, then he faced her. Keeping his features deceptively composed, his burning eyes held hers. Once again, Brooke was struck by his stark good looks. No matter how surly he was, something about him attracted her. Perhaps, like a moth to a flame, she was doomed. She wasn't sure she liked that scenario.

"I was rather expecting or should I say hoped that you'd be leaving with Mr. Jeffries," Travis told her.

Brooke smiled. No wonder he'd been in such a cheerful mood this morning! He was expecting her to be gone. "I just bet you were," she said matter-of-factly. "Sorry to disappoint you, but my business is here not in St. Louis with Mr. Jeffries.

"Plus, there is the matter of the little party you must plan. I wouldn't miss that for the world as I am to be the reason for the ball." Ignoring Travis's smoldering glare, Brooke rose and walked around the table to Mr. Jeffries. "The next time I see you, I shall have had quite an education about running Moss Grove Plantation."

Mr. Jeffries tried to hide his smile, but Brooke saw it in the twitching at the corners of his mouth. "I'm hoping that the two of you will work something out to your dual satisfaction."

"My satisfaction would be for you to take her with you," Travis muttered sourly. "Moss Grove is no place for this woman." Abruptly he turned and left the dining room.

As Brooke watched the irritating man stride from the room, she prepared herself for the battle of wills ahead of her. But first things first. She turned to Mr. Jeffries and took his hands in hers, holding them out in front of her. "I hope you will have a safe and pleasant trip."

Jeffries smiled. "Remember, my dear, Montgomery is still adjusting to you being here," he cautioned. "He's stubborn like his father, but he will come around."

"Miracles do happen, I suppose," Brooke said sarcastically. Of course, this miracle might need divine intervention. "Now, where are the stables?"

"I believe they are to your right when you leave by the front entrance," Mr. Jeffries said. "I shall finish gathering my things, and then I'll leave. I shall see you upon my return. And I sincerely hope that your relations with Travis will have smoothed over by then."

Brooke had grown so fond of the man that she impulsively hugged him, producing an immediate flush on his chubby face. He bade her good-bye, then turned and left.

She strolled out of the dining room to the foyer where she found Travis slipping on his dark brown coat. She swept past the damned man, hating the way he made her feel so stupid.

She hated even more the fact that she needed him. She knew full well that hating him was not going to help her achieve her goal. She had to make Travis so hungry for her that that he would break off his engagement to the mysterious Hesione. Brooke hurried outside determined to find the stables with or without him. She heard the door open and close behind her, but she didn't turn. Instead, she marched across the manicured lawn. The one thing she would not do was bow down to Travis no matter how badly she needed a home.

Chapter 5

Travis stood on the porch, gripping the iron railing as if he could break it in two. The thought had occurred to him. He needed to release some of his frustration. Wringing the lovely lady's neck was another option that had crossed his mind.

He barely noticed the crisp air or the beautiful morning as he watched the woman striding across the lawn. What he did notice was the sun playing in her glorious golden hair until it looked like wheat ready for harvest.

Travis cursed himself for his weakness. Why was he even looking her way? The last thing in the world he wanted or needed was to get involved with this woman. He had a fiancée. And Brooke was a threat to his carefully plotted plans . . . or was she merely another obstacle to overcome . . . and nothing more.

He descended the front steps at his own pace. He'd be damned if he'd race to catch up with the exasperating woman. What the devil was she up to anyhow? He'd hoped that by ignoring Mrs. Hammond she would simply go away, but evidently that tactic hadn't worked. She was still here, worrying him like a thorn in his side.

He did admit that Brooke Hammond was different than other women he'd known, and that bothered him. She disturbed him in every way she could. Not only was he becoming more and more attracted to her, but he couldn't figure her out. However, he was fast learning that she was one stubborn woman. Worse, she seemed to know how to work her way under his skin.

And he didn't give a damn how pretty she was. She was trouble—plain and simple.

At least that's what he tried to convince himself. What he did give a damn about was how much the blasted lady stayed on his mind. Even in his sleep he could see those enticing, glittering gold eyes dancing before him. And the light fragrance she wore seemed to be everywhere in the house. Strange. He paused and thought for a moment. He couldn't recall Hesione's scent.

It was as if he couldn't get away from Brooke. She had infested the very air he breathed. Normally, he could shove thoughts of women completely out of his mind. However, with Mrs. Hammond, none of his usual tricks worked. She was like the plague.

He looked up and came to an abrupt stop. Apparently, he'd reached the stables without remembering the walk. Blast it all, he needed to get hold of his mind and his body.

He could only hope that after the infernal Mrs. Hammond saw how complicated running a plantation was, she'd turn tail and go running back to England and her tea parties and whatever it was she'd done before coming here. Women had no place interfering in the operation of a plantation. Especially his plantation.

Entering the barn doors, he immediately spotted Brooke and knew his short-lived reprieve was over. She was waving her arms in exasperation as she argued with his head groom. Evidently, she was trying to convince Old Sam she needed a horse.

"Why you be wantin' one o' Master Travis's good horses, Missy? Not dat I got a t'ing ag'in you, but I don't know who you are, you hear," Sam said in his thick Cajun accent.

"Why does that not surprise me?" Brooke muttered sarcastically. "I'm Brooke Hammond, part owner of Moss Grove."

Old Sam chuckled. "Well now, you be funnin' me. Ever'bod' knows Master Montgomery owns Moss Grove. Dere he is now. Ask him, you'se'f, you hear."

Brooke swung around and focused her attention on Travis, glaring angrily at him. He almost laughed out loud at the murderous look on her face. Instead, he smiled. Unfortunately, his obvious amusement just made her all the more irritated. Finally, Travis asked, "Is there a problem, Sam?"

Sam shoved his hat to the back of his head. "Ooowe, to be sure," he said. "Dis young lady wants t' ride one o' your horses."

Travis looked at Brooke with a raised brow. "You probably should have asked me first."

"I believe I told you earlier that I wanted to see the plantation."

He smiled smoothly, betraying nothing of his annoyance. "Do you ride, Mrs. Hammond?"

"Of course I can ride, you ninny. Do you think I'd get on an animal if I couldn't handle it?"

Something about the way Brooke spat those words at him made chills crawl up the back of his neck. Travis didn't doubt that she could handle just about anything. There was such an air of confidence about her . . . a determination that he'd not seen in other women. He almost admired her for that. "In that case," he said, turning to Old Sam. "Saddle the gray for Mrs. Hammond."

"I prefer that you call me Miss Brooke or just plain Brooke," she said.

"You can use the gray while you're here, Mrs. Hammond," he said pointedly.

"What a stubborn man you are," Brooke told him. She took a step closer. "Don't think you are getting rid of me. I'm here to stay and have no intention of going anywhere."

Travis waited until Sam was out of hearing distance before he responded, low and quiet, under his breath, "You don't belong here."

Instead of shooting a remark back as he expected, Brooke gave him an odd look, and he could swear tears spiked her lashes. Up until now he had not thought of her as a woman with feelings and emotions. She had merely been a thorn in his side and a warm body to think about during the long nights, which made her the enemy.

"That's the problem, you see. I don't belong anywhere," she said in a soft voice, sounding almost defeated. Her golden eyes seemed to pierce his with the oddest, almost desperate, expression. And she was much too close. "Do you know what it's like not to belong?"

Travis's gut tightened and he slowly nodded. "I know exactly how it feels."

"Then I imagine that we are more alike than you know."

Someone cleared his throat, and Travis and Brooke jerked away from each other.

Sam had returned with the horses and broke whatever spell Brooke had cast over him.

Without another word, Travis waited until Sam positioned the horse, then Travis helped Brooke mount the sidesaddle.

As he closed his hands around her trim waist, he marveled at how small she was. He could almost circle her waist with his hands, and there was no doubt in his mind that she wore no corset beneath her garments. Only thin material separated his hands and her warm skin. Steeling himself to resist the spell he was slowly falling under, he lifted her onto the saddle.

Her fragrance seemed to wash over him, and his body's reaction to it surprised the hell out of him. He didn't need to be attracted to Brooke, so he abruptly tuned and went to mount his own horse. He'd be damned if he'd allow that woman to see his growing attraction to her.

After Travis situated himself on the white stallion, he glanced at Brooke's pure profile. She sat so gracefully in the saddle, and with such dignity, that she certainly appeared to be the master horsewoman. Her habit was cut so perfectly to the contours of her body that he could imagine her completely naked beneath the fabric. An image of her lying in bed, her golden mane of hair fanned out across a pillow, flashed unbidden into his mind.

Travis's bodily reaction was hard and quick, and he cursed himself. Rather than remain there, trapped under her spell, he touched the white's flanks with his heels and urged him forward. He had to put some distance between himself and Brooke.

Once out of the stables, he paused and took a deep breath to clear his head, then spurred his mount on, pushing him harder and faster than he knew he should. Fresh air! That's what he needed.

Only when Travis felt he was safely away did he allow his horse to slow. He guided him to the top of a rise, which overlooked the river below, and then he drew his mount to a halt.

The telltale sound of another horse approaching told him he wasn't going to be alone for long. He didn't want to give her the satisfaction of knowing that she'd chased him away. Travis forced himself to sit still and wait for her to catch up.

"What a beautiful horse," Brooke said as she rode up beside him. "Does she have a name?" She reached up and patted her mare on the neck.

The gray swung her head to the side, trying to nuzzle Brooke's hand. The traitor! Was everyone on the plantation falling under Brooke's spell?

Travis glanced over at the dapple gray mare. He'd always liked that horse because she was so unique, calm yet spirited, far different from the rest of his stable. Much like the woman who now rode her. "Gray Mist."

"I like the name. I've never had a horse of my own. In England, I always had to ride someone else's horse."

Travis couldn't pry his eyes off Brooke. Something in her voice touched him in all the places he didn't want to be touched. "Do you like her?"

Brooke nodded. "Very much."

"Then she's yours."

Brooke felt as if a thousand butterflies had been released in her stomach. Why was the man finally being kind to her? She knew she could point out that half of everything on the plantation belonged to her already, but she didn't want to break the fragile truce between them. It felt much too good to spoil the mood with facts. "Thank you."

Gazing down on the fields below them, she saw what she presumed to be sugarcane. Although it looked like very tall grass, perhaps four to twelve feet high, it appeared to be planted in rows four feet apart. Green leaves, which swayed in the gentle breeze, sprouted at the top of each stalk.

She saw several men in the fields. The workers close to them swung long, curved blades, and the stalks tumbled to the ground in piles.

"I take it," she nodded toward the field, "that is sugarcane?"

"Good observation," Travis said in a condescending tone. "How much do you know about such crops? Or farming for that matter. I take it you grew up in the city?"

Brooke glanced at Travis, who was looking straight ahead, taking in everything that was happening in the field. She chose to ignore his suddenly ill manner. "You are correct. I've never been on a plantation before. Nevertheless, it doesn't make me ignorant of the operation. I did manage to read every book I could find about cotton as I thought that is what would be grown at Moss Grove."

"You expect to learn from a book?" Travis chuckled. "What a novice you are. However, I do applaud you," he said with a nod. "Not many women would bother themselves with such things. They would be more interested in the money coming in."

Brooke made a quick, involuntary appraisal of Travis's features to make sure that he wasn't making fun of her, yet again. "I'm not like most women."

"So I'm finding out."

Brooke's heart hammered foolishly at the thought that such a commanding individual was actually paying her mind. She knew it unwise to be attracted to him, but the fact remained that she found Travis more than a little disturbing. Every time he moved, she could see the tight muscles flex under his shirt. For now, she wanted to learn—no, had to learn—about the plantation, so she steered the conversation back toward business. "Why sugarcane?"

He shrugged impatiently. "It's the future."

Travis kept switching from warm to cold, Brooke thought, but she had begun to detect a softening in him, or so she hoped. She'd made up her mind to be persistent, even if she had to drag every word out of him. "Is that all you grow?"

"We do have a couple of fields planted in cotton, but the rest is cane. There is a great deal of money to be made with a good crop. But it's also riskier."

"Why more so than cotton?"

"Tariffs. And the weather. Sugar coming from other countries carries high tariffs. We can produce it cheaper, and in Louisiana cane grows faster. Cane is a ratoon crop." When he saw her puzzled expression, he explained further. "The cane is cut at ground level so the roots of the plants are left there. Next spring a new plant will sprout from the roots. So I save the labor of planting for three years."

"Well that certainly sounds smart, but why only three years?"

"Thank you," he said with a smile and a nod. "After the third harvest, we plow up the roots and the field is left fallow to replenish nutrients in the soil. In other words, the land is allowed to rest."

Brooke smiled. That was what she'd been doing for the past two years, letting her body lie fallow so she'd be good as new when she found a lover, or a husband, if she could convince Travis to cooperate.

She looked back over the field. "So tell me . . ." she paused ". . . everything."

Travis's brow rose. He hesitated, measuring her for a moment before inquiring, "Are you certain you want to know?"

"Of course I do," Brooke replied quickly, a little too quickly, he thought. But she did look sincere.

"I want to know everything about the plantation operations. You can't image what it's like being cooped up in the city all the time. So far, I've found that I love this country with all its wide-open spaces, and I want to understand how it works."

"All right," Travis said. He hoped by now she would have tired. He'd been wrong. Perhaps once she learned how much work was actually involved, she'd let up on her notion that she could somehow run a plantation. For God's sake, she was a woman after all. "Let's ride down to the fields so you can see firsthand." Travis nudged his mount down the levee. "Follow me."

"The land seems to be below the levee," Brooke observed.

Travis was impressed at her observation, despite himself. At first he thought she was pretending to be interested, but no one could be that great an actress. Perhaps the woman wasn't as empty-headed as he'd first thought. He found this notion very intriguing. "You are correct, madam. The land ranges from five to fifty feet below sea level here, and that is why you see so many levees. One of the most important tasks for those who live along the Delta is to maintain the levee system. As you can imagine, if any one of them broke we could lose everything."

"What a frightening thought," Brooke murmured, almost to herself. She halted her horse in front of one of the fields. "It's so tall," she said, motioning toward the cane.

"A good ten feet."

Brooke pointed toward a group of workers. "What are those people doing? Of course, I can see that they are cutting the stalks with something, but explain what happens next? Explain the process."

Again, she seemed truly sincere, so Travis indulged her in spite of himself. Something about her eagerness to learn intrigued him. It was most unusual in a woman.

He gestured toward the workers who were bent over their arduous task. Some had removed their shirts, their black skin glistening with sweat.

"Those men," he indicated with a nod, "are cutting the cane at the base of the stalks with machetes. They will trim the unripe joints at the top of the stalk and slash downward, removing the dead foliage. The canc will then be stacked on the mule-drawn carts over there," he said, pointing. "Then it will be taken to the mill, which you'll see later on. Many trips will be made before the day is over. It's important to get the sugarcane to the mill as soon as possible because of the deterioration of the sugar. And that is the second reason that sugarcane is a dangerous crop."

Brooke shifted her horse so that she could better see Travis and hear his explanation. She wanted to keep him talking while he was in good humor. She wasn't sure how long his present mood would last, but she much preferred him this way. "Does it take a couple of years to grow?"

He chuckled. Travis's smile was wide, his teeth strikingly white in his tanned face. "Hardly."

She took a quick breath of utter astonishment. He'd actually smiled, and what a difference it made in his appearance. She found it impossible not to return his disarming smile.

"In Louisiana, we cut the cane before it matures. I actually planted early this season, so I could make sure to harvest before the frost. However, this year it has turned cooler earlier, so it will be close."

Brooke nodded. "I heard that frost isn't good for the crops, but why?"

"If we have a frost it will destroy the sugar content. We can't even store the stalks because the sugar turns bad too quickly. Once we start the process, we must work nonstop until it's complete. You'll see workers out in the fields all night at harvest," Travis explained.

"Something wrong, boss?" A tall, thin, middle-aged man rode over to them. He carried a dangerous-looking whip tied to his saddle, and Brooke wondered if he used it on the workers. She hoped not. The man's white straw hat shadowed his eyes and his shirtsleeves were rolled up past his elbows.

"Nothing is wrong, James," Travis said as he leaned on the pommel. "How is it going?"

"We've sent ten carts to the mill already this morning. Looking like it's going to be a good harvest."

"I'm hoping," Travis agreed, "but it's still too early to tell. I'll be back as soon as I show Mrs. Hammond the mill."

Tired of being ignored, Brooke said, "You could introduce me."

Travis turned to her and lifted an eyebrow. He let out an exasperated breath, then finally said, "Mrs. Hammond, this is James, my overseer." Travis turned to him. "James, this is Mrs. Hammond, my business partner."

Brooke could have sworn that Travis gritted out the last words between his teeth, but she forced herself not to smile. At least he was halfway cooperating. It was a small step forward.

Perhaps the man did have training after all.

She did note the surprised look on the foreman's face, but he masked it quickly. Brooke felt uneasy about the man, but she didn't know why. Could be his dark eyes, she thought. They were too small for his face, and they shifted continuously.

Finally, he doffed his hat. "Ma'am," was all he said, then he turned back to the field to continue his work.

Travis led the way through several fields of cotton

and corn, and Brooke noted the many slaves working the fields. What tremendous pressure Travis carried on his shoulders. No wonder he stayed grumpy, she thought. She would probably feel the same way. However, it was a job he seemed to handle well. Everyone looked to him for answers.

Hopefully, one day they would also look to her for the answers.

The midday sun was now high in the sky, baking the earth. Accustomed to the misty days of England, Brooke basked in the warmth. *How different from home*, she thought as she rode.

A slight wind blew her hair. Her hairpins came lose and they began to slip out one by one. Brooke really didn't care. It felt lovely to be riding in the fresh air and wild country instead of boring Hyde Park where the gentry went just to see how one was dressed. Seeing this beautiful country made London seemed like a long-ago memory. Brooke didn't miss anything about the city.

They paused at one of the cotton fields, which looked more like a field of snow than cotton. "I've never seen cotton growing before," Brooke said. "It's amazing that cloth can be made out of something a plant can produce."

Travis nodded in agreement.

"How old were you when you came to Moss Grove?" she asked.

"Sixteen."

She shook her head. "Such a young age to take on so much responsibility."

"Sometimes one has no choice, Brooke."

"That is one thing you don't have to tell me

about," she said with a sigh. "I've been in that situation more than once."

His single statement tugged at her heart. Brooke sensed there was so much more to Travis than he let anyone see, and before she realized what she was doing, she'd reached across and touched his hand. "Your family must be proud of you."

She wasn't sure what she saw in his eyes, but it was quickly masked, and she realized she'd stepped across the invisible line that Travis had erected. He withdrew, back into his shell.

"Let's head for the mill. I have work to do there," Travis said, his tone much sharper than before. He nudged his horse forward, not bothering to wait for her.

To her annoyance, Brooke found herself blushing. She sighed as she muttered to herself, "So much for being nice." She clicked her tongue, flicked the reins, and Gray Mist took off in the direction that Travis had ridden. How could she penetrate the deliberate blankness in his eyes? And more importantly . . . why did she care?

Brooke wondered if Travis realized that he'd finally called her by her given name.

Could his ice be melting just a little?

"Who in the hell is that?" Jeremy Dubois asked as Travis dismounted and handed the reins over to the groom.

Travis didn't have to look. He knew who Jeremy referred to, but Travis turned anyway to see Brooke galloping in from the field. "My new partner," he drawled, his voice heavy with sarcasm. He felt increasing leery of the woman with each passing moment.

"Your what?" Jeremy, who owned the plantation next to Travis, asked.

"It's a long story." Travis brushed him off, signaling an end to the conversation.

"Hello," Brooke said as she dismounted.

The dark-haired gentleman in front of her gave her a sweeping bow. "It's nice to meet you." He had handsome, well-chiseled features and sinfully dark hair, but it was his dazzling smile that held Brooke's attention. His smile was a refreshing break from Travis's ever-present scowl.

"Mrs. Hammond, may I introduce you to Jeremy Dubois?"

"And your partner, I believe you said." Jeremy grinned, as he took her hand and raised it to his lips. "I must say you have excellent taste, Travis. And my curiosity will kill me if you don't tell me how you found such a lovely creature."

Brooke found Jeremy's attitude refreshing after Travis's rude treatment.

"He didn't find me, Mr. Dubois, I found him," Brooke informed Jeremy, enjoying the look of surprise on his face. "Do you work here, as well?"

"Good Lord, I hope not," Jeremy said with mock alarm. He laughed. "I have my hands full with my own plantation."

"Jeremy is a friend . . . most of the time," Travis drawled. "He owns Slow River, the plantation next to mine."

"Once you're settled in, you must bring Mrs.

Hammond over to call. And bring Mr. Hammond, too," he added.

At least this one had charm and manners, Brooke thought. "There is no Mr. Hammond; I'm a widow," she lied. "Calling me Mrs. Hammond makes me feel so elderly. Please call me Brooke."

"I'd be honored," Jeremy drawled, amusement flickering in his green eyes. "So this means that *you* are Travis's partner and not your husband?"

She nodded.

Jeremy threw his head back and roared with so much laughter that Brooke had to wonder what the previous conversation had been about.

Travis didn't join in Jeremy's amusement. Instead he asked him, "What brings you to Moss Grove, Jeremy? I thought you started your own harvest three days ago."

"I did," Jeremy confirmed once he stopped laughing. "My sugarmaker has come down with the grippe, and I've got to find a replacement for him. As you are aware, without a sugarmaker, the end of the harvest is in jeopardy. I thought maybe Morgan might know someone."

Travis nodded. "I can see your dilemma. Let's go and find out," Travis said.

Both men ignored her completely as they walked toward the building, leaving Brooke on her own. Their manners were deplorable to say the least. She was sure that Travis was sending her a message that she wasn't needed. And the truth was . . . she wasn't needed.

Brooke really didn't understand Mr. Dubois's problem, but both men appeared very concerned about this person who they called the sugarmaker. Nonetheless, she wasn't going to stand outside like a child waiting for her parents to return. She'd never learn anything that way.

She tied Gray Mist under a tree so the horse could munch on the green grass, then she followed them over to the sugarhouse.

The sugarhouse, which was nothing more than a simple shed, seemed to be a beehive of activity. Brooke was surprised at the various apparatuses used for crushing the cane. She paused and watched, knowing she needed a firm understanding of how her plantation operated. She realized that it would take her a long time before she could ever attempt to run something the size of Moss Grove. Another reason that marrying Travis sounded better than it first did.

As soon as she stepped into the open end of the shed, the sweet, pungent air from inside felt like a hot breath in her face. She noticed that everyone working under the shed wore their shirtsleeves rolled up or no shirts at all. And she could understand why. Here she was, dressed in long sleeves and full skirts, and her clothing was already damp and clinging to her.

Over in a corner she saw the piles of stalks that had been brought up from the field. A few of the women were hand-feeding the stalks one at a time into a set of rollers, one on top of the other, designed to crush and force the juice from the cane—at least she assumed so since there was a collecting pot underneath. The rollers were turned by mules who plodded around and around in an endless circle.

As she continued her exploration, Brooke saw three huge boiling pots. The fires beneath each kettle threw off tremendous heat. She didn't know how any of workers stayed in here. Three men, one behind each pot, stirred continuously. They glanced up at her for only a moment, then turned back to the task at hand. She wasn't sure what they were doing, but it was obviously important. It was apparent that she would have to wait until Travis had time to explain the process because nobody seemed to have time to speak to her, much less explain what they were doing.

A big black man in a plaid shirt was dragging a bundle of crushed cane over to the pots. He tossed the cane scraps onto the flames. The fires belched great puffs of black smoke up the chimneys, producing heat so intense the air became hazy.

Brooke felt like she was choking. The air stung her nose and her eyes began to water. Her eyes were watering so badly that she didn't see the sparks shoot out from the fire toward her.

"Watch out!" someone shouted.

Brooke heard the warning but didn't know what or to whom they were shouting at. She turned to see why everyone was waving at her, but she couldn't see anything.

The next thing Brooke knew, someone had clamped an arm around her waist and hauled her out of the sugarhouse.

Once outside, she was set on her feet, and she immediately began coughing. She jerked her handkerchief out of her sleeve to wipe her eyes. It took several gulps of clean air before her coughing subsided and she could see again. What had just happened in there?

Travis brushed at her skirts as he swore. "You little fool," she heard him hiss from behind her.

"What are you doing?" Brooke retorted, jerking at her skirt. "I am not a rug." She felt much like a quilt that someone was trying to beat the dirt out of.

"Trying to keep you from setting your fool self on fire," he angrily informed her. "I don't have time to hold your hand."

"I never ask you to!" she spat and then looked down, gaping at the smoke coming from the hem of her skirt. "Oh, no." She had no idea she'd gotten so close to the fire.

"You must be careful around the boiling pots," Jeremy cautioned. "As you can see, they can be very dangerous."

"I'm so sorry. I didn't know, but it was so smoky in there that I couldn't see anything. I must have gotten too close."

"That's no excuse for your carelessness." Travis was quick to point out. "You could have been burnt to a crisp."

"And no doubt that would have pleased you," Brooke snapped.

Travis gave her a slow grin as he came to within an inch of her face. "It might have been one way to rid myself of you."

Even though she wanted to hit him for his remark, she wanted to kiss him even more. And that made no sense at all. But it just might take that smug look off his face.

"You're not that lucky, Mr. Montgomery," she said with a slight smile. "You'll never be rid of me."

Chapter 6

That's what I'm afraid of, Travis thought to himself as he watched Jeremy help Brooke mount. Travis knew he didn't need to touch the woman—it was too dangerous—and he wasn't too sure he wanted his friend touching her, either.

Brooke didn't so much as look his way before she galloped off . . . not that he cared, he tried to convince himself. He was used to getting what he wanted and ignoring what he couldn't get, but in this case he was finding it difficult to put Mrs. Hammond completely out of his mind. He had a sinking feeling that no matter how hard he tried, he'd never be completely rid of Brooke, just as she had warned him.

Jeremy rejoined him. "You have some partner there, I'd say," he said, glancing over his shoulder at the departing woman. He nodded his approval, and that irked Travis further. "What are you going to do with her?"

"Scare her away."

Jeremy chuckled. "I hate to tell you this, but she

doesn't look like the type that scares. In fact, I'd say she looked pretty determined just now when she rode off." He folded his arms across his chest. "So, how did the intriguing lady come to be your partner? I can't fathom you finding her on your own, nor can I believe you actually want a business partner."

"I assure you," Travis took a deep breath, "I have little trouble finding a woman when I want one," he muttered, his male pride wounded.

A slow grin spread across Jeremy's features. "The problem is you don't want one," he said. "And for a man who doesn't want a woman at all, you now have two."

"My father chose Brooke," Travis answered tersely between clenched teeth. "Why in the hell he did such a foolish thing, I cannot imagine. My father might have been many things, but a fool wasn't one of them." Sarcasm lay heavy on his tongue. "I guess it was his going away present."

"Well, your mother chose Hesione," Jeremy pointed out. "Your parents must have figured it was time you got married and each had their own idea of who it should be. I should know." He laughed. "My parents have done the same thing with me in the past. I've just been lucky and avoided taking the plunge yet. However, I do believe your father's choice is far superior to your mother's, and a hell of a lot better than my mother's last choice," he said with a wry chuckle.

Travis furrowed his brow and answered sardonically, "That is my fiancée you are insulting."

Jeremy paid no heed to Travis's warning. It was no secret that Travis didn't have feelings for Hesione.

"And if you were honest, you'd agree with me. Do you love her?"

"Who?"

"Hesione, of course," Jeremy said with a smile.

A number of emotions flickered across Travis's face as he tried to formulate an answer, "What I feel for Hesione has nothing to do with the matter. She's agreeable, so she will suit. Hesione will make a perfect hostess for Moss Grove because she comes from one of the finest families in New Orleans."

"Perhaps once you marry her it will put you back in good standing with your grandfather?"

"My grandfather . . ." Travis actually winced at the truth, though he tried to hide it. Was there any pleasing his cruel grandfather? Hadn't Travis heard more than once how his birth had ruined his mother? "I don't give a damn what the old bastard thinks. It will please Mother and that's enough."

"And that's a reason to get married? What if Hesione is cold? Who will warm your bed? From my observations, I believe the woman has ice in her veins."

"I appreciate your concern, Jeremy, but a mistress will always supply what a wife cannot. And I care for Hesione. She was the best choice."

"Should I remind you that your last mistress has left New Orleans?" Jeremy leveled his gaze coolly on Travis. "Perhaps you can talk your new partner into filling the role."

It was Travis's turn to chuckle, knowing full and well that would never happen. "I consider that an exceedingly slim possibility. As you just said, she is different from the other women I've known. The only thing I want from Mrs. Hammond is for her to sign her portion of the plantation over to me, then she can be on her way."

"Have you asked?"

"Yes."

"And?"

Travis shrugged. "She told me that I would never be rid of her."

Jeremy couldn't resist a wry grin as he slapped Travis on the shoulder. "I'm sorry, but I can't feel unhappy for you, my friend. The last thing I'd want to do is get rid of her. She is one of the most stunning women I've ever seen." A wicked smile touched his lips. "My blood raced from the moment she spoke. Now there's a woman to die for. Perhaps I should try for her."

Travis scowled. "You need to get control of yourself," he warned. "The woman is lethal."

Jeremy could see how tight Travis's jaw had gotten. "You mean you don't want to share?"

"I've nothing to share," Travis snapped. "And I'm damn tired of this conversation. Don't you have a plantation to run?"

Instead of being insulted, Jeremy grinned. "My, my. You certainly are getting angry over the woman you claim not to care about."

"I've been angry since she arrived."

Jeremy saw right away that Mrs. Hammond had gotten under Travis's skin, something no other woman had ever been able to do. "Then maybe you should ask yourself why," Jeremy pressed as he mounted his horse, "because I think that Brooke makes you feel something you haven't experienced before." He turned his horse to the side. "And do send over a sugarmaker if you can spare one," he said, looking back over his shoulder.

"Get the hell out of here before I change my mind about helping you at all," Travis gritted out. He smacked Jeremy's horse on the rump, causing him to bolt. "I'll send Ben over tomorrow."

Travis needed to do something to work off his aggravation. Jeremy had done a good job of needling, and it had done nothing to ease his simmering anger. Turning, Travis gazed at the mill. Maybe heat from the canehouse could make him sweat the woman out of his system . . . he could always hope.

When Brooke returned to the main house, Mammy greeted her with the news that Prosper, the cook, had returned and would like Brooke's input on the upcoming party.

Brooke forgot her irritation with Travis. Finally, she was going to meet the famous cook whose cooking she'd yet to taste. "Lead the way," she said with a sweep of her hand.

Mammy wrinkled her nose. "What's dat smell? Smells like smoke."

"I almost forgot. I singed my riding habit," Brooke said, pulling up her skirt for Mammy to see the charred material. "Perhaps I should freshen up. I will be back in half an hour."

After Brooke had changed, she and Mammy went to the kitchen, located at the very back of the house. The moment Brooke entered the hot kitchen, she saw the cook acting like a petty dictator, giving instructions to one of his kitchen staff who was stirring a big, black pot hanging over the fireplace.

Prosper was tall and thin, his skin was a little darker than Mammy's, and gray streaked his hair in the back. He wore a white apron tied over his black and white clothes. After a few moments, he turned and Brooke saw that he had a kind face. The hair was completely white ringing his head and his eyes were a rich brown . . . eyes that seemed to be studying her as much as she was him. He held a wooden spoon in his right hand, whether it was used for stirring or for smacking hands was yet to be determined.

"Mademoiselle," Prosper said with a slight French accent. "I am Prosper Ernest Fournier at your service," he said with a sweeping bow. His stern expression was all business as he added, "I understand that you, Mademoiselle, are now in charge of the household staff."

Shocked, Brooke realized that Prosper was the first to acknowledge her place at Moss Grove. "I am now part owner of Moss Grove along with Mr. Montgomery," Brooke said. "It is a pleasure to finally meet you."

Prosper nodded. "I am the cook extraordinaire," he said, waving his spoon. "I have been trained in France by the finest chefs, and have cooked for the Montgomerys for the last ten years."

Brooke smiled. He sounded as if he were trying to impress her.

"My requests are simple—the kitchen is mine to rule, and the dinner hour of seven is strictly enforced."

Brooke's first response was to answer, "Yes, sir." But, she reminded herself, wasn't he supposed to be asking what she would like for him to do? Who was working for whom here? She wondered. "Thank you so much, Prosper, for explaining the *rules.* I hope you cook as well as you issue instructions. If so, every meal will be perfection, I'm sure." Brooke saw a smile sneak across Mammy's face before she could hide it.

Prosper stiffened, his eyes widened, and his face might have turned red, but Brooke couldn't tell.

"You will see, Mademoiselle, I am an *excellent* chef. I would like final approval on the menu for the gala this Friday." He yanked a slip of paper from his pocket and handed it to her.

Brooke scanned the list. Everything appeared in order and the dishes he had selected sounded heavenly. "You have excellent taste, Mr. Prosper." She looked toward Mammy. "Have you seen the list?"

"Oui."

Turning back to Prosper, Brooke said, "If Mammy approves, then it is fine by me. Thank you for your help." She returned the menu to Prosper.

"As you wish, mademoiselle," he said with a stiff nod. Then he turned and went back to the stove. Brooke knew when she'd been dismissed, so she left the man to his kitchen.

No wonder Travis liked the man. They both had the same sour dispositions.

Once in the hallway, Brooke turned to Mammy and asked, "Is he always so pleasant?"

Mammy gave her a sideways glance. "Well now—

dat's a question." She chuckled. "You see, Prosper don't want nobody messin' in his kitchen."

"Oh, he made that perfectly clear," Brooke said with a smile.

"He's always been uppity, not associatin' wit de others," Mammy said, stopping once they were in the foyer. "It's not his fault, yes. Sometimes folks are not as dey seem. Prosper worked under a great chef in Paris. Dat is w'ere His Grace first sampled Prosper's cookin', yes. Montgomery persuaded Prosper t' come and work fo' him. So he worked fo' His Grace in England fo' a year, yes, until Montgomery purchased Moss Grove and broug't Prosper wit' him."

"I wonder why Jackson didn't take Prosper back to England?"

"Mebbe 'cause the Duchess didn't get alon' none wit' Prosper. An' Prosper he liked it in Nawlins." Mammy shrugged, then added. "I always t'ought His Grace would make Moss Grove his home, yes. He loved dis place," she finished with a sigh as she looked off. It was as if Mammy were talking to herself and forgetting that Brooke stood near. "Somet'in' went wron'. Shouldn't have been messin' with Miz Margaret—" Mammy stopped short.

Brooke reached out and touched Mammy's arm. "I understand. I think you were fond of Montgomery, and so was I."

She nodded. "He was always good t' me. Den he sent me his fine son, t' be sure."

"You mean he has another son?"

Both women looked at each other, then burst out laughing.

That's how Travis found them when he strolled in through the front entrance.

"Have I missed something?" he asked.

"Not really," Brooke replied. "Just something between the two of us." She gestured between herself and Mammy, then turned abruptly and left him in the foyer, wearing that peculiar expression of his. She might still have work to do on Travis, but Brooke felt that she and Mammy had reached a new understanding, and that cheered her. Finally, Brooke felt that Moss Grove was truly her home.

Travis remained in the foyer, wondering what the two women had been talking about before he walked in on them. It bothered him that Brooke seemed much too comfortable in *his house.*

Rubbing the back of his neck, Travis leaned on the newel post as he watched Brooke climb the stairs. Her long blond hair, having escaped most of its pins, swayed across her slender back, and that is where his gaze should have stopped, but it didn't.

She'd changed out of her sooty clothes and wore a green day dress without her crinolines. His eyes shifted to her perfectly rounded derriere. He found himself extremely conscious of her sensual appeal. He wanted to reach out and touch her, and that was one thing he knew he must not do. His feelings for her had nothing to do with reason.

Brooke's luscious body was made for love and there was something provocative about her that made his loins tighten at the mere thought of entering her soft flesh, and feeling her warmth surround him.

Travis jerked straight up as if he'd been slugged

in the stomach. And to tell the truth, he wouldn't care if somebody beat the shit out of him right now. Evidently, he needed some sense knocked into his thick head, something to erase the thought of Brooke and make him forget how much he wanted her.

The woman was poisoning his mind.

"Where you at?" Mammy said from behind him.

Travis swung around, feeling much like a child being caught doing something he shouldn't. "What makes you ask a question like that?"

"Well, now," Mammy said, tilting her head to the side and placing her hands on her hips. "I've already been t' de dinin' room and back here t' find you in exactly de same spot starin' up those stairs. Did you forget t' tell Miz Brooke somet'in'?"

"Of course not," Travis responded, his embarrassment quickly turning to annoyance. "I'm tired and my mind was wandering."

Mammy's eyebrow rose as she said, "Uh huh." And then she left him.

Travis started up the stairs, thinking Mammy only thought she knew more about him than she really did. "What I need is a good stiff drink and a hot bath." Yes, that was exactly what he needed to get his head straightened out, he decided. On second thought, what he really needed was a woman. But that wasn't going to happen anytime soon. He was too damn busy with the plantation.

Perhaps, once he was married to Hesione, he'd be able to push Brooke from his mind completely. After a year, Brooke would be more than willing to sell out to him, and then he'd never have to see her again.

But what would she do? Did Brooke have family? Would she have some place to go? From the few things she'd said, he didn't think so. Then an even more terrifying realization washed over him. What if she married someone on a nearby plantation, and he would constantly see her at parties? Travis reached for the doorknob of his room, but his thoughts stopped him.

No. She couldn't marry and stay around here—near him.

Entirely caught up in his own emotion, he shoved open the door.

"Do you need assistance with your bath, sir?" his valet Lucien asked.

"What I need is Scotch, make it a double. And then you may draw my bath. I need a long, hot soak."

Hopefully he would drive the golden-haired witch from his thoughts.

When Brooke came down to dinner later that night, she was surprised to find Travis waiting for her. Normally he wouldn't even be present, and she would dine alone with Mr. Jeffries. Now she was glad that she'd dressed in her white lace dress with the small white cap sleeves. The better to seduce him with, she thought.

Brooke noticed that Travis's hair was still damp, from a bath, she presumed. Had he come in from the fields just to dine with her? She wanted to laugh at that silly thought. Surely she'd been out in the sun too long and was beginning to imagine things.

Travis hadn't done anything for her since she'd been here.

Brooke nodded in greeting. "I'm surprised to see you at dinner."

Travis's smile was courteous as he pulled a chair out for her. The chair was at his end of the table instead of the opposite end. "Prosper has returned," Travis told her. "Only a fool would miss one of his meals."

So much for thinking that he'd wanted to have dinner with her, Brooke thought sourly. She should have known he wasn't going out of his way for her. Any woman with common sense knew men always thought of their stomachs first.

A commotion sounded in the foyer, drawing both their attentions. Feminine voices grew louder as they approached the dining room. A moment later, a lady entered the dining room.

"I'm home."

Chapter 7

Brooke jumped, startled at the sudden intrusion. She had thought she would have more time before the other woman returned. Now, Brooke held her breath as the intruder entered the room and ran straight to Travis, wrapping her arms tightly around his neck.

"Have you missed me?" she asked, then kissed him on the cheek.

"Not a bit," Travis answered as he gave the girl a warm hug in return.

Slowly, Brooke let out the breath she'd been holding. The young woman swung toward her, and Brooke realized that the newcomer was a child and not a woman.

"I see we have company," the child said.

"You might say that," Travis said with his usual smirk. "If you'll have a seat, I will introduce you."

The servants had already appeared and were setting a place for the girl across from Brooke. When they finished, the young lady took her seat with a cheerful flounce.

"Brooke Hammond, may I introduce my second cousin, Eliza Bordelon," Travis said with a wave of his hand. "She is a headstrong twelve-year-old who needs a firm hand."

Brooke smiled. "And that is why she was sent to you?"

Travis's eyebrows rose slightly. "I guess you could say that. Eliza has lived with us for the last year, but she has been visiting her parents for the past month. Now I see the brat has returned."

"I love you, too, cousin," she said, cutting her eyes at him with a frown. "I'll have you know I am almost thirteen," she stated firmly.

"You're still a child," Travis quickly pointed out, "and as such you should be seen and not heard."

Eliza ignored him and turned her attention to Brooke. "You're very pretty. I know your name, but I still don't know who you are or why you're here."

The child was so engaging that Brooke couldn't help wondering if she really was a member of this family. Eliza was also pretty, in a childish way, with a light dusting of freckles running across the bridge of her pert nose. Her hair was a lustrous shade of brown and pulled up on both sides in ringlet curls. Eliza's inquisitive eyes were also a lovely shade of light brown. She studied Brooke with frank curiosity from across the table.

"This is Brooke Hammond, my new business partner," Travis said simply. "I believe her room is located next to yours."

"So she's staying with us?" Eliza asked.

Travis nodded.

"Oh, what fun," Eliza said clapping her hands

delightedly. "I didn't know that Travis had a partner," Eliza said. She had been addressing Brooke, but Travis answered.

"Neither did I," Travis quipped, but Eliza appeared more interested in the new lady than in paying him any attention.

Brooke smiled at the child. "I hope you don't mind company at your end of the hall."

"Of course not. I just love your English accent. Are you really from England?"

"Yes, I am," Brooke said, nodding. "It was a very long trip over."

Eliza linked her fingers together, then perched her chin on top of them. "I bet you know all the latest fashions. Did you have a coming-out party and everything? I can't wait until I get to attend all the balls and parties. I'll dance the night away." She sighed and for a moment was lost in her own world. "You'll have to tell me all about the famous London parties you've attended."

The child was as fresh as a whirlwind and Brooke found herself drawn to the bundle of energy. "Well, I didn't have a coming-out party, but I have been to many balls, so perhaps I can entertain you with stories."

"Oh that would be lovely."

Travis listened to his cousin chattering to Brooke, and he realized he didn't know much about Brooke's life in England. Then he quickly reminded himself that he really didn't care. She was here now, and she was in his way. "My goodness, Eliza, you are a chatterbox tonight. Were you not allowed to talk on your trip back home?"

"Of course," she said with a frown. "But my brothers and sisters are *so* boring." She rolled her eyes.

"Well, my dear, I don't think anyone will ever say that about you." Travis rang the small bell beside his plate. "How about if we start dinner? You must be famished after your long trip."

On cue, the servants came through the door with platters laden with food and a large soup tureen.

"It must be seven o'clock," Brooke said with a laugh.

"Precisely," Travis confirmed.

As he chuckled, the lines around of his face soften. He appeared almost boyish, she thought. A current of excitement raced along her spine ending in the pit of her belly. Wait a minute, she reminded herself. She wasn't supposed to be the one lusting. Travis was. Glancing at him from beneath her lashes, Brooke found he was more interested in the soup than her.

Evidently she had lost her touch for enticing men.

Travis glanced up. "Are you not going to eat?"

She nodded, then reached for her soup spoon, stirring the mixture to see what ingredients this dish consisted of. It smelled wonderful. It seemed to be a thick soup with okra and potatoes and some kind of white meat. She noticed Travis didn't have to tell Eliza to eat. She'd already dug into the steaming concoction with great gusto.

The first taste of the aromatic soup absolutely enchanted Brooke's mouth. "This is wonderful!"

"They don't have gumbo in England?" Eliza asked, seeming surprised.

"Afraid not. The flavor is very, very different from the food I'm used to. What is it?"

Travis paused, his spoon in midair, before taking another taste and smiling. "It's crab gumbo. I'm glad that you are enjoying it."

Brooke blew on her spoon before placing the next spoonful into her mouth. Travis and Eliza were talking, so Brooke could observe the man from beneath her lashes. He seemed more relaxed tonight. Maybe having the child in the house was a good thing. She certainly seemed to do Travis some good.

Each spoonful of broth seemed to be better than the last. "I can taste the crab and many spices, some of which I do not recognize," Brooke commented.

"I must admit it's one of my favorite dishes," Travis said as he reached for the long loaf of freshly baked French bread. He offered it to the ladies before he took a slice off the end.

As each course was brought in, Brooke discovered that Prosper wasn't boasting about his culinary abilities. He had merely stated the truth. He was a superb cook.

Finally, the last course was brought in. Dessert, a cake with butter-cream frosting that was at least four layers high, was placed before them. Just looking made Brooke's mouth water. And tasting the confection only confirmed her first impression.

When Brooke had finished the last bite, she sighed. "I think that is possibly the most delicious meal that I've ever eaten."

"Prosper is the very best," Travis admitted. "He is the one good thing my father left to me."

"And I was the second," Brooke quipped.

Travis didn't bother to comment.

"I heard about your father," Eliza said. "I'm so sorry. Are you sad?" she asked, assuming Travis possessed an affection for his father that Brooke knew he didn't.

"Thanks, brat. I'm fine," he said, dismissing her question. "Now, tell me, how did you find your family when you visited?"

Brooke noted how quickly he changed the topic of his late father. He was obviously very uncomfortable with the subject when it came up.

Eliza shrugged. "The same."

"Do you have brothers and sisters?" Brooke asked.

"Do I?" Eliza giggled. "I have eight brothers and sisters."

"Really?" Brooke was surprised at such a large family. "I'll wager you can't name all of them."

"I bet I can," Eliza asserted. Then she began to count them off by name. "There is Constance, Marguerite, Felicite, Maria, Nicholas, Jean, Hortense, and Gertrude. So you see, there isn't much room left for me, and that's why I asked to come and stay with Cousin Travis and Aunt Margaret."

"I can't imagine having so many in a family," Brooke commented.

Eliza dabbed at her mouth with the linen napkin. "You don't have any brothers and sisters?"

Brooke shook her head. "None at all," she said, feeling a twinge of regret. "Just myself." Would her life have been different if she'd had a family to care for her? It was something she'd never find out.

"That sounds heavenly to me," Eliza said with a sigh. "I think I was meant to be an only child. I must have ended up in the wrong family." She laughed merrily.

Travis realized his cousin's conversation was providing him with a wealth of information about his uninvited guest. That was why he hadn't calmed her down with a reminder that all her questions were impertinent. Even twelve-year-olds were expected to act like ladies . . . not hoydens.

"May I be excused?" Eliza asked, placing her napkin across her dinner plate and breaking into Travis's musings.

Travis didn't realize that he had been staring at Brooke until Eliza reached across the table and touched his arm. "Cousin Travis?"

His gazed switched to the child, who had her chin propped upon her hand, apparently waiting for him to respond to something. "What?"

"I asked," she said, pausing to give the impression that he'd kept her waiting, "May I be excused? It's been a long day and I'm very sleepy."

Travis nodded his assent.

Eliza stood, then kissed Travis on the cheek. "Good night, Mrs. Hammond," she said, then she turned and left Brooke and Travis alone.

"Sometimes I forget how much noise she can make," Travis commented, more to himself than to Brooke.

"I think she is adorable," Brooke told him. "And definitely a breath of fresh air around here."

Travis's lips twisted into a cynical smile. "I believe you just insulted me."

Brooke gave him a sweet smile. "Only if you consider the truth an insult. You have to admit that the mood of this house is far too serious."

"You always have the option of leaving," he threw back at her.

Brooke really didn't want to get into a sparring match with Travis tonight. She'd had a long day as well, so she ignored his barb and asked, "Will you call Prosper in?"

For a change, Travis did as she requested. When Prosper came through the door, he looked at Travis for instructions, "Sir?"

Travis swung his hand toward Brooke. "I believe the lady would like to speak with you."

Prosper glanced at her and executed a curt, but shallow bow. "Mademoiselle."

"I just wanted to tell you that was possibly the best meal I have ever had the pleasure to eat," she said, placing her right hand on her heart. "And from this day forth, you have my undying devotion, Prosper. You must be the greatest chef alive."

"Thank you," he said with a confident smile and a slight nod. "I believe there may be one, possibly two, better than I."

Brooke laughed. "They would have to prove it to me."

Prosper actually chuckled this time. He turned to Travis. "Anything else, sir?"

"That will be all," Travis said with a shake of his head. After the chef had gone, he added, "I do believe you've won him over."

Brooke stood. Then she moved around the table to where Travis was sitting. "But not the master of the house?"

He drew back and peered at her. "Do you want to win me over?"

Brooke thought for a long moment. "I would like for us to be"—she paused—"friends." She reached out to touch his arm. The instant she did, a cracking shock ran up her arm and she snatched her hand back. She noted Travis's puzzled look and knew he'd felt the same thing. In the same instant, she felt herself losing ground. She could sense he was drawing away from her, putting up that shield that he used so well. And his next words confirmed exactly that.

"I'm afraid it's too soon, Brooke," he said with what she could hope was a note of regret. "You'll have to give it time."

Brooke didn't respond. Was he regretting that it would take time, or that he was beginning to want to know her? Or worse still, was he wishing she were completely out of his life? With something new to consider, Brooke turned and left the room, all the time thinking, *but I don't have the time. Don't you understand?*

Later that night, a thunderstorm rolled in off the Gulf, bringing with it blustery winds, torrential rain, and brilliant flashes of light. A bolt of lightning struck somewhere close by.

The crash was so loud it brought Brooke straight up in bed. She clutched the covers in front of her as if they would protect her from her childhood fears. Her heart pounded in her chest. Wildly, her gaze darted around the darkened room as she tried to calm her breathing.

"Don't be foolish," she whispered to herself. "It's only a storm."

It took several moments before she was able to make herself stop gasping for air. She always told herself the same thing. It never did any good.

How foolish to be afraid of storms when they were nothing more than wind and rain. But every time a storm came upon her, she was transported back to her childhood, and many unpleasant memories.

Brooke's mother had brought her to the boarding school during a thunderstorm, leaving her there without so much as a hug. After that, Brooke was pretty much on her own. She could remember huddling in bed many nights, with her special blanket wrapped around her, praying the storm would go away. From that time on, storms always seemed to bring trouble in her life.

Of course, the other girls were not afraid and they'd teased her about being so silly. Everyone but Jocelyn, who'd taken up for Brooke. But as much as she tried to convince herself that there was nothing to fear, Brooke had never gotten over them.

Even now, she wondered what terrible thing would happen to her next, though she knew it was silly to think such nonsense. The only thing that came to mind was the fiancée could return early. Of course, she'd already had that scare once tonight. Brooke looked upward. "Oh, please don't let that happen. Give me a chance."

She tossed back the covers and went to the hearth. With trembling fingers, she took one of the wood splinters and placed one end to the hot coals. As soon as it caught fire, she took another splinter and lit the candle on the bedside table. The flame sputtered but finally sprang to life. Next, she removed the globe from the kerosene lamp and lit the wick. The soft glow made her feel a little better. Then the next rumble of thunder rolled in.

She knew she had to do something to distract her mind from the storm. Perhaps she should fetch a book from the library. There had been times when she'd been able to escape into another time and place when she had a good story to read. It might just do the trick this time, she thought.

Brooke grabbed her pink satin wrapper and slipped it on, tying it snugly at her waist. No one could possibly be up this time of night, so she wasn't worried about her appearance. She shoved her long wavy hair over her shoulders, picked up the pewter candleholder, and stepped out into the hallway.

Carefully, she slipped down the stairs, her bare feet not making a sound. Seeing that no one was up, she continued down the hallway to the library where she pushed open the door just as another lightning bolt struck a tree nearby. She jerked, causing hot wax to splatter on her finger, and the flame sputtered out.

"Damn," she swore, then quickly placed her sore finger in her mouth, feeling the coating of wax that clung to her finger.

She hadn't taken more than two more steps into the dark room when someone said, "Such language from a lady. I see you couldn't sleep either."

Brooke gasped, startled. Between the storm and having Travis to contend with, she was turning into a bag of nerves. "I—I didn't realize you'd still be up.

And I definitely didn't expect to find you standing here in the dark."

"It's hard to sleep when one realizes that this bloody storm has brought the cane harvest to a halt." Travis turned back to the window where he'd been leaning against the sill.

She could see his hard physique in the window now that her eyes had adjusted to the darkness. "Come and see how the wind and rain is ruining our harvest," he said.

"I—I—"

He glanced back at her. "You're not afraid, are you?"

Hell, yes, she wanted to cry, but she'd never let him see her weakness. As she stepped closer, she could smell the light scent of cherry from his pipe. "I just came down for a book," she said. "I don't want to bother you."

"Now there's a first," he said, his tongue heavy with sarcasm. "It's your crop, too."

When she reached him she could feel the breeze from the open window brush her face with a fine mist of water. It felt good on her flushed skin.

Evidently, Travis had a different opinion of the storm than she did. However, the window was protected by the veranda, she noticed as she peered out the window, and no rain came inside. She felt a little safer as she watched the steady downpour. "Are all your storms like this?"

"Sometimes," Travis said, leaning against the window frame. He placed his pipe on the ledge and picked up a glass. She could detect the brandy on his breath before she noticed his glass. She won-dered how long he'd been drinking.

Travis saw the direction of her gaze and held the brandy snifter up, offering it to her. "It will warm you."

To his surprise, Brooke took it from him and sipped the reddish-brown liquid. She handed the snifter back to him and murmured her thanks.

A flash of lightning provided enough light so he could see a glistening drop of brandy lingering on her bottom lip. Before he could reach out and remove it, Brooke flicked out her tongue and stole the temptation from him.

Outwardly, he remained expressionless.

Inwardly, his blood raced.

Travis hadn't believed his eyes when he'd first turned and found her standing in his study wearing nothing more than a wrapper. A pink silk wrapper that was cut low in front provided him a good glimpse of creamy skin. The candlelight made her flesh appear as white as alabaster, as if she were a perfect statue instead of a thorn in his side.

Instead of squealing and tuning away from him like a virgin, she hadn't seemed the least bit embar-rassed about her lack of clothing. Of course, Brooke was a widow, so she would know a man's touch. But she should have some sense of modesty.

The question plaguing his mind was whether she like a man's touch. Or did she lie there like a statue in bed and simply endure? Had she loved her husband?

Travis's jaw tightened at the thought. And of course, it irritated him that he'd care. He needed to get his mind on something other than the lus-cious body before him. He felt a prickle of uneasiness inside him, instead of the numb feeling he wanted so much to achieve.

"Did the brandy help?" he asked, detecting a strange tone in his voice. He hoped Brooke did not notice.

"Yes," she said, looking out the window instead of at him. She was too damn close, Travis thought. He could smell her freshly washed skin. Then she added, "It warmed me."

It sure wasn't the brandy that was warming him, Travis thought ruefully. He was on fire with desire that needed to be extinguished. "Would you care for more? I have several bottles."

She laughed softly before looking at him. "That would be one way to get through the storm," she quipped and took another sip of brandy. "I've never thought of drinking as a solution." Travis liked the sound of her silky, smooth voice, even through he detected that she was a little nervous.

Lightning struck somewhere close to the veranda. Brooke jumped back, bumping into him. She gasped at the contact. "I'm so sorry," she said and tried to move away.

Travis caught her and felt her tremble against him. He placed the brandy snifter on the window ledge and pulled her to him, wrapping his arms tightly around her. "You are shaking. You're afraid, aren't you?" he asked gently.

Brooke nodded as she pressed her face against his chest. "Go ahead and tell me I'm a coward. And if a storm frightens me, how do I expect to run a plantation."

"The storm can't hurt you in here," he murmured

into her fragrant hair as he tried to reassure her. "I like storms."

"You would," Brooke said with a half-laugh, and he smiled.

He hadn't noticed until now that Brooke was the perfect height, fitting nicely into his arms. He also hadn't noticed how delicate she was until he had her soft body pressed against him.

Thunder rumbled. She clutched him tighter. Somehow they were no longer enemies. They had become simply two people in need of comfort. And he had to admit she brought out a streak of tenderness and protectiveness within him that he'd never known existed.

"Shh," he whispered.

After several moments she murmured, "I'm such a coward."

Travis lifted her chin. "I don't think so. Tell me why you are afraid."

"I don't want to bother you," she said, her face resting against his chest."

"I wouldn't have asked if I considered it a bother."

"I'm not really sur—" Brooke paused as the thunder rumbled angrily through the sky. "Sure," she finished. "But I think it started when I was young. My mother sent me to boarding school when I was five. She said it was the best thing for me. But I didn't want to go. I was afraid and wanted to stay with her, but she wouldn't listen."

"What about your father?"

"Remember I told you that we are a lot alike," she reminded him of their conversation at the stables. "The difference being that you got to meet your father, I never did. He paid for my school and clothing, and I suppose I should be grateful for that." She laughed, a bitter chuckle.

Travis tightened his arms. A gust of wind whipped around them, bringing a sprinkling mist of rain, and for a moment there was silence. He felt as though he'd been slugged in the stomach. God help him, he knew exactly how she felt. "I'm sorry I interrupted," he said in a whisper. "Finish your story about the storm."

"Are you sure you want to hear this?"

He had his cheek resting on top of her head and he brushed his lips against her hair. "Yes," he said simply.

"The first day she left me it was raining. I think I forgot to say that earlier. Funny, nothing important ever seems to happen when the sun is shining. Then later, when I was twelve, my mother returned to see how I was faring in school. Perhaps she was curious. I'm not sure. But she did tell me things about herself, and when I asked if I could go with her, she said no. At least she seemed sad that she couldn't take me. I do remember sadness in her face when she refused. It was stormy that day, too. She asked if I'd walk with her to the door, and I did. When we opened the heavy oak doors, a gust of wind blew in and got us both wet. She laughed, and I remember what a pretty sound it was.

"I stood in the doorway, watching her walk away, the wind whipping her cloak to the side. A bolt of lightning struck in the distance, causing me to jump back and shut my eyes just like I always did when we were having a storm.

"When I opened my eyes again, she was gone."

"You were young," Travis pointed out. "I can see how you would have been frightened, but surely you got to go home on holiday visits to see your mother."

"No. I never returned home again. All my holidays were spent at Spencer Girls School, and I only saw my mother but one other time."

"When was that?"

"I had just turned sixteen, and she came to school to visit. She said she wanted to see me, and see how I had turned out. Then she told me about my father. It seemed the lord duke had a wife." Brooke drew in a deep, shuddering breath. "I can see it all as if it were yesterday," she said in a small voice.

Travis said nothing because he didn't want to interrupt, but he felt her anguish.

"My mother stood up to leave, but before she did she reached over to kiss me on the cheek. I drew back. After all that time, the woman was a stranger to me. I felt nothing for her."

"She said she understood, and then she reached for her cloak and fastened the frog under her throat. Believe it or not, it was yet another stormy day.

"I walked with Mother to the front door and opened it for her. She tugged the hood of her cloak over her hair. Just before she stepped outside into the rain, she reached into her purse and handed me a slip of paper, and told me if I ever needed help, this woman would help me.

"I thanked her and watched her walk out into the rain, and somehow I knew she was walking out of my life. The thunder rumbled and I trembled just like I always had. But I was determined to not move this time.

"Out of nowhere a bolt of lightning stuck the oak tree next to the walkway. It exploded. I screamed to warn her. But it was too late. The tree fell, crushing my mother beneath its weight," Brooke said, her voice so soft that Travis strained to hear what she was saying.

"I ran to her," Brooke said in a dead-sounding voice. "I was too late, though. All I could do was hold her head in my lap until somebody came to drag me out of the storm. Before I left I bent down and kissed her on the cheek."

Travis didn't know what to say. Most women would have been in tears, but Brooke hadn't made the first whimper. What kind of woman was she—not the pampered lady he'd first thought her to be.

Gently, he lifted Brooke's chin. Her eyes sparkled with unshed tears as he gazed into them.

Travis told himself to walk away.

He told himself to leave her.

But found he wasn't too good at listening to his own advice. What was it about Brooke that made him burn . . . made him want to touch her . . . made him want to taste her? He could usually get any woman out of his system, but this one was different. Maybe if he kissed her, it would frighten her enough to leave and also satisfy his curiosity.

Unable to resist her poignant sweetness any longer, Travis lowered his mouth to Brooke's. Her eyelids fluttered shut, and her arms wound inside his jacket and around his back. She yielded with a sigh of surrender as he moved his mouth over hers and devoured its softness. God, she was sweet.

Vaguely, he could hear the distant thunder and the rain splattering as it hit the railing of the veranda, but his thoughts were more on the storm that brewed within him than the one outside.

Brooke was caught off balance. She usually knew when a man was going to kiss her and from there everything would be planned. But for just a moment, before Travis kissed her, his blue eyes had been so warm and understanding as his gaze drifted down to her lips. The feeling stunned her, sweeping all logical thoughts completely from her mind.

His kiss was tender, more so than she could have imagined coming from a powerful man such as Travis. He was so gentle with her that she wanted to cry. Brooke had never felt so out of control in her life as a jolt of wild desire shot through her body.

Somewhere in the back of her mind she felt like a virgin, as if she'd never made love before. He parted her lips, and she moaned with pleasure. She touched her tongue to his and a delicious shiver slid down her spine.

Travis jerked back for a just a moment. "Damnation," he swore. Then he crushed her to him again, taking her mouth with urgent hunger. He brushed his hand down the length of her back until it came to rest on her hips.

Brooke had him where she wanted him, and he had definitely made her want him as well. She wasn't used to that.

But somehow over the past two years she seemed to

have forgotten everything she knew about handling men. Or maybe she'd lost the desire to seduce a man.

Maybe she wanted more.

Travis had, in the short time she'd been here, managed to turn her head to mush.

Her body was molded to his and she could feel how much he wanted her. All she had to do was make a move . . . to encourage him . . . but she couldn't. She couldn't!

She shifted, and Travis's mouth slipped lower. He placed kisses along the curve of her neck, delectable kisses that were driving her wild. The reasonable side of her head told Brooke to reach out and take what she needed, but some little voice, one she'd never heard before, kept saying "I want more." She pushed Travis away, surprising herself as much as she did him.

The change in his face was immediate and he quickly regained control of his body.

Travis had never held anyone like this woman. She fit him much too well. His chest tightened and ached as his senses returned to him. At least her senses had returned first. "This was a mistake," Travis rasped out. "I'm sorry, but I'm marrying someone else."

Brooke stared at Travis, knowing she'd lost her mind. She had had him right where she wanted him, yet she had stopped, and she had no idea why. There was nothing left to do or say, so she left him.

Damn her conscious for interfering.

She didn't remember her steps as she walked out of the room. The only thing she could hear screaming in her head was *Why*.

Brooke could only hope to God her sanity returned soon.

Chapter 8

What in the hell was the matter with her?

That one question had been raging through Brooke's mind over and over again. Last night she'd forgotten everything she'd ever learned about seduction. She knew how to turn off her emotions—she'd taught herself to feel nothing years ago, and it had worked perfectly all this time. It was the only way she had survived.

After dismissing Millie Anne, Brooke wandered over to the window although she had no intention of looking out. She needed a few minutes to herself. Glancing out the window, she could see some of the servants picking up the debris from last night's storm. The wind might have ceased, but the storm inside Brooke still raged with all its fury.

She closed her eyes and drew in a deep, wistful breath, feeling the magical kisses she'd shared with Travis last night. She could still taste them.

Brooke had kissed many men before, but they'd been sloppy, wet kisses or mere pecks. Travis made her feel things she'd never felt before. She'd never imagined it possible to feel such deep desires, not only for lust but for some unknown emotion she couldn't put a name to.

That was the problem.

She'd lost control of the situation. And now she didn't know what to do.

Brooke closed her eyes again and shook her head. How could she be so stupid? The first lesson she'd learned years ago was never to let any man get too close. Never let them know what you are thinking, and always keep then at arm's length. It was the one rule she always followed.

That way, when the time came, she could walk away and never look back with regrets. A few admirers had begged her to stay with them, but she'd pushed them aside. She had done everything on her own terms for so long that she truly believed she had ice in her veins.

Brooke could remember a certain Russian prince who'd written to her. "I've been traveling in my carriage through the Ural mountains, with your portrait on the seat opposite me. I long to see you, Brooke. Please come back to me." She could have had anything she wanted from the prince, but she never went back to him.

Maybe she did have ice in her veins.

So what had happened to cause the ice to melt?

She didn't even like Travis. She couldn't possibly like the man . . . or could she? No, she didn't like him, she told herself firmly. It should be easy to brush him off. She'd just slipped off course and forgotten the business side of the affair. Perhaps she needed to have a talk with Travis. Then she could calmly point out that they were both business people and, being such, they should be able to tackle their situation with a decision that would benefit them both.

A knock sounded on her bedroom door, interrupting her thoughts. "Come in," Brooke said, turning toward the door.

"Good morning," Eliza said as she bounced into the room. "We missed you at breakfast."

"I wasn't very hungry this morning," Brooke said, knowing the child spoke for herself. "Is your uncle still downstairs?"

"No. Cousin Travis went to see how much damage the storm did last night. I can't believe I slept through the whole thing."

"I can't believe you did either. It kept me up most of the night," Brooke admitted. She still felt unnerved by the ferocity of the storm, but she didn't feel it necessary to go into details with the child.

"You should have come to my room," Eliza said as she perched on the end of the bed. "I would have kept you company."

Brooke felt her face flush. "I didn't think about it at the time." She hadn't really been capable of thinking. She didn't add that it would have been much safer than where she ended up.

"Guess what?"

"What?" Brooke asked, seeing that Eliza was trying to tell her something.

"Cousin Travis said I may go to the party tonight for a little while. So I need your help to pick out the perfect dress."

"I'd love to," Brooke said, strolling over to the child

and offering her hand. At least this was a distraction that would set her mind on something other than Travis. "Let's go see what we have to work with."

In Eliza's room, they went through her wardrobe, examining each garment carefully. Brooke would hold up a dress and then they'd promptly reject it, quickly moving on to the next gown.

"They all look too childish," Eliza fretted. "I will be thirteen years old in three more months, practically a woman. I don't want to look like a little girl."

Brooke smiled. Eliza was in such a great hurry to grow up, just like all girls her age. "I have an idea." Brooke pulled out a soft pink dress of watered gauze. "This one is lovely," she said, holding the dress up to the girl's face. "I have some dark rose feathers in my room that we can use to accent the gown. We can ask Mammy to find us someone who can sew the feathers around the bottom of the dress. With a little lace across the top it will be quite fetching. What do you think?"

Eliza clapped her hands. "That sounds lovely. You are absolutely wonderful. I'm so glad you are here instead of Hesione."

Brooke turned. "You don't care for her?"

"No." Eliza sighed. "Not really."

Brooke placed the dress on the bed and busied herself with the adjustments. She tried not to act interested, but she was dying to know about the other woman. "Your cousin obviously has a different opinion."

"I think Travis has motives."

"Motives?" Brooke arched an eyebrow as she considered the girl's statement. Then she said, "You mean you don't think love is his reason for marrying her?"

"I guess he likes Hesione well enough, but I think he's marrying her because she comes from an affluent Creole family."

"Travis doesn't impress me as someone who cares about affluence."

"You know him quite well already, I see," Eliza said with a smile.

"I'm not too sure how well I know him, but he doesn't impress me as someone who can be forced into doing anything he doesn't want to do."

Eliza shrugged. "True, and I shouldn't be gossiping, but I think he is marrying Hesione to please my aunt.

"You see, her father disowned her when she had Travis out of wedlock. I heard my mother talking about it once. Of course, she didn't know I was listening. She said my grandfather had plans for Aunt Margaret to marry a respectable Creole, but she met the duke and fell madly in love with him. She thought he'd leave his wife and stay with her, but that wasn't to be.

"Instead, he left Aunt Margaret and returned to England. The scandal that came upon the family turned my grandfather into a bitter man."

Brooke didn't want to care, but found she couldn't stop herself from commenting. Besides, the more she knew about Travis, the easier it would be for her to bend him to her wishes. "I can see how that would have caused a scandal, but when Jackson claimed Travis as his son and gave him the plantation, didn't that change things?"

"No." Eliza shook her head. "You see, Creoles are very proud people and not very forgiving. I shouldn't say this, but my aunt is also a bitter person. She's always been good to me, but she constantly reminds Cousin Travis how he is to blame for her ruined life."

"But Travis had nothing to do with it. He didn't ask to be born," Brooke quickly jumped in to defend him. "He was only a child. Margaret was the one who behaved badly. She was to blame."

Eliza gave Brooke a funny little smile before saying, "I think you like my cousin."

For a moment, Brooke gave Eliza a stunned look. Why would the child think such a thing? She was only asking questions because she was interested. And, perhaps, just a wee bit curious. "Let's just say that he's growing on me. I must say, you seem to bring out a different side of him."

"I love my cousin—most of the time," Eliza said with a giggle. "Unless he's being grumpy. Then I try and keep my distance."

"I know the feeling well," Brooke admitted wryly. She reached for Eliza's dress. "Let's go find Mammy and see if she can find someone to perform a miracle with this dress."

Travis made sure he stayed away from the main house, and Brooke in particular. He'd been a fool last night. How in the hell had he let the woman get so close to him? Now, having tasted her, he found he wasn't satisfied, as he hoped he'd be. Instead, he wanted more.

But at what price?

Travis wondered how Brooke would feel about being his mistress. Dare he ask her?

He reined in his horse. There was no time to think of that now for he had reached the sugarcane field. The plantation came first. It always came first.

What Travis found in the sugarcane field didn't please him one bit. He'd lost half the crop from the way it looked, and if the workers couldn't get back into the field quickly to salvage the rest of the crop, the entire harvest could be in jeopardy.

Was even the weather conspiring against him? He railed inwardly as he watched the hands struggling to get the carts unstuck from the mud.

"Damn," he muttered as he dismounted and stepped up to a cart, shouldering the wagon as he pushed against the clinging mud. He might as well get dirty, too.

Brooke stood wrapped in a bath sheet, gazing into her closet. She wanted to make just the right impression tonight. It would be the first time she'd meet her neighbors, and she wanted to look her best.

Millie Anne swung into the room. "Sorry fo' bein' late, Miz Brooke, but I had to takes Miz Eliza's dress to her. You ready to start gettin' dressed? Folks be arrivin' soon."

Finally, Brooke pulled out a royal blue dress of silk and satin. "I think this is what I'm going to wear."

"Ooowe, that color will suit you just nice," Millie Anne said as she shook out the cream-colored petticoats. "I wants you to lie on de bed so I can rub you with de almond oil. Mammy said to make sure I did dis so you'd look your prettiest tonight."

Brooke smiled. Maybe Mammy was beginning to like her after all. That would certainly be a major accomplishment, she thought.

By the time Millie Anne had finished, Brooke was so relaxed she thought about going to sleep and forgoing the party, but she knew that wouldn't do. She got up and slipped into her French corset, holding it together while Millie Anne pulled the pink ribbons tight. Then she slipped the petticoats over Brooke's head.

"Dis here's de finest gown I've ever seen," Millie Anne commented as she carefully lowered the blue gown over Brooke's head, the rustle of silk filling the room as the gown fell into place.

Brooke held the back so Millie Anne could fasten the rows of tiny hooks, then she adjusted the top so that it fell fetchingly off her shoulders. The bodice was cut low, revealing a tempting glimpse of cleavage beneath a froth of creamy lace, giving her a very seductive appearance.

"My, my, my," Millie Anne exclaimed. "You is goin' to be de finest lady at de whole ball."

"Thank you. This dress is one of the latest French fashions. I had it made just before I left England. This is the first chance I've had to wear it." Brooke ran her hand through her hair. "Can you tame these curls?"

"How abouts we sweep your hair to the side? I can twine de curls with gold and blue ribbons. De gold will match your eyes."

Brooke smiled her approval. "Work your magic,"

she said as Millie Anne began to finger her rich, thick tresses.

Brooke was well pleased with her maid's finished coif. She opened her jewelry box and selected a sapphire necklace Jackson had given her. The necklace was a fine gold rope that wrapped around her neck, a dark blue sapphire dangling on the end. The gem rested seductively in the cleavage between her breasts. It was perfect, Brooke thought with a satisfying smile.

"Ooowe, Mister Travis ain't goin' to be able to take his eyes off'n you," Millie Anne said with a grin.

That's the idea, Brooke thought as she left the room.

She could hear the soft music wafting up to the second floor and the murmur of the guests' conversations as she started down the stairs, her blue gown swishing about her as she walked.

Travis stood at the bottom of the stairs, apparently waiting for her, but engaged in conversation with Jeremy. Jeremy noticed her first, his eyes widening with admiration as he nudged Travis, who slowly turned her way.

Travis was impeccably dressed in black with a white waistcoat and shirt. His sandy hair was wavy where it brushed his collar, the white contrasting beautifully against his tanned skin. There was an air of strength and confidence about him.

Travis was so handsome it took her breath away. When he turned his crystal blue eyes on her, Brooke felt her cheeks heat to what she could imagine were two red spots on her face. His gaze was so hot she wanted to look away, but she couldn't. She didn't even remember taking the last few steps.

Jeremy politely held out his hand. "You look lovely tonight, my dear," he said, not trying to hide his admiration.

"Thank you," Brooke replied, barely noticing that Jeremy was almost as good looking as Travis. She'd bet he'd broken several hearts.

"Madam," Travis said, drawing her attention back to him. He offered his arm so she could place her hand upon his sleeve. Evidently, he wasn't going to comment on her gown, much less give her a civil greeting. At least she had the satisfaction of knowing that he had noticed her, even if he refused to acknowledge it. There was no denying the lust she'd seen in his eyes before he quickly hid it.

With her head held high, Brooke strolled into the ballroom where the guests were waiting for the dancing to begin. Travis stopped once they reached Eliza, and guided Brooke to the receiving line so that they might greet their guests.

"You are so beautiful," Eliza whispered beside Brooke. "How do you like my dress?" The child whirled around for her.

"If we were in England," Brooke said, pausing for a moment, "I would think that you were at least fifteen."

Eliza beamed with the compliment.

There was no more time for conversation as the guests started filing past them and the introductions were made. Though she struggled to keep them straight, their names and faces became a blur: all but two. The first was Travis's grandfather, who looked down his nose at her as if she were dirt. Brooke pretended not to notice, although she longed to give him a good setdown for being such a snob.

Then another gentleman escorting his wife glared at her so intently that for a brief second, Brooke thought she'd glimpsed hatred in his eyes.

Once the couple moved on, Eliza leaned over and whispered, "Those were Hesione's parents."

Well, no wonder they were so cold, Brooke thought. Before she could comment, Travis asked, "Are you ready to go into the ballroom? I believe we are required to begin the dancing."

"You mean you can dance?" Brooke teased. Travis didn't reply. He simply gave her a mocking look in return.

Travis didn't know how he was going to resist this bewitching creature. Every inch of his body was tense, and had been since he'd turned and saw her floating like a spirit down the long, curved staircase.

The last thing he needed was to be this close to Brooke, but the first dance was required. Maybe the quicker he got it over, the quicker he would be done with her. Travis guided Brooke out onto the dance floor. She was so close that he could smell her unique fragrance. It reminded him of gardens and marzipan candy. She may have smelled sweet, but he *knew* Brooke wasn't sweet. She was a woman after something that he didn't want to give up.

Travis gave himself a mental shake, turned the woman toward him, and fitted his hand at her slender waist. He felt all the men's eyes on them, though he knew they were really looking at Brooke. It annoyed the hell out of him, but seeing the cut of her gown—which was much too low—how could he blame them?

Travis nodded toward the musicians and they began the soft melody of a waltz.

Sweeping Brooke into his arms, he whirled her around the dance floor, noting the surprised look on her face. Her cheeks were flushed, and he'd give anything to read her thoughts. "So, how am I doing so far?"

She laughed, her golden eyes twinkling like stars. "Quite nicely, I must admit. I see you've waltzed before."

"Many times, I'm afraid. I learned when I was taking my tour of Europe."

Brooke tilted her head to the side and said, "And broke many hearts, I'm sure."

Travis didn't bother to comment. Instead, his eyes kept going to the sapphire that teased the tops of her breasts. "Don't you think your bodice is cut a little low?"

"It is the latest fashion in Paris."

"You're not in Paris anymore," he grumbled.

"Well, I'm sorry to embarrass you, but my fashions are European," Brooke said. His jaw tightened.

"That's beside the point," he ground out between clenched teeth, censure strong in his tone. "I request that, in the future, you adjust your bodice before appearing in public."

Brooke tried to bite back her anger. "You speak to me as if you were my husband," she retorted. "What right do you have to tell me anything? We are partners in business only. Nothing more."

A lazy grin swept across his face. "Point taken, madam."

They didn't speak again as they waltzed. The

music eased their angry tension and soon they were lost to the gentle rhythms as they gazed into each other's eyes.

Brooke was conscious only of him. His arms around her, his dark, handsome face above her, and those glorious blue eyes that seemed to command her to his will. But she had a will of her own, too. "How did you find the cane fields this morning?" she asked, needing to get her mind on something else.

Travis felt as though he were staring into pools of pure gold. He'd enjoyed looking at her so much that he'd momentarily put the cane field completely out of his mind. Brooke had jerked him back to reality. "Not good. I'm not sure we will have a crop. Most of the cane was destroyed by the storm and now the fields are too muddy to move the carts."

"I told you storms were no good."

Travis chuckled. "I'm beginning to agree with you."

She found it impossible not to return his disarming smile. "Well, that's a first."

Much to Brooke's regret, the waltz ended and Travis escorted her to the refreshment table. He'd just handed her a glass of punch when his grandfather, Archie deLobel, approached him.

"I would like a word with you," the old man said. It might have sounded like a request, but it was obviously a command. He glanced at Brooke. "Alone," he added. "I am ready to leave."

Travis took a slow sip of Scotch before answering, "So soon?"

Brooke noted that Travis didn't sound the least bit disappointed.

"Walk me to the door," his grandfather ordered as if he were a general.

Travis nodded toward Brooke, "If you'll excuse me . . ."

Seething, Travis accompanied the head of the family to the foyer. Once there, they stepped into a side parlor where they could talk privately.

The old man stared at Travis, an odd expression on his face, before he spoke. "Do not disrespect this family."

"What have I done this time?" Travis said wearily, having had the conversation many times before. He'd been doing everything wrong since he was born, including the fact that he was born.

"I don't like this woman you have living with you."

"You know nothing about her," Travis countered. "You make it sound like I went out and picked her up in the street."

"I know her well enough," Archie deLobel informed his grandson. "I expect you to do the correct thing." With that, he turned and left, much like he always had after reprimanding a child.

Several hours went by in a blur of music and idle conversation. Brooke had danced with everyone. Her neighbors were polite, but she could tell they were holding back on accepting her. *I guess some things never change*, she thought.

She was so tired that she didn't even remember the last time she'd seen Travis.

Travis, however, definitely had his eyes on Brooke, especially when she waltzed. The men couldn't seem to keep their eyes off her. Each time she accepted a dance with a new partner, Travis felt as though someone were twisting the air out of his lungs. And for the first time, he realized he was jealous of anyone who touched Brooke.

"I will have a word with you," George D'Aquin demanded.

Again. Travis thought. First his grandfather and now Hesione's father. What the hell did he want? Of course, he knew, but that didn't make him feel any better. Travis finally answered the demand, "On the veranda," he said tersely.

Once outside, they stepped to the side by the railing. Travis turned and waited for the man to speak.

"What is the meaning of this, Montgomery?" D'Aquin snapped. "You are engaged to my daughter, and now you have brought this other woman into your home to live."

Travis really didn't care for the man's accusatory tone. "First, I didn't bring her to Moss Grove. My father's solicitor did. Second, Brooke now owns part of Moss Grove. It is as much her home as mine."

"I am appalled that you let this happen. It is not proper to have the woman living here."

"I can't very well evict her from her own house now, can I?"

D'Aquin's face turned beet red. "What about my daughter?"

"What about her?"

"Do I need to remind you that you are engaged to my daughter?"

Travis was fast losing his temper. He was getting fed up with both men badgering him. He was old enough to make his own decisions, even if this situation hadn't been exactly his own. "I suggest you get out of my face," Travis warned him. He then left the man gaping after him as he stormed down the stairs and out into the flower garden. Did the old bastard think he was going to bow down and beg his forgiveness?

If he did, he was delusional.

Brooke was tired of dancing.

She was also tired of smiling and making polite conversation. The only sure place she knew to escape was outside. At least there she could get some fresh air and rest a moment before rejoining the party.

Thank goodness she'd escaped without an escort, Brooke thought as she walked down the veranda steps to the gardens. A slight breeze caressed her skin, a refreshing relief after the hot and stuffy ballroom. Torches that had been placed throughout the flower garden provided just enough light that she didn't trip.

When she reached the rose bed, she leaned down to smell a perfect red rosebud. She wasn't disappointed with the light rose scent. Soon, the weather would turn cold and there wouldn't be any more roses until spring.

Carefully, she snapped the stem, but a thorn caught her finger and she yelped.

"Sometimes you have to be wary of beautiful things."

Brooke jumped, startled at the voice coming from what seemed like nowhere.

She swung around. "Must you always appear out of the darkness to scare me?" she tossed back at him. Not waiting for Travis's reply, she moved over to the gray stone bench and sat down, the rose still clasped in her fingers. She remembered seeing Travis a few times across the room as she'd danced, and she was puzzled why he'd not waltzed with her again. However, he didn't seem to have a problem dancing with another lovely lady who'd laughed at everything he'd said. Strange, she'd never found anything he said particularly amusing.

For the first time in her life, Brooke found she was jealous. And she didn't like that feeling.

Travis moved closer. "I just can't seem to get rid of you."

"Apparently. I was here first," she was quick to point out. "What are you doing out here ignoring all our guests?"

"I might ask you the same thing," Travis shot back.

Evidently he was in the same mood as she, Brooke deduced by his tone. "I needed some fresh air," she finally said.

Travis propped a booted foot up on the stone bench and leaned his forearm across his knee. "The air is much better out here, I admit, but I figured you loved parties and would want to enjoy every moment."

She gazed up into his cool blue eyes, which looked much darker in the dim light . . . and stormy. "There you go again, trying to figure me out. And, as usual, you're wrong."

"Wrong," Travis repeated with a mocking smile. "I seem to recall that you were having a marvelous time, dancing with every man in attendance."

Brooke couldn't believe what she was hearing, not that Travis had actually noticed anything at all about her. "So you were counting?"

"Not necessarily counting," he said. "Just being observant."

"You could have very easily asked me to dance again. Or were you too busy with more important things?"

"And ruin your fun of capturing every man's heart?" he said as he straightened and glared down at her.

Well, this conversation wasn't turning out as expected, Brooke thought. He didn't look in the mood to be seduced. He was angry. Or was he jealous?

That notion pleased her immensely. "So, why did you come out here, Travis? Surely it wasn't to irritate me."

Instead of answering, he lit a cheroot. He inhaled then blew out a white puff of smoke that circled and floated into the air. "I needed to calm down after speaking with Hesione's father."

Brooke's curiosity was piqued and she arched an eyebrow in question. She wondered if Travis would reveal any of the conversation.

"He doesn't seem to be a very pleasant man."

"More like a pain in the ass," Travis snapped, then added, "Pardon me."

Brooke had to laugh. He'd never been that concerned about proprieties before. "What did he want?"

"He wanted me to get rid of you," Travis informed her.

Brooke pushed to her feet. "Well he has some gall. I'm sure you told him that you wish you could."

Travis gave her a slow smile. Brooke's eyes reminded him of an angry cat the way they glittered in the sparse light, and at this very moment they were full of fight. He liked that. What would it be like to tame this wild tiger before him?

Without another word he pulled her to him.

"What are you doing?"

He noticed she didn't put up much of a fight. "The very thing I've wanted to do since I saw you coming down the stairs tonight," he said softly. "I'll not have you flirting with other men in my house."

"It's my house, too," she informed him as she always did.

"I hate you."

Brooke gave him a sweet smile before she purred, "I know." Then she reached up and placed a feathery kiss on his lips. Apparently that had more of an effect on him than a slap on the face.

His warm breath mingled with hers, but Brooke sensed that Travis was trying desperately to resist her. *Too bad*, she thought. She removed the cheroot from his hand and tossed it away. Then she slid her hands inside his jacket and felt his chest muscles tense and heard his short intake of breath. "I believe you mentioned earlier you wanted to do something. Do you want to show me what that something is?"

Chapter 9

Travis's jaw tightened. "Damn you."

Roughly, he jerked Brooke into his arms. His mouth claimed hers before she had a chance to say anything. Slowly, his lips parted hers. She dropped her head back and moaned as she felt his tongue, wet and hot, enter her mouth in a devouring kiss.

Immediately, fire roared through Brooke's blood from the wild excitement of his mouth on hers. His hands shifted possessively across her back as he kissed and caressed her with very skillful hands.

Finally, she thought. *I haven't lost my touch.*

I'd merely been rusty, that's all. He was doing just what she wanted him to do.

The seduction of Travis Montgomery was going to be pure pleasure. She would make him beg before the night was through.

Molding herself to his body, Brooke became aware of Travis's hot masculinity throbbing against her belly. Knowing she needed to shatter the hard shell he'd built around himself, she touched her tongue to his, giving into the passion of the kiss.

Travis went rigid.

Brooke pressed her advantage, teasing his tongue with wild and free abandonment as she truly gave of herself for the first time in her life. With other men she had been merely going through the motions but never felt anything.

A needed hunger that had long lay dormant sprang to life and made Brooke want to strip off both their clothes and make love to Travis. What a powerful opponent she'd chosen. Now she understood what lust was, having seen it in many men's eyes. She was lusting after the only man who had the capability of producing this wild heat between her legs.

She couldn't deny the evidence any longer. She wanted Travis Montgomery.

Travis tore his lips from Brooke's and placed kisses down her throat, moving to Brooke's cleavage, something he'd yearned to touch all night. *Damn this woman,* he thought. She'd somehow managed to rouse his passion, and other parts of his body, as well. He tugged on her bodice. Her breasts sprang free of their restraints, and surged at the intimacy of his touch.

Wasting little time, he teased her nipples with his fingers, preparing them for his love-starved mouth. He intended to suck each nipple until she cried out his name.

I've found heaven, he thought.

"What is the meaning of this?" a voice shot out of nowhere.

Travis jerked up, startled by the sudden intrusion. Slowly, he turned, hiding Brooke behind him as he faced the intruder he was ready to murder for this interruption.

"I knew she was a whore the moment I saw her!" George D'Aquin shouted.

Protected behind Travis, Brooke cringed as she crossed her arms to cover her bare breasts. She didn't need to be caught like this. Her reputation would be ruined.

"If you want to live to see another day," Travis warned, "you'll apologize to Mrs. Hammond."

"I will do no such thing," D'Aquin informed him. "Have you forgotten that you are engaged to my daughter? Apparently so," he answered his own question with a wave of his hand. "I find you out here with another woman in your arms," he shouted with a wild look in his eyes. "You bring disgrace to my family and to yours! Your grandfather shall hear of this immediately!"

Travis was actually defending her, Brooke thought with a pleased smile. She was thankful that Travis blocked her from the man's view as she adjusted the bodice of her gown. Then she tried to move beside him.

He caught her and shoved her back behind him, saying under his breath, "Stay where you are." He switched his attention back to Hesione's father.

Travis resented the old man who had spoken to him as if he were still a child. Is this what his life would be like if he married Hesione? Not only would he have his grandfather and mother hounding him, he'd have D'Aquin and Hesione on his back as well. Not that Travis would pay attention to any of them, but he could certainly do without the constant badgering.

"You can tell my grandfather anything you wish," Travis informed his opponent, his voice courteous but patronizing. "But, first, you can start by telling him that I'm no longer betrothed to your daughter."

"You cannot do this." D'Aquin growled. "Your grandfather owes me."

Brooke had her hand on Travis's back, and felt every tense muscle as he spoke. She listened with growing trepidation.

"I'm not sure what my grandfather owes you, nor do I care, but I can assure you that Hesione is a free woman," Travis punctuated each word carefully, before adding, "I am not chattel to be used as money for paying debts. I'm marrying Mrs. Hammond in two weeks. I'll be sure to send your family an invitation."

What? Brooke nearly blurted out, but clamped a hand over her mouth before she could. Travis was going to marry her? She seemed to have missed a step here. Wasn't she supposed to have convinced him to marry her? She didn't remember convincing him yet.

D'Aquin lunged forward and swung at Travis, but Travis quickly stepped aside and caught the older man's arm.

Brooke moved away from both men, fearing she'd get caught in their disagreement.

"I demand satisfaction for this insult to my family!" Even in the dim light, she could see D'Aquin face had reddened.

Travis released the old man's arm and snarled through his gritted teeth, "Name the time, place, and weapons."

"Pistols at dawn. Who is your second?"

"Jeremy Dubois."

"The arrangements will be made," D'Aquin told Travis, before storming off.

"Until tomorrow," Travis said to D'Aquin's back.

Brooke felt nailed to the spot. Travis whirled and glared at her as if everything had been her fault. His eyes were so stormy she couldn't read them.

"What just happened?" she finally asked when it became evident he wasn't going to speak.

"It seems that I'm going to duel under the Big Oaks tomorrow morning."

"But you could get hurt."

"I didn't think you'd give a damn, my dear." Then he added, "You have little faith." Travis grasped her elbow firmly. "I could also be killed, and the plantation would be yours just that much faster."

"I don't want it that way," Brooke admitted.

"I believe," he paused, his tongue heavy with sarcasm, "you wanted me to leave the moment you first saw me."

"Yes, but alive, not dead."

Travis nudged her chin upward with his finger, mockery invading his eyes. "Your concern is touching. If I survive, I assure you I will be very much alive, and I'll be forced to marry you in two weeks as I told D'Aquin."

So Brooke had heard him correctly. Now she had what she wanted, but somehow it wasn't as satisfying as she'd imagined.

"What is this? Silence from the condemned?" Travis taunted.

She really didn't care for his superior attitude. "Are you asking me to marry you?"

"No. I ask for nothing," he clarified. "I'm telling you that we will marry in two weeks. After all, it's what my father wanted. So Mr. Jeffries should be happy. We can look at it as a business arrangement. After a year, when the obligation is met, you'll be free."

It was a good thing she wasn't the sentimental sort who believed in love, because that was certainly not what she was getting. Travis was making himself very clear on that topic.

"I thought you wanted to succeed on your own," she reminded him.

His mouth thinned with displeasure. "The storm destroyed most of our crop. We can't survive another year of just getting by, nor do I want to. There are many people who depend on this plantation for their livelihoods. My father's money will save the place."

Ignoring the mocking voice inside that wondered why she should care, she snapped, "It's always the plantation with you." Brooke twisted away from him. "Is there nothing else?"

"And what else is there?" he asked her. "If you don't have the land, then you have nothing."

"What if I don't want to be free?"

"Oh, you'll want your freedom to find someone who loves you," he told her when she looked up at him. Travis regarded her with impassive coldness. "For you see, Brooke, I'm incapable of loving anyone. You're nothing more than an obstacle on my way to getting what I really want."

Strange, it was exactly what she'd thought of Travis

more than once. He was standing in her way of getting what she wanted. However, it didn't sound that good when it was said to her.

Brooke knew what he really wanted, and it wasn't her.

Each of Travis's words felt like a slap across her face. All these years she'd been a calculating businesswoman, and now the tables were turned. Nonetheless, she wasn't going to let him get away with his last remark. Even if he was giving her everything she'd wanted . . . a business arrangement.

She took a step closer to him, balancing on her toes so she could see into his cold, blue eyes. She whispered, "I don't think you really know what you want, Travis Montgomery."

"That is where you are wrong, my dear. I know exactly what I want," he rasped before turning away.

Brooke watched the arrogant bastard leave, but she was determined to have the last word. "Travis Montgomery, you'll regret those words one day."

Someone woke Brooke by shaking her arm. She opened her eyes to find that it was barely dawn.

"Look what time it is," Mammy said as she nudged her again. "Wake up, Miz Brooke, you hear."

Brooke wasn't used to Mammy waking her. When she finally understood and was in some sort of conscious state, she shoved herself up with her elbows. "W—what's wrong?"

"Mr. Travis done and left fo' de Duelin' Oaks."

Everything that had happened last night came flooding back to Brooke. Her first thought was to wonder why she should care after the rotten way Travis had proposed marriage. She assumed that after a good night's sleep everything would have cooled down between the two men.

Brooke flung back the covers. "I thought maybe they wouldn't go through with the duel. It isn't as if anyone was hurt," Brooke said, slipping out of bed. She headed for the washstand. "I can't believe they are going to try and shoot each other. Dueling is outlawed in England."

I should probably let D'Aquin shoot Travis, Brooke thought as she poured water into the washbasin. But then again, she needed him.

After splashing water on her face, she turned to Mammy, "Where is Millie Anne? I need to get dressed so I can stop this foolishness."

"I sent her t' have de carriage ready, figurin' you'd want t' go t' de Oaks. I'll help you dress, but tell you de trut', you ain't goin' t' stop de duel. And I intend t' go wit' you. Got me too much time vested in raisin' dat boy t' see holes shot in him, yes," Mammy said as she pulled out a black skirt and white blouse for Brooke.

"I hope Eliza isn't going."

"She is much too youn'. Millie Anne will stay wit' her."

Brooke slipped the garment over her head and held it for Mammy to fasten. "Tell me about American duels. There were a few in England, but none that I was privy to. It was considered a crime back home. Are there very many duels fought in New Orleans?"

"*Oui.* Youn' men fight over de sli'dest affront fo'

such absurd reasons as dere honor. Mos' happen at soirees such as last nig't. I hear tell a duel was foug't fo' de honor of de Mississippi River, yes. In Nawlins ever'bod' is hot-blooded, yes."

After Mammy had fastened the last hook, Brooke rushed over to her dresser and snatched a hairbrush and ribbon. "I can brush my hair in the carriage. Let's hurry."

In no time, they were in the foyer. Mammy handed Brooke a shawl as a servant opened the door. Brooke turned to Mammy, "You don't suppose Travis will get hurt, do you? Is he any good with a pistol?"

Mammy more or less nudged Brooke out the door, the concern evident in her face. "He's better wit' swords, t' be sure. Mebee why his opponent choose de pistols."

"A life is a big price to pay for honor," Brooke commented while she climbed into the carriage.

"Exactly, what are dey fightin' over?"

Brooke frowned. She felt guilty and couldn't look Mammy in the eyes, but she had to answer the question. "Me," she whispered softly.

When Mammy said nothing, Brooke glanced up, expecting to see a look of disapproval. To her surprise, she saw none. Instead, Mammy asked, "Someone mus' have insulted you, yes?"

The carriage began to move. Brooke leaned back against the soft cushions and began to brush the knots out of her hair. "That was part of the reason."

"So I figured. Mr. Travis would never take an insult lightly, you hear. But who's he fightin'?"

"Hesione's father."

"Lordy, Lordy," Mammy mumbled as she shook

her head back and forth. The creases in her forehead seemed to have doubled. "What has gotten
into dat boy?"

"Travis didn't issue the challenge, Mr. D'Aquin
did."

"And why dat be?"

Brooke finished brushing her hair. She tied the
yellow ribbons she'd brought around her hair to
keep it out of her face, then placed the hairbrush
on the seat beside her. She really wasn't sure what
Mammy's reaction was going to be, but Brooke had
to tell her. She felt as though she and Mammy had
reached a mutual trust, and she didn't want to destroy what they'd built.

"It probably had something to do with the fact
that—" Brooke paused. "Travis told Mr. D'Aquin
that he wasn't going to marry Hesione, but would
marry me instead."

Mammy looked to heaven before saying. "Dere
goin' t' be a big ruckus when Miz Margaret and Miz
Hesione return, t' be sure. If Mr. Travis survives dis,
his mother just may shoot him herse'f."

"Are you disappointed?"

Mammy clicked her tongue then said honestly,
"Depends. What you marryin' him fo'?"

"Because it suits both our needs," Brooke finally
said. "We both own the plantation, so it makes
sense. What other reason would there be?"

"Well now . . . dat's a question. Mebbe cause you
should love de man you are marryin'."

"I gave up on love a long time ago, Mammy,"
Brooke told her. "I'm not sure I even believe in it
anymore."

Mammy shook her head but said nothing more.

Brooke gazed out the window, wondering what would happen when they arrived. And then it dawned on her that the person challenged usually chose the weapons, but that had not been the case last night. Why had Travis let the older man choose? Did he want to die? No, that wasn't even a plausible thought. He had too much fight in him. Maybe it was out of respect for the man's age. Travis did have a strange sense of decency.

Fifteen minutes later they arrived at the edge of New Orleans. The carriage rumbled down Decatur Street to Jackson Square where they turned. It was still very early and extremely foggy, so it was hard to see, but Brooke could make out the streets where vendors were just beginning to emerge for a days work.

A steeple jutted heavenward though the fog like a beacon. Once they reached Saint Louis Cathedral in St. Anthony's Garden, the coach started to slow. They went on around the church to a parklike, grassy area with two large oak trees.

Brooke turned to Mammy, "I guess this is it."

Mammy nodded.

The driver opened the door and helped them out. Through the fog, Brooke could see two groups of men separated by a few yards. She spotted Travis about the same time he saw her. He immediately headed toward them.

"I don't think Travis is glad to see us," Brooke whispered to Mammy.

"Tell you de trut' . . . I t'ink you may be rig't."

Chapter 10

Like a menacing silence, the fog swirled, waiting for the unknown. The scene before Brooke seemed much too eerie—the huge oak trees, their drooping arms covered in Spanish moss, jutting across the field.

Through the thick, gray haze Travis marched toward them, looking like the devil coming up from the depths of hell to pounce on her. There were times that she truly felt that way.

"What the hell are you doing here?" Travis snapped the minute he reached them. "This is no place for a woman."

Brooke pulled her cream-colored shawl around her shoulders to ward off Travis's frosty stare, but she stood her ground. "We're here to stop you. We don't want you to go through with this madness."

"You're wasting your breath and my time," he informed her. "You have no say in the matter." Then he gave Brooke a peculiar look. "I see you're dressed in black. How appropriate."

Travis's tone infuriated her. She'd gotten up

early to come here and try and stop this idiocy, and now she had a good mind to tell him to go to the devil. For a brief moment, she didn't give a damn if he were shot or not. It would solve her problem of ownership of Moss Grove. However, that wasn't her only problem. For whatever reason, she really did care. Even if she didn't want to. So she took a deep breath and tried again. "Can't you just apologize?"

"No," he replied sharply. "If you remember, this wasn't my idea. It was his. So I can't call it off." For a brief moment, Brooke thought she detected a trace of fear, but Travis swallowed it quickly. She shook off that notion—she couldn't imagine him being afraid of anyone. "Since you are both here, you might as well be witnesses."

Brooke had been prepared for another argument. However, he'd given in much easier than she'd expected. Glancing down, she noticed the pistol dangling from his hand. She knew little of firearms other than there were many different kinds. The one he held appeared to be specially made for someone because initials had been carved into the smooth, English oak. The long gun barrel was made of cold, blue steel and looked deadly.

She tore her gaze away from the weapon and back to Travis. "Who are all these people?"

"The two gentlemen standing next to D'Aquin are his second and a witness. The two men over there," Travis said as he pointed, "are doctors. And, of course, you know Jeremy, who is acting as my second."

"It's time," D'Aquin's second announced.

"Ladies," Travis said with a curt bow.

"Be careful, you hear," Mammy whispered, wringing her hands.

Travis smiled fondly at Mammy, then glanced at Brooke briefly. "What? No good wishes?"

Brooke had noticed the smirk on his face, but she wasn't about to give Travis the satisfaction of hearing her tell him to be careful. She'd already tried to talk him out of this nonsense, for all the good it had done. She tipped her chin up stubbornly, but he had already turned away.

In the middle of the field the two men took their positions. Neither of them offered to shake hands. Both were deadly serious.

A semblance of daylight began to sift through the thick fog as the referee issued his instructions, "On the count of three, you both will walk out twenty paces, then stop. When I yell fire, both of you will turn and take your best shot." He looked from one man to the other. "Do you understand?"

Both men nodded.

"Mr. Dubois and I will watch to make certain the rules are followed." The referee stepped away from the men.

The opponents turned to stand back-to-back, pistols pointed upward in the air, ready for the deadly confrontation. The click of the hammers being drawn back broke the silence.

The weak sunlight pressed the fog low to the ground so Brooke could see well enough. Both men had removed their jackets and now wore only white shirts and black trousers. Since D'Aquin faced her direction, she could see his features. His eyes lacked the luster of youth. His skin was dark, and he had heavy jowls. At the moment he leveled hate-filled eyes directly at her. He must see her as the cause of all this.

The referee began the count. "One, two, three . . ."

Travis and D'Aquin stepped precisely to the count as if they were performing the steps of a dance. Fog swirled around them as they strode across the field.

Brooke couldn't take her eyes off Travis. He advanced, so tall and proud, appearing not the least bit frightened. With each step that Travis took, Brooke's chest tightened. Soon she could barely breathe. Reaching over, she gripped Mammy's hand.

"Lordy, Lordy," Mammy murmured under her breath.

As the count reached eighteen, Brooke whispered a short prayer that nothing would happen to Travis. She didn't want to think of him getting hurt. Who would she have to argue with?

"Nineteen."

"Watch out!" Jeremy shouted at the same time a shot rang out.

D'Aquin had fired early.

Frantically, Brooke jerked her gaze back toward Travis, but she didn't see him. There was nothing there.

Nothing but fog.

"No!" she screamed, scarcely aware she'd voiced her fears aloud. Surely Travis couldn't be dead.

That wouldn't be fair.

"Oh, my God," Brooke said over and over again, her hand coming to her mouth. She took a step toward him but Mammy held her back.

"You cheated, D'Aquin!" Jeremy shouted, leaping toward the guilty man.

A harsh, hoarse "No" came from out of the fog. Everyone turned as something, someone, slowly emerged from the fog where Travis had been.

Brooke's legs turned to mush, and she would have fallen if Mammy hadn't taken hold of her arm.

Slowly, Travis struggled to his feet, a bright red stain on the upper portion of his white shirt, proclaiming that he'd been hit. Travis had fallen to the ground, but he was still alive.

Relief filled Brooke.

"Mr. Montgomery, fire your shot at will," the referee instructed.

Travis slowly raised his arm, gun in hand.

"What?" Brooke turned to Mammy. "What's going on here?"

"Both men are allowed one shot," Jeremy explained.

"Mr. D'Aquin mus' stand his ground or be labeled a coward, yes," Mammy added.

Travis leveled the weapon at D'Aquin. If he pulled the trigger, it would mean certain death for the old man. The pistol was aimed squarely at the middle of his chest.

"Shoot, damn you," D'Aquin shouted.

Travis held his pistol in position. Tension mounted. At the very last moment, Travis pointed the pistol up toward the sky and fired.

"I believe your satisfaction has been met this day," Travis rasped. "I'll not take your life, coward that you are, so that you might remember your shame." Then Travis's knees buckled and he sank to the ground.

D'Aquin's shoulders sagged and he hung his head. There was a fury of murmuring all around as the men conferred about what had just occurred. But Brooke's eyes were only for Travis.

Before she realized what she was doing, Brooke was halfway across the field to the spot where one of the doctors examined Travis.

"It's lodged in your shoulder," the doctor said, "but you'll live. I'll have to remove the bullet, but I cannot do it here. Let's get into my carriage, and I'll take you to my office."

Travis glanced up at Brooke, his eyes sharp and assessing. Her pulse skittered alarmingly.

After a moment, he reached up and drew Brooke down to him. Then he whispered in Brooke's ear, "Disappointed?"

"Shut up," she snapped, her voice deceptively brittle. How could he think such a thing? She didn't want to care. And right now, she wasn't sure she did. Brooke had a good mind to leave him there. But she didn't instead she helped him stand. Even wounded, the man was insufferable. If the gun were still loaded, she would shoot him herself.

"Jeremy, my friend, I've kept you long enough from your harvest." Travis patted him on the back with his good hand. "Thank you for the warning. It could have been much worse if you'd not shouted. I didn't know that D'Aquin was such a coward."

"You realize now that by not shooting him, you've made an enemy." Jeremy pointed out. "I'd be careful, if I were you."

"I know," Travis said. "I've caused enough scandal by not marrying his daughter."

"Are you going to stand here and bleed to death?" the doctor interrupted. "Why don't you let me fix your wound while you still have some blood left in you, son?"

"I'm ready," Travis said, his voice beginning to show the weakness he was loath to admit. He allowed the doctor to help him to the buggy.

With that, everyone dispersed to their respective carriages, and Jeremy escorted Brooke back to Travis's carriage where Mammy was already waiting inside.

"Why didn't Travis take the shot?" Brooke asked.

"If he had killed D'Aquin, there would always have been talk of a younger man taking advantage of an older man. By Travis not shooting him, D'Aquin remains a coward because he cheated. Even worse, with Travis having spared D'Aquin's life, it's a blot against his character. The Creoles are not forgiving in matters such as this."

"I see," Brooke said. "Thank you for being here for him today."

"There isn't much I wouldn't do for Montgomery. We have been friends since we were children." Jeremy smiled down at Brooke. "I hear that congratulations are in order. He told me that you are planning to wed in two weeks," Jeremy said, grinning. "Personally, I think he has finally made a good choice."

Brooke found herself blushing, something she'd not done recently. "Thank you. I think."

Jeremy chuckled as he walked away.

* * *

The doctor's office was located on Toulouse Street. Their driver wasted little time getting Brooke and Mammy there. He parked the conveyance behind the doctor's buggy, which had arrived only a few minutes before they had. Brooke leapt to the ground even before the coachman had time to help her out.

Once inside the building, Brooke glanced about at the neat, clean room. There were several chairs scattered against the walls. She presumed this was a waiting area.

Since there was no one there to greet them, Brooke was ready to fling open doors until she found where Travis had been taken. But before she had a chance, the doctor stuck his head out of the back room and shouted, "I'm going to need somebody's help. My nurse isn't here and we don't have time to send for her. Mammy, get me some bandages and hot water. And you, young woman . . ."

"My name is Brooke."

"Brooke, I'll need you to hold Montgomery down, so I can dig out the bullet. Can't have him moving about."

"But I don't know anything about nursing."

"It doesn't matter. All you need to do is hold him down. Let's go." He motioned impatiently for her to come into the back.

As Brooke followed him, she asked, "What is your name?"

"Doctor Smart or Smarty as a few refer to me," he

said with a chuckle. Then he switched to all business as he placed his instruments on a small, white table.

Travis sat slumped on a table, his booted feet dangling over the edge. He had a bottle of Scotch that he'd evidently been drinking propped on one leg.

"Don't be shy," the doctor said without looking at her. "Help the man get his shirt off. Can't do a thing to him with his clothes on."

Brooke laughed. "Shy is one thing I'm not, Doctor," she told him as she bustled over to Travis.

"Glad to hear it," Travis said to her, his eyes raking boldly over her.

She got the general impression that he'd rather be removing her top instead of the other way around.

Brooke positioned herself between Travis's legs, bracing herself against the edge of the table in case he should weaken and fall. Wasting little time, she unbuttoned his shirt. Her fingers brushed his collarbone, lingering there for just a moment before she continued her task. His muscles flinched each time she touched him. She was glad to know she had an effect on Travis. Finally, she reached the bottom button and glanced up at him from beneath her lashes. A vaguely sensuous look passed between them.

In response, Travis drew his legs closer together, trapping Brooke between them. The jolt of his thighs brushing her hips made Brooke gasp at the unexpected tingle. But the fact that he was purposely trying to make her squirm brought out her devilish side.

"Here, let me push the shirt from your shoulders," she purred as she stepped up on a small stool, her breasts pressed against his chest as she peeled the shirt from his body, careful not to hit his wound and the temporary bandage the doctor had applied.

Travis's entire body tensed. His breath was warm on her neck and she was very conscious of where his warm flesh touched hers. Even wounded, Travis radiated a vitality that drew her to him.

"There," she said as she stepped back down. She gazed into blue eyes that held her captive. The smoldering flame she saw there pleased her. There was a maddening hint of arrogance about Travis that she liked way too much. An undeniable magnetism was building between them. However, she must be the one in control.

"I want you to lie on your stomach, Montgomery," Doctor Smart said, interrupting the moment they were sharing. "And you, young woman, take that bottle away from Travis and stand by his head. I need you to hold his shoulder firmly."

Brooke did as instructed while Mammy assisted by fetching water and fresh linen bandages for the doctor who had told her where to look for the supplies.

The doctor placed a pillow under Travis's shoulder so he could better do his work. "This is going to hurt like a son-of-a-bitch," the doctor warned without bothering to apologize to Brooke.

Brooke stood on Travis's right side while the doctor sponged off the wound. Then he took the bottle of Scotch and poured some in the wound.

"That's good Scotch," Travis hissed with pain and tensed as the liquid hit the gaping wound.

Feeling his pain, Brooke cringed. She touched his shoulder to keep him still. His skin was smooth and hot beneath her hand. She didn't like seeing him in pain.

"I'm going to have to dig the bullet out," the doctor said.

Travis nodded. "Get it over with," he rasped.

"Here." He handed Travis the bottle of Scotch. "Better take a few more swigs."

Travis pushed his body up and propped himself on his elbow. He grabbed the bottle and gulped the amber liquid down.

"All right, Doc," Travis muttered, his voice slurring as he handed the bottle to Brooke, who, not thinking, tipped the bottle up and took a swig herself. Very unladylike, she scolded herself when she realized what she done. But she wasn't sure she could stomach seeing the doctor cut Travis without the extra fortification.

Travis chuckled. "Didn't realize that you were a Scotch drinker, my dear."

"There are many things you don't know about me," she informed him.

"Hold him down," the doctor instructed. "Mammy, be ready to hand me some bandages after you give me that knife." He pointed.

Brooke pressed down on Travis's good shoulder just as the tip of the knife slid down into the wound. She expected Travis to scream or shout, but he never made a sound. He tensed and clenched the edge of the table for dear life. As the doctor probed deeper, fresh blood seeped out, and Brooke couldn't watch any longer. Instead she let her gaze dart to Travis.

He was staring up at her from his position lying on the table. She saw the pain etched in his clouded blue eyes. He reached for her hand and clasped it tightly. Something inside of Brooke melted. Travis was in pain, yet he was trying to comfort her. He really did have a heart buried in that arrogant, stubborn chest.

"There it is," Doc said.

Brooke pressed down on Travis's shoulder with all her might as the doc extracted the bullet. He held it up for her to see. Only then did she let out the breath she didn't realize she'd been holding.

"Just a couple of stitches and we're all done," Doctor Smart said as he threaded a needle with horse hair. The stitches were made quickly. He cleaned the area with another generous dose of liquor, then began to bandage the wound. Doc had Travis sit up. Mammy brought over the fresh bandages, and they began to wrap Travis's shoulder while he continued to drink.

Brooke knew Travis had to be in a great deal of pain, but there wasn't much she could do for him that he wasn't already doing for himself. Perhaps if he passed out it would be better for all of them.

Doctor Smart looked at both Mammy and Brooke as he gave his final instructions. "Watch for infection. You can tell by the purple and red which spread away from the wound if it becomes infected. The redness should go away. Not get worse. If that happens, you'd better send for me immediately."

With the help of Smarty and the driver, they managed to get a staggering Travis into the carriage. Brooke sat beside him and Mammy across

from them. Travis was quiet as the carriage rolled
out of town, only showing some life after they had
ridden several miles.

"Well, Mammy," Travis said in a drunken slur.
"Have you heard that I'm getting married?"

"*Oui*, I believe your mama is shoppin' wit' your
fiancée, yes."

"You've not heard the latest news, then," Travis
said. He seemed to be having a difficult time holding his head up. It felt like a brick and hurt like a
son-of-a-bitch. He slumped over, placing his head
on Brooke's shoulder. *Much better*, he thought as he
rolled his eyes up at Brooke. "You didn't tell her?"

"We had more pressing matters to deal with. I
don't think the subject came up," Brooke lied.

Travis rolled his head back to Mammy. "I've
changed fiancées," he said drunkenly. "I'm going
to marry Brooke in two weeks, so you're going to
be very busy planning the wedding."

"Ooowe," Mammy said, shaking her head. "You
goin' to get married wit'out Miz Margaret?"

"Yep," Travis tried to nod, but the only thing he
accomplished was to make his head slip lower
against Brooke's breast. *So soft*, he thought with a
grin before he continued. "Under the circum-
stances, I think it's best. Do I have your good
wishes?"

Mammy looked uncertain at first, but finally she
broke into a wide smile. "I t'ink you've made a
good choice. But Miz Margaret, ooowe, she goin' t'
have a fit."

Travis smiled. "Yes, she is." He realized his words
were beginning to sound slurred, and Mammy was

becoming a big blur. She was kind of sideways, he thought as he slumped further down until his head rested in Brooke's lap.

Brooke placed her hand across Travis's arm. Was he really going to marry her? "I think he has finally passed out," she told Mammy.

"Dat's best. He goin' t' be hurtin' both in his shoulder, yes, and his head when he comes to." Mammy chuckled. "And we go'n' be busy gettin' t'ings ready fo' a weddin'."

The next week disappeared in a flurry of activities as they made preparations for a wedding. Brooke watched everything as if she were in a daze. Was any of this real? She wondered more than once.

She never thought she would be getting married, had never really desired to. She hated to admit that she had been swept up in the excitement of the thing.

Travis's wound healed quickly, though not soon enough to suit him. Still, he wasn't as grumpy as the first day when he'd remained in bed. After that, when he'd bitten her head off, Brooke had stayed clear of him. Let Mammy handle him. She wasn't going to put up with his foul mood. Perhaps he was regretting his quick decision to marry her.

Travis had managed to tell her that a telegram had been sent to Mr. Jeffries informing him of the impending wedding. Brooke hoped that Mr. Jeffries received the message in time to make the wedding. It would be nice to have someone in attendance that she actually knew.

She would love to see Shannon and Jocelyn. It would be perfect if they could come, but Brooke knew it was impossible. However, they would be surprised that she was marrying first. Of course, they wouldn't know that this wasn't a true love match, but more a marriage of convenience.

Eliza burst into Brooke's room with a swirl of petticoats. "Good morning," the child said cheerfully as she sat down on the edge of the bed. "Mammy said to tell you that you need to decide on what kind of dress you're going to wear for the ceremony."

"I haven't given it much thought," Brooke admitted.

"Well, you should. Cousin Travis said he wants to do the wedding in Creole tradition."

Brooke turned away from her dressing table. "I don't know anything at all about Creole tradition. What do the brides usually wear?

"Usually silk muslin trimmed in pearls."

Brooke went over to her wardrobe. "Maybe I have the perfect dress." She searched through her numerous gowns until she found what she was looking for. A cream-colored silk dress trimmed in delicate lace. She couldn't remember what she'd had the dress made for—most certainty not a wedding—but Brooke felt it would work.

Pulling out the garment, Brooke held it up for Eliza to see. "This gown was made by a *haute couturier*, Charles Worth. The demand for his clothing was all the rage when I left London."

"It's beautiful," Eliza said with a sigh. "Look at that beautiful lace, so delicate. Maybe you can hand it down to me for my wedding dress one day."

Brooke smiled at the child. "You'll have to do some growing first, but I'd love for you to wear the same dress that I'm wearing when the day comes for you to marry. We can start a family tradition."

"I dream about that day," Eliza said with a sigh. "Tell me what love is like."

Brooke gaped at the child and her innocent question. She was unprepared to answer. She had no idea what love felt like. "I—I'm sure it feels different for everyone," she stammered, hoping her flimsy answer would satisfy the child.

"But tell me how you feel about Travis," Eliza persisted.

Brooke felt like she was trapped in a corner. "Sometimes, I feel a little sick when I'm with him," Brooke finally said.

"So being in love is like being sick in your stomach?" Eliza drew her brows into a frown. "That doesn't sound wonderful at all."

Brooke laughed, easing some of the tension knotted in her stomach. "No, it doesn't, but it's like butterflies." Maybe that made it sound a little better. "Then there is this excitement when he comes into a room." Brooke thought for a moment. "I guess I don't know how to explain love to you, but you'll know when you fall in love," Brooke finished lamely.

"When did you know that you loved Cousin Travis?"

When I found out I needed him to get this plantation, Brooke wanted to say, but she couldn't disappoint the child looking at her with such wide-eyed wonderment. "From the very first minute I saw your cousin, I thought he was so handsome. I guess I was attracted to him from the beginning, and as the days went by my feelings became stronger."

"Does he kiss good?"

"Yes, he does," Brooke answered honestly.

"Well, I'll keep dreaming," Eliza said, then added, "You'll get to meet my family tomorrow at the engagement breakfast."

Brooke swung around. "Travis hasn't mentioned this breakfast. Isn't it a little late to announce our engagement since we are to be married next Friday?"

Eliza's brown eyes grew big. "You can't be married on Friday. That's Hangman's Day. You'll be married next Tuesday."

Brooke glanced at the child in surprise. "It seems that you know more about my wedding than I do," she said, more than a little aggravated with Travis. The damn man could tell her something. He'd appear very foolish if the bride didn't bother to show up because she hadn't been given the correct time and place.

Eliza giggled. "I know our customs."

Brooke hung the gown on the door of the rosewood wardrobe and fluffed the skirts. It looked so plain hanging there, but once the crinolines were placed under the skirt it would be fine. She turned back to the child. "Tell me something. Did Travis have an engagement breakfast for Hesione?"

Eliza scooted off the edge of the bed. "No. Hesione wanted to wait until after her shopping trip." Eliza giggled. "Now she will have a wardrobe and no husband. She'll be in for a surprise when she returns."

"I actually feel sorry for her," Brooke commented

thoughtfully. She hadn't met the woman, but she couldn't help empathizing with her. "Especially if she loves Travis."

"Pshaw," Eliza said. "Hesione is in love with herself." Eliza started for the door. "I'm going riding. You want to come?"

"Thank you. I'd like that. Perhaps I'll get to see Travis while we are out. Lately, he never seems to be home in time for dinner."

Brooke enjoyed the freedom and the crisp air as they rode. Ever since they had returned from the duel, she had been tethered to the house, first tending to Travis, then preparing for the wedding. This change of scenery helped her mood.

She felt free when she rode. For just a few moments, she would enjoy the fresh air and the peace and quiet. Unfortunately all that ended when they topped the next hill that overlooked the sugarcane. Fires burned everywhere, and deceptively sweet-scented smoke drifted toward them. The workers were burning the ruined sugarcane and trash. Among the men, she spotted Travis. He'd gotten off his horse and seemed to be issuing instructions like a general.

Now she saw for herself what the storm had done. The once-healthy crop was destroyed. No wonder Travis had decided to marry her so quickly.

That was why she must always remember that this marriage was a business agreement. Brooke could never let her heart get involved where Travis Montgomery was concerned.

Chapter 11

Travis wasn't really looking forward to seeing some of his relatives over breakfast.

So what else was new?

Some he'd just as soon never see again. But this time it was necessary. There would be plenty of whispering about his sudden change in marriage plans, so he would try his damnest to do everything in the correct Creole manner. Getting his relatives on his side would take some maneuvering; he just hadn't come up with the perfect plan, *yet.*

The more Travis thought about it, the more this unusual marriage was growing on him. There could be many things worse than being married to a beautiful woman . . . a beautiful and very desirable woman.

He knew Brooke desired him as much as he did her, so perhaps this business deal wasn't such a bad idea. He'd have the money, and a woman to enjoy for a year.

Feeling a tightening in his loins, he readjusted his trousers. Lately, just the thought of her seemed to produce this annoying reaction. He could picture Brooke lying on his bed with her hair fanned out across the pillows. Perhaps in the next year he could get the woman out of his system. He would buy her out and send her on her way.

What could be simpler?

Travis knew Brooke didn't want this marriage any more than he did, so maybe they were both alike. He'd set down a few rules and the rest would be easy, he thought just as he reached up to knock on Brooke's door.

The door jerked opened and Brooke jumped back with a surprise gasp.

"Sorry," Travis said with a smile. Brooke's skittish reaction amused him. He couldn't imagine her being afraid of anything.

This morning she looked lovely, dressed in a deep plum. Her cheeks were peach color and those golden eyes of hers glittered as she watched him. "I came to escort you down to breakfast."

"Thank you, but I think I can find the dining room," Brooke returned dryly.

Travis smiled and offered his arm. "No doubt that you can, but this is our engagement breakfast. We should look like a loving couple in front of my relatives."

Brooke glanced at him as they made their way to the dining room. Travis was teasing her—something he'd not done before.

"That means you'll have to remember to smile at me every once in a while, and perhaps a kiss on the cheek wouldn't hurt."

Travis paused just before they turned the corner.

"I assure you that I can play my part. But I'm not sure how good an actress you are." There was a trace of laughter in his voice. She found this Travis much more dangerous than the other one.

Brooke reached up and placed a light kiss on his lips. He shot her a quizzical look. "Darling, I assure you that I can act," she said softly, letting her hand slide down his chest. "Do tell me, exactly what is an engagement breakfast?"

"You'll see," he said, steering her into the dining room. "Good morning," he greeted the crowded room.

Brooke was surprised at the crowd gathered. Travis definitely had relatives.

"They're here!" Eliza called out.

"Travis, my dear, you have simply taken us by surprise," a woman walked up to Travis. She hugged him.

"Aunt Anne, it's good to see you again. I can understand your confusion," he said with a shrug, "but what can I say other than I fell in love." Travis gave her a ready smile as he dropped his arm around Brooke.

Brooke smiled at the woman to keep from laughing at Travis's blatant lie. "You must be Eliza's mother," Brooke said as she extended her hand. "I can see where she got her lovely smile."

"Yes, my dear, I am," Anne confirmed, but she glanced back at Travis. "Well, young man, are you going to introduce us, or shall this lovely woman remain nameless?"

"Of course," Travis said with a nod. "I would like for everyone to meet my fiancée, Brooke Hammond.

I hope you'll welcome her into the family. Brooke," he tugged on her arm and she leaned lightly into him, "I'd like to introduce Aunt Anne," he said, then continued down the line, introducing her to aunts, uncles, and cousins. Most were cordial but not accepting.

Brooke noticed that Travis's grandfather wasn't present, and she thought that was just as well, but his grandmother was in attendance. After the introduction, Mrs. deLobel took Brooke's hand and gave it a gentle squeeze, but she addressed Travis. "Are you going to change your mind in the next two weeks and present us with yet another female?"

"No, Grandmere," Travis said patiently. "Brooke is the one that I will marry."

"Your mother is not going to be happy," deLobel said then moved over to her place at the end of the table without another word.

As Travis escorted Brooke to her chair beside his, Brooke whispered, "I can see how enthusiastic they are for us. Perhaps I should check the food for poison."

Travis actually chuckled, causing more than one of his relatives to gape at him.

Once they were seated, the servants started serving piping hot coffee. Next they brought trays of pastries; one that Brooke particular liked was a tasty pastry called a beignet. It was served warm and dusted with white powdered sugar. There were also omelets, sausage, and bacon.

"Mother, you should see how beautiful Miss Brooke's dress is. Tell her," Eliza said, but added quickly, "Brooke said I could have the dress after her wedding. Isn't that grand, Mother?"

"That is wonderful, my dear, but let's hope it will be a while before you are getting married. You are my baby, after all."

"Oh, Mother. I'm not a baby anymore," Eliza protested.

"In my eyes you are," Anne pointed out.

"We can save the gown for you, Eliza. It will be your first French fashion, no?" Brooke asked.

"No—I mean yes." Eliza giggled.

Aunt Anne finished eating and placed her fork on the plate, turning toward Travis, who'd been very quiet during the meal. "Travis, have you contacted your mother?" she asked but didn't let him answer. She shook her head before adding, "You know she isn't going to be happy that she isn't in attendance for your wedding."

"Grandmere pretty much said the same thing," Travis told her. He looked around at his stone-faced relatives. They didn't seem to be accepting Brooke like he'd hoped. Only Aunt Anne and Eliza were talking to her.

There would be enough talk among his neighbors about the broken engagement with Hesione. If his relatives were also standoffish, it would make for a long year. Finally, an idea struck him. There was one way to get Brooke into the family's good graces quickly.

"Mother was traveling to several cities up North, so I have no idea how to get in touch with her. Hopefully she will be pleased with my decision," Travis said, though he knew she'd be anything but pleased.

He pulled a small box from his pocket and addressed the crowd. "Since this is my engagement breakfast, I'd like to continue the Creole tradition of presenting my future wife with a ring. I know this has been sudden, but Brooke simply left me breathless the first time I saw her." He reached over and took her hand in his, wanting to laugh out loud at the doubtful look in her eyes. She always seemed to be waiting for something to happen, like she was constantly on edge. "I hope you will wear this ring with the pride of my family, and I'd like to tell them our little secret."

"Secret?" Brooke repeated as she took the box from him. What was he up to? she wondered.

"Yes, darling," he said. "Brooke is going to have my baby, which is the reason for our hasty marriage."

Everyone started talking at once. Brooke gaped at her future husband as if he'd grown horns out of the top of his head. She was so stunned that words wouldn't come out.

Travis had just taken her new reputation and destroyed it with one outrageous sentence. His relatives would think she was a loose woman. And she wasn't a loose woman . . . anymore. For God's sake, she hadn't had sex in a couple of years. She had a good mind to hit him! Maybe it would knock some sense into his thick head.

But before she acted upon her thoughts, all the women were gathering around her chair, congratulating her and offering advice on how she should take care of herself. She couldn't believe that these people were treating her like a queen when they had barely spoken to her a few moments ago.

She glanced at Travis, who sat there grinning like a fool. "Are you not going to look at your ring?" he asked.

Brooke stared at the small, black box in her hand, all but forgotten. She turned the box around and removed the top. There, nestled in black velvet, was a large ruby surrounded by twinkling diamonds. She'd never expected anything like this. After all, it wasn't a real wedding. Yet Travis had made a point of getting her something nice. Then again, it could be the ring he purchased for Hesione. She peered at Travis to find him still smiling. He seemed to be enjoying all of this way too much. Where was that scowling face she'd grown accustomed to seeing? Perhaps he was a good actor after all.

He reached over, removed the ring from the velvet cloth, and slipped it on her finger. It fit perfectly. Sitting there twinkling at her was the biggest gem she'd ever received.

Travis shoved up from his chair and moved over to help Brooke to her feet, "To our future," he said before he kissed her on the cheek, playing the game with perfect pretense. Brooke smiled at him, determined to play her part as well. They must have succeeded because all Travis's relatives applauded.

When everyone had left, Brooke clutched Travis's arm. "I would like to speak to you."

"I thought you might," he said softly, then escorted her to his study. Once they reach some privacy, Brooke whirled around. He ignored her and went over to his desk, leaned against the front, and folded his arms. "Well?"

She was so angry she gritted her teeth as she paced back and forth. Now everyone would think he had to marry her.

"You don't like your ring," he drawled with a smirk she didn't care for. He seemed to be amused by the entire situation.

"It is probably a hand-me-down from Hesione!"

"That is where you're wrong, my dear. I purchased this ring two days ago, choosing a ruby because it seems to suit your fiery personality. Like the way you just looked at me, as if you wanted my blood."

"Yes, that thought did cross my mind after the lie you just told." She smiled sweetly. "Just what are you going to do when there is no baby forthcoming?" She didn't wait for him to answer. "I can't believe you just told a blatant lie. And how does that make me look? I'll tell you—like a whore. Your grandfather already thinks I'm a whore, so why not let the rest of the family think so?"

Travis reached out to stop Brooke's pacing. "I did it for you."

She glared at him and spat, "And you expect me to believe that?"

"I know how my family thinks. By telling them you're pregnant, they immediately accepted you into the family. Rest assured they will not breathe a word to anyone. It would tarnish the family name." Travis gave a half-laugh. "Believe me, they put great store on how the family is perceived."

"But I'm not expecting," she told him.

Travis gave her a slow smile as he allowed his

gaze to rake over her. "It's only a small technicality. You will be before long."

She could feel the sexual magnetism that made Travis so self-confident. "This could be a marriage in name only."

Travis caressed her check with the back of his finger. "Do you really want to miss all the pleasure we'll have?" His question was quite seductive.

"It's a terrifying possibility," she finally said. He drew her into his arms. Her heart skipped a beat, then began to hammer. "You might regret it," she warned him.

"I'll risk it," Travis murmured huskily.

The shock of his mouth on hers inflamed her. His tongue flicked over her lips, teasing her to part them as his hands moved down her back, molding her body until it fit the curves of his own. She felt ripples of excitement.

Their closeness was like a drug, lulling her to euphoria, leaving her trembling. Her quivering lips parted and Travis took advantage, kissing her endlessly. His body imprisoned hers in a web of growing arousal. Her vow not to become involved with this man shattered into a thousand little pieces.

With a supreme effort, Brooke jerked back, a little stunned at how fast Travis could rule her emotions. She wasn't used to that happening. "I—I think we need to wait until after the wedding." Since he had volunteered to marry her, she wanted to do it the correct way. She didn't want to feel cheap or dirty.

It took a moment for Travis to think straight and his vision to clear. Brooke seemed to be an itch he just couldn't scratch. The more he scratched, the more he itched. It was both exciting and irritating at the same time. "You sound like a virgin." He couldn't stop the cynicism in his voice; he wanted her so badly. "And I do believe that you're a widow, unless you've lied to me."

He thought he saw a guilt-ridden expression flash across her beautiful face, but it was gone in an instant.

"I might not be a virgin, but it has been a long time. And it's going to be a while longer for you." she said sweetly, then smiled at his frown. "I intend to do this correctly."

Travis raked his hand through his hair. "You've picked a fine time to have morals, my love."

Brooke reached up and kissed him on the cheek. "Better late than never," she whispered.

She then had the audacity to walk out, leaving him with an ache that needed relief. *One more week,* he told himself. Then he was going to satisfy his lust with that woman one way or the other.

Later that night, Brooke lie awake trying to understand the consuming emotions Travis was able to arouse in her. She was not finding any answers. He had purchased the ring for her, that fact pleased her until she remembered what he'd just told his relatives. She'd been cold for so long that to feel anything scared her. Brooke couldn't deny that she wanted Travis, and he knew it.

So had she been better off in England, her other world? She wondered. Why hadn't Jackson prepared her for all this? She sighed and rolled over, still staring out into the dark.

Strangely enough, she could still remember her last conversation with Jackson. It seemed like it was only yesterday. The duke had been frail, but his voice still thundered when he spoke.

"For once in your life, do as you're told," Jackson had snapped.

"By now you should know I don't take orders," Brooke informed him.

"Ah, my feisty girl," he said with a slight smile as she adjusted the pillows behind his head, *"just try and humor an old, dying man."*

"Please don't say that," Brooke insisted. *"You've just had a setback. I'm sure you'll be your old self in a few days."*

"The word is 'old', my girl, and I've had many good years, but I feel my number has been called." He paused, catching his breath. *"That is why I want you to listen to me. You might not take orders, but you are still a courtesan, and as such you'll never have complete control of your future."*

Jackson's words had stung. *"Do you think that this is the life I chose for myself? If I'd had any other options, I'd surely have taken them. I had no hope until you found me."*

Jackson reached out and took her small hand in his. She compared the young skin of her own hand against his thin, weathered skin. Some day her skin would look the same, withered and old, and she'd be robbed of her youth. Who would she turn to to hold her hand? Would she be all alone?

"If I had been younger, things would have been different between us. Of course, I still couldn't have married you." He paused and took a deep, rattling breath. *"That is the reason I want you to get away from here. You deserve so much more than this life you lead."* He watched her, and she could see that he did care a great deal. She had

always known that. Jackson had been the father she'd never had.

"Our relationship has always been platonic, but when I'm gone you'll have to choose another. I want you to have a chance to love."

"I don't believe in love. There is too much hurt involved. My mother was a perfect example. She gave her heart to a man, and he walked all over her until he finally walked out of her life, leaving her with nothing," Brooke said.

"Tsk, tsk, my girl." Jackson shook his head. "You have seen the bad side of love, but there is another side of love that can last a lifetime. Just think of Shannon and Jocelyn. They have had their problems, too. But the three of you together have bonded. I appreciate everything you've done for them."

"If you say so," Brooke said with a frown, "but I can't believe in something I've never experienced."

Jackson started to cough those racking coughs that always made her shudder. After a few moments, his attack eased, and Brooke gave him a sip of cool water. As he relaxed back on his pillows, it was very apparent that the coughing spell had left him weaker than he'd been before.

After a moment, Jackson continued, "I'm going to give you the chance to find what I tell you is out there. What you do with it is up to you. I'm going to leave you my plantation, Moss Grove, in America. There you'll be able to start a new life and have all the things you should have."

"I—I don't know what to say," Brooke paused, for her voice had caught in her throat. When had someone given her something and not expected something in return? "You've been so good to me. I couldn't have asked for a better friend."

"And you, my dear, have been a joy to me. I've done

some things in the past I'm not proud of, so this is the first step to right one of the great wrongs in my past."

"What wrongs?" Brooke asked. But she never received her answer. The Duke of Devonshire slipped into a deep, sleep, and two days later he was dead.

When Brooke opened her eyes, it was still dark. She fumbled on the bedside table until her fingers felt her handkerchief. She dabbed the tears from her eyes. She would always miss Jackson. He was such a good man. But now she wondered what Jackson had been up to when he'd planned this entire thing. He had to have known that Travis would never give up the plantation. So why did Jackson give it to her?

Somehow Jackson wanted her to right his wrong. She wasn't sure what that wrong was, but she'd bet it had something to do with Travis, and so far she'd made him miserable.

Brooke rolled over in bed and stared into the darkness. "Jackson, whatever you had planned—it isn't working," she said, hoping he was listening somehow. "And I still haven't seen this love you speak of—you know, the one that can last a lifetime. There is no such thing," she said with a sigh and then she shut her eyes. Still, the tears trickled down her cheeks.

Chapter 12

The day of Brooke's wedding brought cooler weather and the first frost. Fall had finally arrived. It also brought Mr. Jeffries, who arrived while she was eating breakfast.

Travis had told Brooke the night before that he wouldn't see her until the wedding at Saint Louis Cathedral. It was said to bring bad luck otherwise. Of course, Brooke knew that already.

Eliza had gone home so she could attend the service with her family, so Brooke was all alone this morning. As she drank her hot tea, she wondered what kind of turn her life was about to take.

A commotion in the hallway dragged her out of her deep thoughts. She couldn't imagine who could be here. It was with great pleasure that she looked up to see Mr. Jeffries being shown into the dining room.

Brooke squealed with delight as she scrambled to her feet, nearly tipping over her water goblet. She met him halfway around the long table and gave the man a big hug.

"I can't believe you are here," she said, stepping

back from him. "It is wonderful to see you," she added, noting his blush. There was something about Mr. Jeffries that comforted her, someone familiar in a place where things were still very alien to her. Perhaps it was because he was her one link to her past. Then again, it could be because he was older and wiser.

"Have you had breakfast?" she finally asked, remembering her manners.

"Afraid not. I had to travel all night to make it in time," he said, removing his hat. "Let me assure you that these old bones are not accustomed to riding like a madman over hill and dale."

"Come sit down." Brooke waved him over to the table, laden heavily with all manner of breakfast foods, far too much for one person to consume. "I hope you are hungry. As you can see, there is more than enough."

Mr. Jeffries settled himself gratefully into a chair. Brooke rang a tiny brass bell that was set in front of her plate and a kitchen maid scurried in. "Please bring a plate for Mr. Jeffries."

As the maid scuttled away, Brooke turned back to the solicitor. "Eat now. You'll have plenty of time to rest and freshen up. The wedding isn't until this evening."

The maid returned carrying a plate of fresh sausage and eggs. Brooke ordered another pot of tea as well. After the servants had gone, Mr. Jeffries said, "An evening wedding is a bit unusual, isn't it?"

"I know." She smiled, remembering as she reached for cup and saucer that she'd said those very words herself when Eliza told her the time. "I would have thought the ceremony would have been around midday, as it is in England, but this is yet another Creole tradition, or so I'm told."

"I would imagine there are many different traditions in this country. I'm pleased to see that you seem to be adjusting well." He smiled as he placed a napkin on his lap before adding, "His Grace would have been pleased."

"Would he?" She knew she sounded doubtful. "I've often wondered why he sent me here. I thought it was to give me a new start in a new life without any problems. However, I encountered one very big problem when I arrived here." She gave a half-laugh and gestured to indicate the room and the rest of Moss Grove. "Why did he give me only part of all this? Especially when he could have given Travis the entire plantation, and rightfully so."

"I'm sure he had his reasons. You'll find life will always be full of unexpected turns," Jeffries said as he spread a liberal spoonful of jam on his toast. "And its share of problems," he added. Then, seeing her frown, he explained, "I wish I could give you the answers that you need, but His Grace did not see fit to explain his logic to me, either. I think in time that you will know what he intended for you." He took a big bite of jam-covered bread, then reached for his cup. "Tell me, are you unhappy?"

Brooke stared at Mr. Jeffries for a moment, wondering how to answer his strange question. "I really haven't thought about it," she finally admitted.

"Perhaps you should."

Brooke took a deep beneath. "To be truthful, I don't know how I feel. I came here expecting to run a plantation I thought was mine. But once I arrived, I found I was both an unwanted guest and part owner."

"Could you run the plantation by yourself?" Mr. Jeffries asked rather pointedly.

"Perhaps in time," Brooke reluctantly confessed with a shrug. "Travis does a wonderful job here, and his workers admire instead of fear him. I have heard stories of what occurs on other plantations. Some of the stories would make you sick to your stomach." She paused. "I want to contribute, but I have so much to learn."

"I've heard such stories, as well," Mr. Jeffries commented, then wiped his mouth with the linen napkin. "But you still haven't answered my original question. Are you happy?"

Brooke's shoulders drooped as she admitted the truth, "I'm not unhappy. It's just that I had so wanted to plan my own future. And, quite frankly, that future did not include getting married. Now I find myself doing exactly what I'd declared I'd never do." Brooke sighed with long pent-up frustration. "But then I remind myself that it's only temporary. In a year we can go our separate ways."

"Indeed." Mr. Jeffries arched an eyebrow and gave her a funny kind of smile. "So, you are working together as business partners. I think that is a good start. Who knows how you will feel after a year has gone by?"

"I'm sure we'll feel the same as we do now," Brooke answered quickly.

Why would we want to stay married when we don't love each other? she thought to herself. No sense in telling Mr. Jeffries, however. And just what was love, anyway? She hadn't been able to explain it to Eliza, and for some reason that made Brooke sad. She had never experienced the one thing that most people seemed to cherish above all others. Somehow she had been deprived of this wonderful thing.

"I'm truly sorry," Jeffries said. "I seem to have made you sad. That was not my intention."

"It's not you," Brooke told him. "It's the sad truth that I do not truly know what love is. I tried to explain it to a child the other day, and I could not."

Mr. Jeffries pushed his chair back from the table. "I beg to differ," he said, plucking his napkin from his lap. He continued once he had her attention. "Few of us can explain love. It is an intangible thing," he said with a shrug. "You can't hold it, you can't see it, but once you find it, it's worth a fortune in gold."

"You speak as if you know of such," Brooke remarked thoughtfully. "Do you? Have you found love?"

"When I was younger," he said with a wistful smile.

"And?"

"She was young and beautiful, perfect in every way," Jeffries said, a faraway look on his face as he recalled. "She brought joy into my life and showed me how to appreciate the simple pleasures."

"And did you marry her?"

Jeffries smiled. "As quickly as I could," he said, obviously thinking fondly of the mystery woman. "We spent many wonderful years together."

"What happened then?" Brooke couldn't help

her curiosity. Mr. Jeffries had changed completely as he spoke of his wife. "If you don't mind me asking."

"She died of consumption, I'm afraid," he said sadly.

"I'm so sorry," Brooke murmured, glimpsing his pain.

"Don't be sorry for me, my dear. For I have my memories," he said, reaching across the table and patting her hand. "I will say, however, that you do know what love is like."

Brooke frowned, and Mr. Jeffries went on. "Remember how you felt when you had to say good-bye to Jocelyn and Shannon?"

"It was very sad to leave my friends. But is that love?"

"Well, my dear, if you hadn't loved them you wouldn't have cared that they were leaving, nor would it have mattered what happened to them."

"This is true. But surely it must be different between a man and woman."

Mr. Jeffries patted her hand again. "It is the same, yet different—more powerful. Don't fret over this, my dear. You'll know when you're in love," he assured her before he stood. "If you will excuse me, this old man must rest his weary bones. I assume I have the same room?"

Brooke nodded.

"Then I shall retire, and I will see you when we are ready to leave for the church." He headed for the door but stopped and reached for something inside his coat. He extracted an envelope. "I almost forgot. Jocelyn sent you a letter."

Brooke smiled with anticipation. In fact, she

couldn't stop smiling. Her melancholy suddenly vanished as she took the envelope from him.

"Thank you so much for bringing this to me," she said as she hurried out behind him, seeking her room before reading the letter. Now that she had an address for her friend, she'd finally be able to keep up with Jocelyn and share with her everything that had happened.

Once in the privacy of her room, Brooke scurried over to the rose-colored chair. Barely containing her excitement, she opened the letter, unfolded the parchment paper, and began to read.

Dear Brooke,

I hope this letter finds you well. I picture you as a queen in her new home without a care in the world. If anybody deserves something good to happen to her, you do. Shannon sends her love. Yesterday, she boarded the train that will take her part of the way to her new home. From there, she'll have to travel by stagecoach, which her new employer arranged.

However, you will not believe what she told me before she left . . . it seems Mr. Griffin stated in his advertisement that he wanted an older woman to care for his children. So Shannon lied about her age to get the position. Can you believe she did such a thing? Sometimes I wonder if she has a brain in her head. I worry about what will happen once she arrives and the man discovers that she isn't the old woman she claimed to be.

"Oh, my goodness," Brooke exclaimed to the empty room. "What has that child gotten herself into?"

Shannon would be too far away for either her or Jocelyn to help, Brooke realized. Then Brooke thought of something else. How could any man with blood in his body send Shannon away? And Shannon was feisty, with a lot of fight in her. She would **most** certainly stand up to the man, despite her lie about her age. Brooke shook her head. Knowing there wasn't anything she could do, she went back to reading the letter.

As for me, I have found a room in a nice boarding-house. The lady who runs the place is a bit bossy, so I have to ignore her. She is also very nosey. I choose not to answer her personal questions, though she has many. However, the good news is—tomorrow I'm going to talk with a Mr. Peter Parley about working at his small magazine. He seems to need help as he suffers with gout, so wish me luck.

I will write more when I can. In the meantime, write to me at my new address and let me know what is going on in your new life. I'm sure it's wonderful, and not nearly as disorganized as mine. You always knew what you wanted from the start.

I miss you so much and look forward to the day the three of us can see each other again.

Love,

Jocelyn

Brooke sighed and placed the letter in her lap. She might have known what she wanted, but what she got was far more than she had bargained for. She'd give anything to be able to talk to Jocelyn and Shannon and tell them about all her doubts and fears. They had always looked to her as if she had the answers to everything, and yet Brooke lacked any of the answers she needed for herself.

Since there was time before she had to dress for the wedding, Brooke sat down to write to Jocelyn. Brooke poured her heart into the letter . . . all her doubts and fears, and then she told her friend about Travis.

When she finally placed the pen down, she realized that some of her jitters had fled. She also realized that she hadn't reported one bad thing about Travis.

Could the man be growing on her? Surely she wouldn't be so foolish as to fall in love with him?

"It's time t' gets ready, Miz Brooke," Millie Anne called out as she knocked on the door.

Brooke had been lolling in a hip tub, trying to relax. It felt as if every muscle in her body was tied in a knot. Never would she have dreamed that she'd be nervous about getting married. The closer the time drew near, the more the butterflies multiplied in her stomach. "Come in, Millie Anne."

The girl hurried in and held out a bath sheet. Brooke stepped out of the tub and wrapped the sheet around herself.

"Aren't you real excited?" Millie Anne asked.

Brooke half laughed. "Is that what all these butterflies are?"

"Yes'um," Millie answered. She strode over to the wardrobe and fluffed the skirts of Brooke's gown. "Dis is real pretty. Mr. Montgomery is gonna be speechless when he see you."

Brooke slipped into her satin chemise trimmed

with pink ribbons, then stepped over to the dressing table. "I can't imagine me ever striking Travis speechless." She chuckled. "He seems to find an abundance of words when I'm around."

"But he's mighty taken wit' yo' just the same," Millie Anne persisted. "I can tell."

Brooke let the comment pass. She would let the girl have her illusions because she knew better.

"Let's fix your hair," Millie Anne said, grabbing the hairbrush from the table. She brushed Brooke's hair until it shone like gold threads.

As Millie Anne fussed, another knock came on the door, followed by Mammy carrying a basket full of flowers and a bouquet, drawing Brooke's attention. "I broug't de orange blossoms fo' your hair and your bouquet."

"The flowers are beautiful, but where did you find them?" Brooke asked as she held an orange blossom to her nose, breathing in the soft fragrance.

"To be sure, we've our own greenhouse. Su'prised you've not seen it yet, no."

"After this is over, I'll make sure to see it. Are you coming to my wedding?"

Mammy shook her head. "I'll be servin' at de reception. Prosper's been fixin' food all day. And, tell you de trut', I better get back t' help him," she said, smiling. "You look real pretty, you hear. Don't you worry. Ever't'in's gonna be fine, yes."

Brooke gave her an affectionate smile. "I'll try." For just a brief second, Brooke thought she saw a tear in the old woman's eyes. Then Mammy turned and left.

Millie Anne began to weave orange blossoms into Brooke's hair as she twisted the long curls onto the crown of her head and fastened them with pins. "I gots a short veil t' pin on your head, but you'd best slip on your gown first," Millie Anne suggested.

Brooke didn't argue. She felt like a puppet going thought the motions of a play. None of this seemed real. She felt that any minute someone would burst into the room and tell her that Travis had changed his mind and wouldn't be at the church. God, what a thought. What if she went to the church and he wasn't there?

She'd kill him!

No, wait! Calm down, she told herself. It was just the jitters. And it wasn't as though she really cared for Travis, she reminded herself. She looked down at her hand and saw the ruby ring twinkling up at her. He had purchased the ring for her, not Hesione, and something inside Brooke felt good and special every time she looked at it. The ring had been purchased just for her. She liked that special feeling, and she needed to hang on to it to get her through the day.

She put on the cream-colored silk slip, smoothing it over the petticoats. Brooke settled the bodice just off her shoulders and shrugged it into place. The top fit snugly, showing off her small waist, something she always been proud of. Tiny pearls had been sewn into the lace across the bodice, down the front of the dress, and into all the folds.

Millie Anne pinned on the short veil and Brooke was ready. Millie Anne kept telling her how beautiful she was until Brooke finally began to believe that she had made a lovely bride. Still, she really needed to do something about these jitters.

She thought about stopping for a stiff drink of

something, but then chided herself for being such a coward. Instead, she walked down the stairs like a queen, with her head held high.

The carriage and Mr. Jeffries were waiting for her out front of the plantation house. The carriage was sleek, black, and pulled by four white stallions. It made a splendid slight, reminding her of something Jackson would have done. Perhaps Travis was more like his father than he was willing to admit.

Brooke had to sit on one side of the carriage to keep from crushing her full gown. Mr. Jeffries sat across from her. He beamed at her as if he were pleased everything was turning out as though it had been planned from the start.

Brooke leaned against the seat back and kept her thoughts to herself as they rode to the church. Her mind tumbled thought over thought as she stared out of the window. She was excited, in spite of herself. But what if Travis should find out about her previous life? Of course there would be no way he could possibly find out, she tried to convince herself. She certainly wasn't going to tell him.

She wondered what tonight would bring. She might as well be a virgin, she was so nervous. Tonight, she was going to allow herself to feel and enjoy her new husband, because he would be hers after today.

"We're here," Mr. Jeffries announced, breaking into her musings. "Would you like for me to escort you down the aisle?"

"That would be wonderful," Brooke said, breathing a sigh of relief. "I'm not sure my legs will hold me."

Jeffries laughed. "My dear, you look like you are going to your execution instead of your wedding," he chided before she left the carriage. "Perhaps you should try to smile as you walk down the aisle to your new husband."

Brooke drew in a deep breath, pinched her cheeks for color, and nibbled at her lips for the same reason. Then she lifted her skirts and allowed Mr. Jeffries to help her as she climbed the several steps to the covered doorway.

As soon as the doors were thrown open and the music began, Brooke pasted a smile on her face and clutched Mr. Jeffries arm as if it were the only thing that kept her from turning around and running out of the church.

Everyone turned and watched her enter, but Brooke saw none of them. What she did see was a tall, handsome man waiting for her at the altar . . . and he was smiling . . . at her.

Travis was dressed all in black except for a snow-white vest to soften the color. He presented a compelling figure—she couldn't deny that. But it was his blue eyes that held her with each step she took. There was a naked hunger in his eyes that fascinated her, frightened her, yet made her want to find out more about what the man was hiding behind his ice-blue eyes.

No matter how compelling he was, she vowed that she would not allow him to walk all over her. Brooke tossed her head defiantly, shaking out long, golden tresses that should have stayed pinned up. Her hair was just too heavy to behave, and instead scattered around her shoulders.

* * *

God, she is beautiful, Travis thought with apprecia-
tion as his gaze lingered on Brooke as she advanced
down the aisle toward him. She looked nervous,
and that pleased him. Tonight, Brooke would
belong to him. Tonight, he'd taste those full lips
until he had his fill.

It was about time Brooke learned that he would
be the master in this marriage.

As Travis watched her come toward him, he recognized that stubborn chin lifting. *Defiant as usual,*
he thought with a wry smile. Did she have any idea
how bewitching she looked at this moment?

And then Brooke was standing beside him. Her
hair had tumbled down, he noticed. So like her, defiant to the end. He liked that, but he wanted to see
her face, so he lifted the gossamer veil.

Dark lashes caressed her cheeks just for a second,
teasing, before she opened her eyes and caught
him with those golden eyes that he loved so much.
She revealed nothing of what she was feeling or
thinking, much like himself.

It didn't matter, Travis's body responded against
his will, and tonight he would finally get to taste
what he'd yearned for since she'd waltzed, uninvited, into his life.

Somehow, Travis managed to hear what the priest
was saying and to answer at the appropriate times.

The priest called for the alliance ring, a double
ring of gold, which was a tradition in New Orleans.
When opened, the ring became two interlocking
bands revealing the initials of the bride and groom
and the date of the wedding.

He opened the ring so that Brooke could see their

initials, then he slipped it on her finger in front of her ruby ring, a ring that had set him back a pretty penny. Yet he knew she was worth every cent.

Brooke softly repeated her vows as she slipped the smooth gold ring on his finger.

She was surprised that he'd taken the time to have their initials engraved in the rings, but she tried not to let it show. Travis was making her feel as if all of this was real, instead of the sham it really was. Could he possibly be gazing at her with something that looked like affection? As much as she wanted to believe it, she knew that couldn't be true.

Perhaps he was putting on a good show for his gathered relatives. Why else would he do it? And yet, knowing that, her heart still gave a little twist at the way he made her feel.

An even more terrifying realization washed over her . . . she feared she was beginning to care for Travis.

A few minutes later, the priest pronounced them man and wife, and Travis pulled her into his arms. He whispered for her ears only, "This time it's legal." Then he kissed her so tenderly that Brooke began to feel like a real bride.

They turned.

"May I introduce Mr. and Mrs. Travis Montgomery," the priest announced. "May no man tear them apart."

Travis tucked Brooke's hand into the crook of his arm and they proceeded down the aisle as man and wife.

Brooke didn't remember any of the faces they passed. She was simply relieved that the farce was finally over. Still, there was more to get through.

All the relatives signed the register as the bride and groom made their way to the great reception.

When they entered the parish hall, Brooke was astounded at the food that had been set out on two long tables. Huge hams dotted with cloves and dripping with brown sugar syrup were stationed on each end. Pheasant, mutton and, of course, a large pot of gumbo, were there as well. A white wedding cake graced a smaller table.

"Look, a cake," Brooke whispered to her new husband.

"Of course," Travis said as he escorted her over to the cake. "You are a bride, after all."

"It's just—" she paused. "I wasn't prepared for anything like this."

"After we have eaten, you are supposed to cut the cake so every young woman present can receive a slice of cake."

"I assume this is another Creole tradition," Brooke said, her lips twitching with laughter.

"Of course," Travis replied with a grin. "They will place the cake under their pillow with the names of three eligible young men. Tradition has it, that the one she dreams of will be her future husband."

Brooke gave Travis a devilish grin. "It's exactly how I found you."

Chapter 13

Travis's eyes gleamed with surprised laughter. "I wondered how you managed to catch me."

"On the contrary, I wasn't trying to catch you," she said smugly. "You merely fell into my lap."

Travis's brow jerked up. "Is that so?"

Brooke wanted to laugh at Travis's shocked expression, but before he could retort, his relatives began filing in to the parish hall to greet them.

Brooke nodded and smiled as everyone wished them well. Today's event was so much different than the wedding breakfast, she thought, where no one even spoke to her.

Just as she began to relax and congratulate herself for getting through everything, Brooke turned and found herself face to face with Travis's grandfather. He was just as unsmiling as the last time Brooke had seen him. Who did this man think he was, sitting in judgment of his grandson? Hadn't he ever done anything wrong in his lifetime?

Brooke smiled to herself. She'd wager there were a few skeletons in the old man's closet that he kept hidden. It was a shame that she didn't know any of them. She wondered if she might be able to uncover any of those deep, dark secrets.

Travis had stepped away from her for a few moments, so Brooke was left alone with the head of the family. They regarded each other, two fiercely indomitable wills clashed in silence.

"So you are the one," Archie deLobel said, making his statement sound more like a question.

"Yes," Brooke replied with false confidence.

DeLobel stiffened. "I have been after my grandson to marry for years," he said, his voice snapping like a whip.

Brooke wasn't intimidated by his gruffness. "Then you should be happy that he has finally heeded your advice."

"But you are not Creole," deLobel said as if she carried a lethal disease. Then he added, "This marriage is too sudden. After all, Travis was engaged to another."

Brooke shrugged. "I understand that they were not formally engaged because Travis had yet to present her with a ring."

"Formalities," deLobel said gruffly. "It makes our family look bad."

She started to tell him that she really didn't care, but he held his hand up.

"However, now that I know the reason, I can see why he changed his mind so quickly and did the proper thing. You're fortunate that the man did his duty." He nodded, though his stone-faced expression did not alter. "I give the boy some credit on that point. His mother never did correct her mistake."

So, his grandfather was really angry with Travis's mother and he directed that anger at Travis. What a shame. Brooke would store that tidbit of information away for future use.

She didn't care for the man's snide attitude one bit, but his comment was telling, whether he'd intended it or not. "Yes, it was gallant of Travis, wasn't it?"

"I just said so, did I not?" the man snapped. "At least you have gotten what you wanted?"

Brooke gave the tyrant a sweet smile and said softly, "Have I?"

Archie deLobel's face screwed up into a frown as if he couldn't decipher what she meant. As a lull in the conversation lengthened, Travis strode back over to them, keeping his grandfather from saying any more.

"Grandfather, I see that you are getting acquainted with my wife."

"Yes, I am." He scowled. "You will have to teach the woman to curb that sharp tongue of hers," he told Travis as if Brooke wasn't even in the room much less standing in front of him.

Travis just smiled. "There will be plenty of time for that," he said lightly. "Now if you'll excuse us, we've been instructed to take a seat at the head table."

Travis tucked Brooke's hand under his arm and led her away from his grandfather. "I see you and the old man got off to a good start. So, how did you find my grandfather?" Travis asked as they made their way to their special seats.

"He's rather a pompous ass," Brooke commented, keeping her voice low and smiling sweetly in greeting to another wedding guest.

Travis burst out laughing, causing many heads to turn. "At least we agree on something, my dear," he said as he pulled the chair out for her.

The feast began as soon as everyone was seated. Brooke was hungry and she didn't hold back. She'd barely picked at her breakfast, so everything tasted wonderful, especially the savory gumbos.

She glanced up and caught Travis looking at her. "Most brides are too nervous to eat and just pick at their food," he said. "I see you are not having that trouble."

Brooke smiled at his comment. "I would think you would have noticed by now that I'm not like most women," she informed him, using a napkin to hide her smile of triumph.

"So I'm finding out."

"Perhaps you should explain the difference between Cajun and Creole," she suggested, lowering her napkin. "That way I can understand what is so great about being Creole. Your grandfather makes me believe that if you are not Creole, then your blood is tainted."

"That is precisely the way he thinks," Travis said with a wry smile. He placed his fork on the side of his plate. "The Cajuns trace themselves directly to the Acadian French who were expelled from Nova Scotia. By your people, I might add. And Creoles trace their heritage from the French and Spanish who came here directly from Europe. My relatives, being French, are very proud people."

"So I've found out, and also rather rude, I might add." She smiled sweetly. "I hate to tell you, darling, but you are also English on your father's side."

"That I know, and my grandfather misses no chance to remind me of that. That's why I'm an outcast," Travis said matter-of-factly. However, I do have Creole in my blood. As far as he is concerned, there is no hope for you." Travis chuckled. "You are entirely English."

"An entirely unacceptable state of affairs," she concluded.

"Precisely."

As the celebration continued, champagne corks popped and bubbly liquid flowed freely. Every time Brooke turned around, someone was there to fill her glass. Soon she felt light-hearted and, yes, she had to admit, happy. It scared her to admit that, even to herself. How could she be so happy when she knew Travis didn't really love her? He lusted for her like many men had. That's why she needed to be careful and distance herself—because she could care for this man.

Travis was a complex man, and it would take considerable effort for her to completely understand him. Surely, the result would be well worth the challenge. Perhaps once she got to know him better, they might actually be able to pass a peaceful year together.

But then what? Brooke didn't want to think about that now. She had a year to decide what to do. For now she wanted to enjoy the moment.

Travis took pleasure in watching his wife when she didn't know he was looking. Despite his intention to treat her indifferently, he found he truly enjoyed his new wife's company. She was everything a man could desire in a woman. Not only was she beautiful, but she was intelligent as well, and he enjoyed talking with her and being in her company.

Perhaps this hadn't been such a bad arrangement after all. He'd always intended to marry one day, so why not to Brooke? She was certainly more desirable then Hesione. However, he most definitely wouldn't give up the plantation in a year, nor did he think Brooke would be willing to sell her portion, either. And so they would return to a stalemate.

Maybe at the end of the year they just might stay together. All he had to do was remain in control, and make sure not to fall in love with the head-strong woman. He had enough problems without risking his heart as well. That was, if he had one. Of course, if Brooke were pregnant by then she couldn't leave.

The music began, and Travis took Brooke's elbow and escorted her to the dance floor. "I believe the first waltz is reserved for us, my dear," he said, placing his hand lightly on her waist and guiding her across the floor.

For a few minutes, all Travis thought about was the soft music as he whirled his new wife around the dance floor. It gave him time to drink in the beauty of his bride, so blushingly radiant that she made men turn and look her way.

"Are you enjoying yourself?"

The champagne had relaxed her so that Brooke was indeed thoroughly enjoying herself as she whirled gently around in the arms of her husband, watching the crowd over his broad shoulders.

Her husband, she thought. What was she going to

do with a husband? Well, she knew *one* thing. She smiled to herself, anticipating the wedding night. After that, what would their lives be like?

Brooke looked up at Travis and found herself gazing into his ice-blue eyes. She could feel the sexual magnetism that made him so self-confident and irresistible. He seemed to have mesmerized her, and she couldn't think clearly. She did manage a small tentative smile. "What did you say?"

He tightened his grip, pulling her closer to his body. *Most indecent*, she thought, enjoying every moment of it. Travis's gaze moved down her face as if he were memorizing it, and finally rested on her lips. "I asked if you were having a good time."

"Yes, I am," she admitted fuzzily. There was something lazily seductive in her look. "Everything has been very lovely. And you?"

He gave her a devilish smile. "It wasn't nearly as painful as I had imagined it might be," he confessed dryly.

Brooke laughed. "Thank you, I think. I'm surprised at how well you dance," she commented gaily. "Some still believe that the waltz is a scandalous dance." She pointed out. "When I was a child, my mother told me that the Prince Regent held a ball in London where the participants danced the waltz, and a few days later *The Times* stated: 'We remarked with pain that the indecent foreign dance called the Waltz was introduced at the English court on Friday,'" Brooke said with a very heavy accent. "'We feel it a duty to warn every parent against exposing his daughter to so fatal a contagion.'"

Travis threw back his head and laughed. "I take it you did not heed the advice?"

"I rather like the dance, as well as doing things that will shock others," she said with a flippant smile. "Besides we have on all our clothes, so how indecent could it be?"

"You'll not have on your clothes much longer, my dear," Travis informed her with a devilish grin as the waltz came to an end. Brooke felt her pulse suddenly leap with excitement.

He took Brooke's elbow to escort her over to the refreshment table. "We will be leaving in just a few moments."

Well, he is most certainly making his intentions clear, Brooke thought with a delightful tingle of anticipation. She'd caught the anxious sound of his voice and couldn't resist the opportunity to tease. "Really?" Brooke said. "And where, may I ask, are we going?"

Travis drained a flute of champagne, tipping it high to get the last drop, before answering. "One of the Creole traditions is that the bride and groom do not leave their bedroom for at least five days."

Ooo, I like that, Brooke thought to herself. She smiled, thinking of yet another Creole tradition . . . they had many, and she wondered if someone had to actually watch to prove they had consummated the marriage. "You cannot be serious."

"Oh, but I am," Travis nodded. "So I have booked passage for us on a riverboat for a small cruise up the Mississippi. I thought you might enjoy the trip." When he saw the look of concern on her face, he added, "The paddlewheel ride is very different than the ship you sailed over on. This way, we'll be away from my family and we can relax."

"What about the plantation?"

"Ah, a true businesswoman," he remarked, smiling. "I like that. I asked Jeremy to look after everything, or at least the rest of the crops. The storm did so much damage that there is not much to do but prepare the soil for next season. And Mr. Jeffrics said he would stay and take care of the financial arrangements at the bank while we're gone."

"It sounds like you have taken care of everything," Brooke said, not sure whether to be pleased or annoyed at his taking charge. Then again, it felt good to let someone else take care of decisions. She'd never had anyone to lean on before. It was nice.

"I try to. Now you're the only task left on my list."

Brooke feigned a sigh. "And that would be?"

He gave her a wolfish grin. "I believe you know the answer to that question, my dear."

"Task, you say." She tilted her head. "You make it sound like a chore," she whispered.

"Yes," Travis replied. "And a delightful chore it will be."

Travis and his new bride arrived at the levee and boarded the *Natchez* around ten in the evening. The boat was a magnificent creation of wood and metal, shrouded and mysterious in the darkness.

Captain Leathers was there to welcome them aboard. Brooke couldn't see the man clearly in the darkness, but Travis had told her on the way over that riverboat captains were treated almost like gods in Louisiana society. Most had designed and built their own boats, and knew the river as well as their own bodies. Travis had told her that Leathers was one of the toughest captains he knew, and the best on the Mississippi River.

"Welcome aboard the *Natchez*, ma'am," the captain said in a slow southern drawl. "Most of our passengers will be boarding in the morning," he told her. "Since this is a special day for you both, I've made an exception."

Brooke smiled her thanks before the porter took Travis's bag. "This way, ma'am."

The porter showed Brooke to their stateroom, which he volunteered was the largest cabin on the ship. It was certainly ever so much nicer than the cramped space she had shared with Jocelyn and Shannon on the trip over from England.

Telling Brooke that he would be along shortly, Travis stayed behind to speak with Captain Leathers. Brooke supposed that he wanted to give her some privacy, and she appreciated that. It might not be her first time making love, but it would be her first time as a married woman.

Brooke stepped quietly into the stateroom. Once inside, she was surprised by its elegance. It was spacious. There was a huge Tester bed in the center of the room, and there were real windows that provided a splendid view of the Mississippi River. The windows were dressed with white, billowing, lace curtains. In the corner sat a chair, and a large looking glass flanked a small vanity. Cream-colored carpet covered the floor. Next to the door, Brooke spied her trunk. Evidently, Millie Anne had been privy to the secret and had packed her things.

Brooke smiled as she crossed to the trunk and opened the lid. On top was a snow-white nightgown, a favorite of hers. She picked it up and gave it a good shake clear the wrinkles. The top was constructed of fine, transparent lace that fit snuggly over her breasts in an Empire style tied with pink and blue ribbons. Yards and yards of fine sateen would swing seductively around her hips.

Brooke wanted to make sure she was wearing the gown when Travis came in, so she began to work on the many hooks on her dress until she was finally free of its restraints. She placed the wedding gown over the back of the chair and slipped into the nightgown. She loved the way the fabric felt smooth and cool against her skin.

Plucking the hairpins from her hair, Brooke shook her head, making her hair flow, wild and free, all around her shoulders and down her back. She stood in front of the mirror and admired the way the material shimmered when she mowed. It seemed to cling to her body in just the right places.

She looked around, smiling with satisfaction. The room was bathed in soft candlelight . . . everything was perfect.

She was ready. All she needed now was a groom.

Travis paced the deck until he figured he'd given Brooke enough time to prepare for bed. He knew how shy and timid most women were when it came to taking off their clothes in front of a man. He just

hoped that Brooke had left at least one candle
burning so he wouldn't break his fool neck entering the room.

Pausing outside the door, he reached for the
brass handle and drew in a deep breath. He'd
dreamed of this night. The knob turned easily
under his touch. *This is a good sign,* he thought. At
least he hadn't been locked out of the room. He
shoved open the door.

Stepping inside, he found not one but several
candles burning. The room was bathed in light, not
dark like he expected, and the bed had been
turned back.

Everything looked inviting.

Opening the door wider, he saw Brooke sitting at
the small dressing table brushing her long, golden
hair. The first thing that struck him was that her
gown was cut so low in the back that every time she
moved, he caught an enticing glimpse of creamy,
white skin. A lot of skin . . . no high-necked gowns
for her.

She must have seen his reflection in the mirror,
for she smiled at him and asked, "What are you
thinking?"

"I'm thinking how ravishing you are, and how
much I'm going to enjoy this night," he admitted,
his voice husky with desire. He placed a hand on
her soft shoulder.

Brooke leaned into his caress, then pushed away
from the table and turned around to face him.
Travis could see a body of pure perfection outlined
by the delicate fabric. His body burned with desire,

and he felt like a man trapped in the desert as he started unbuttoning his clothes, suddenly clumsy.

He felt as though he'd been struck deaf and dumb as he stared at the lovely creature he'd married. Her gown left nothing at all to the imagination. The way it clung to her in all the right places made his heart beat twice as fast. Her nipples strained invitingly against the lace bodice.

By God, she's going to kill me before I get my damn clothes off, he thought desperately, still fumbling with the buttons.

"Here, let me help you," Brooke purred. She pushed his clumsy hands out of the way and made short work of the task.

Travis drew in a deep, relieved breath. Brooke smelled so fresh and clean, and her hair smelled like flowers.

After she'd freed the buttons, she slowly pushed the shirt away from his body, her small hands teasing him with her touch. All he could do was to stand there, helpless, much like a young boy. Next she ran her hands over his chest, causing his breath to catch in his throat. That snapped Travis out of his stupor, and he hastily undid his trousers and disposed of them.

Now it was his turn. He wanted to see all of Brooke. However, she was distracting him by placing kisses on his chest. If she kept that up he'd surely go mad, he thought, so he placed his hands on her arms and pushed her a step away from him.

"Now, I want to see all of you," he told her thickly as he slipped his fingers under the thin straps and slipped them off her shoulders. Her gown slid seductively down her naked body, landing in a pool of shimmering satin on the floor.

For the second time tonight, Travis's breath caught in his throat as he gazed upon pure perfection. Why did he feel like this was his first time making love?

Perhaps it was because it was the first time with Brooke.

There was just something about her that was different from the other women he'd known. And she most definitely was not bashful.

He gave that to her.

She stepped brazenly into his arms then tilted her face up to him, her golden eyes glowing like a cat in the dark. He had a vague sensation of being stalked—she was the cat and he was the bait. Feeling a tightening in his loins, he knew he wanted her more than he'd ever wanted a woman before. He wanted to kiss those sultry lips into submission. And do many more indecent things with her.

Her flesh was creamy and soft beneath his fingers. Her breasts were round and firm and they stood waiting, inviting his touch.

Brooke turned into his arms. The moment she did, Travis wrapped his strong arms around her, molding her soft body to his hard one.

Brooke reveled at the feel of him. There were muscles everywhere she touched. She deliberately pressed her breasts against his chest, and the responding shiver she received told her **he** wasn't unaffected by her. He may not love her, but he wanted her, at least for now. His body's response told her it was the one way she would be able to control him.

Standing on her tiptoes, Brooke placed a soft kiss on his chin, then strained to reach upward until she found his lips. He responded, kissing her tenderly at first, but when she slid her arms around his neck, she found she'd awakened the beast within him.

And how she loved that beast.

Travis crushed her lips in a fevered kiss. He parted his lips, tender and insistent, and stroked hers with his tongue. He molded and shaped them into a perfect fit to his. With a little pressure, she opened her mouth to receive him, and he thrust his tongue into her mouth, kissing her deeply as she clung to him. He was insistent, relentless as he robbed her of every sense she possessed.

Brooke burned with a yearning need that she'd never experienced before. This was so different from all the other times.

She leaned into him as Travis trailed kisses down her throat. She moaned, lost in the intimate, sensual way he made her feel.

"Move your hair for me," he whispered.

Brooke pushed her heavy golden hair aside, exposing her neck, and Travis took advantage. She clung to him to keep from falling. Her knees felt like water.

But Travis still had more in store for her. He hadn't finished with his exquisite torture.

He bent lower until he reached her breast. He took one of her budded nipples into his mouth and teased her, circling it with his tongue. Then he sucked her nipple until she felt as if she were going to scream out at any moment.

Brooke reached for him, tangling her hands in his blond hair, pulling him closer against her breast. He responded by playfully biting her nipples, then sucking each one until she was moaning with pleasure.

She was on fire.

Brooke gasped but she couldn't catch her breath, for he reared up and took her mouth with a vengeance. She felt the hard, manly boldness of him resting against her belly, and now more than ever, she wanted to feel that hardness within her. She wanted to ride the magnificent beast until he, too, moaned her name. "Please, Travis."

Hearing his name on her lips started a raging fire within Travis. He needed relief. Since they were already so close to the bed, he bent a leg, kneeling on the mattress, and pulled Brooke with him as he rolled her over and onto her back. That long golden hair fanned across the sheets just as he'd envisioned so many times before.

As Brooke gazed up at him, she was overwhelmed by the intensity of her feelings. She'd thought she'd understood what desire was before. Now, having met Travis, she discovered that she understood nothing about what she felt for him. Could it be something more than lust?

The gentle strength of his embrace was sweet perfection as he held her to him, kissing her with such a tenderness that it made Brooke's heart swell with gladness.

He wanted her.

Travis was smoldering. The heat within him had built to such a tremendous state that he knew he had to have her now. He moved his hand down between her thighs to the warm wetness that waited for him there.

Good, she was ready, he thought as he enjoyed the warmth of her tongue on his.

He felt as though he were going to burst for want of fulfillment. His yearning to enter the sweet-hot flesh overwhelmed him as never before. It took a lot of restraint to ease himself slowly into her incredible warmth, but he wanted to feel her surrounding him before he began to move, slowly at first. "I want you so much," he said in a choked whisper.

Her hips arched beneath him in response as he plunged deeper. Her legs entwined around his waist. She moved with him as he held back, wanting to give her as much pleasure as she gave him. Her fingers bit into his skin as he felt her shudder. Travis drove deep and hard, shuddering with his own release as she called out his name.

Through the all-consuming heat of their passion, Travis realized that it had never been like this before. God, she was wonderful, he thought as he tried to catch his breath.

Finally, Brooke began to spin back from the abyss. An unfamiliar feeling of tenderness welled up in her breast as tears threatened to overwhelm her.

She tried to tell herself that she shouldn't be so emotional. Emotions had never been a part of her . . . until now.

Then realization hit Brooke right between the eyes. Travis meant something to her. How had this happened? She hadn't wanted him to mean anything at all.

Was this love?

She didn't know. Nor did she know how to handle it.

What was Travis feeling at this very moment? He certainly wasn't proclaiming his undying love.

Brooke was wise enough to know that one night of stormy lovemaking wasn't necessarily true love. The one thing she did know—Travis was her husband, and she had all of him.

At least, for now.

Chapter 14

The next morning, Travis told Brooke that Captain Leathers would give her a tour of the boat while Travis played cards in the salon. She wondered why Travis himself wasn't going to show her around, but she supposed that he didn't want to be bothered.

It occurred to her that she should possibly be put out that her husband didn't want to spend every little moment with her, especially since this was their honeymoon. However, Brooke reminded herself that their marriage wasn't built on undying love; theirs was strictly a business arrangement. So she gave her husband a little smile and told him to enjoy himself. This produced a frown from him as he left the cabin. Brooke was at a loss for how to interpret his expression.

Travis couldn't wait to get out of the cabin, and he wasn't sure why. Perhaps it was the fact that Brooke's every movement reminded him of her sexual attractiveness. Last night had been satisfying. It was damn good sex and something more, and it was the *more* that disturbed him. He needed time to come to terms with his newfound feelings. As long as they were together he'd never be able to think straight, so he had to get away to clear his mind. Maybe over several games of cards, he could relax long enough to think.

He passed several fetching women who smiled and flirted as they bid him a good day. Travis nodded a greeting, but kept going. The women were attractive, but they didn't have golden eyes and hair the color of fresh wheat.

Damn, he needed a drink.

He entered the salon with its inviting red interior and many windows positioned to allow plenty of light. Over in the right corner was what he was looking for—diversion—something to get his mind off his new wife. Four men sat playing cards and a fifth chair sat open and inviting, waiting for him.

Brooke dressed in a warm walking dress of purple cashmere trimmed with cream-colored lace. It had a high bodice with draping folds from the shoulders, down the back. She selected a cream-colored shawl to ward off the fall air, then left her cabin.

The weather was pleasant, typically fall-like with a chill in the air, accented by a light breeze. The sky was a clear crystal blue. Stationing herself by the rail, Brooke looked out over the vast expanse of the Mississippi River, which stretched as far as she could see. Apparently the rest of the passengers had boarded earlier that morning, and she and Travis had slept through the commotion. Brooke smiled, thinking how tired they had been after a night of making love. She wondered how she compared to Travis's other conquests. Hopefully he had the same sense of fulfillment that she did.

The water was as smooth as silk and the sun shimmered across the translucent, olive-green surface. Behind her loomed two tall, fancy-topped chimneys, belching black smoke that drifted behind them in the wind. The splashing of the trundling paddle wheel was slow and rhythmic as it turned, almost relaxing, she thought.

The pilothouse sat in front of the two smokestacks. The white gingerbread work that adorned the cabin promenades suggested an opulent hotel set afloat. Glass windows fronted all four sides of the rectangular cabin, providing the captain with a panoramic view of the river. A big, wooden steering wheel stood regally in front of the windows. Brooke raised her hand to shade her eyes so she could get a better view of the impressive structure.

The captain saw her and waved in cheerful greeting. He motioned for Brooke to stay where she was, then he exited the pilothouse, coming quickly to join her.

"Good morning, ma'am," Captain Leathers said as he strode purposefully but gracefully along the hurricane deck. He was tall and massive, looking like an advancing storm front in his coat of gray. His blue eyes were large and full of fight; his lips stern, a dense fringe of dark red beard ringing his jaw. There was such an air of confidence about the man that Brooke automatically liked him.

"I see you are enjoying my river," he said.

"Your river?" Brooke said, arching an eyebrow. "Yes, I am," she agreed. "I've never seen a river so large."

"You bet it is! It's the longest river in the world—two thousand three hundred miles," Leathers boasted. "It discharges three hundred and thirty-eight times as much water as the Thames."

"Really," Brooke commented, "I'm impressed. I always thought of the Thames as quite a large river. Tell me, how long have you been on this river?"

"Long time. Started as a deckhand when I was a boy," he answered proudly as he nodded to a knot of passengers strolling past them.

The women were dressed in deck-sweeping skirts and flounced jackets, and their hair was coiffed into elaborate whorls and fringes. Some wore hats with veils that protected them from the brilliant sun. The men were dressed just as fancy with coats, high hats, and varnished boots.

Brooke asked many questions as the captain showed her around the boat. She'd always enjoyed learning new things, and the captain and his ship were quite fascinating. Talking to him also kept her mind off of Travis and the wonderful way he had made her feel last night.

They walked leisurely along a promenade that stretched outside the staterooms on either side. Next they climbed a set of stairs that led to the passenger cabin, then on to the hurricane deck where the officers' quarters were grouped in the Texas house. The pilothouse was located on top of the Texas deck, three decks above the boiler deck.

When they reached the pilothouse, Leathers said, "This is where the pilot guides my ship. This river might look like it is easy to navigate, but there are sandbars everywhere, and if we hit one, we're stuck. Or worse, it could tear a hole in the underside of the boat. There are also reefs and islands and snags that are constantly changing, not to mention the abrupt ox-bow turn."

Leathers placed a hand on the shoulder of the pilot who was watching the river. "This is Edwards. The job of keeping us safe is on his shoulders."

"It sounds like you have a very important job, Mr. Edwards," Brooke commented.

Edwards turned and smiled at her, then glanced back to the captain. "Just like I've been trying to tell you, Cap'n. I'm very important to this paddleboat."

Leathers chuckled. "Let's go. My pilot already has a big head to go with the big price I have to pay him."

"The boiler room is the life of the boat," the captain explained. *It's very noisy*, Brooke thought. There were five boilers lying horizontally, side-by-side. Stacks of fuel lay opposite the furnace. The heavy iron doors were open, and sweating firemen fed the furnaces with pitch pine. As she watched, one man even threw in some rancid bacon.

Brooke looked to Captain Leathers for an answer.

Leathers chuckled. "Believe it or not, the grease is good for the fire. Makes it burn hotter."

Brooke wasn't sure it needed to be any hotter. It was so stuffy and dry she could hardly breathe. She wanted no part of this room. "If you don't mind, Captain, I'd like to go back up."

"The boiler room is no place for a lady, I agree," Captain Leathers said once they were on deck, "but I thought you'd like to see what makes this boat run."

"It was extremely interesting," Brooke admitted. "But, it was too hot and steamy in there. It almost felt like the depths of hell.

"I do appreciate the tour; however, I think I'll go and see what my husband is doing with his time. Travis said he was going to play cards. Do you know where that would be?"

"The salon. Of course, I'll show you how to get there."

The Grand Salon was a large room with crystal chandeliers providing enough light to read by. Rich, opulent furniture was scattered around in clusters so that men and women could lounge and talk. In one corner, however, there was a table where five men sat hunched over their cards. One of them was her husband.

Brooke waited a few moments to see if Travis would look up and notice her, but she might as well have been holding her breath. When he didn't glance her way, she strolled closer to the table.

She stood back, fascinated by their concentration, while the men played. Captain Leathers stood beside her and watched as well.

They were playing poker, and she could see the cards in Travis's hand. He had a full house, but was betting conservatively as he watched the pot grow. Finally, there was a call and Travis laid down the full house, much to one of the other gentlemen's disgust. He had three of a kind. Travis raked in the pot and began sorting his money.

"That was excellent strategy," Brooke said.

Travis turned around, his arm on the chair. "And you know something about the game?"

"I played a little back in England. It was all the rage in the salons in London."

One of the taller men stood. "I've had enough for today. Why don't you take my place, little lady?"

"I don't want to intrude," Brooke demurred.

"Gentlemen, this is my wife, Brooke," Travis introduced her. "Do you mind if she plays a few hands? I'm sure she will bore quickly," he added.

The men laughed but nodded their approval.

Brooke thought that her husband really didn't know her well enough to make such a statement, but that was all right with her. She could very easily show him. She moved around the table and took the recently vacated seat.

"Gentlemen," Captain Leathers said. "I see that Mrs. Montgomery is in good hands. However, I hope that you'll be gentle.

"And you might want to save some of your money to make wagers on the boat race," he added. "I received word that the *Annie Johnston* is waiting at Baton Rouge and would like to race us to St. Louis."

"Good news," the gentleman to her left said. "It's been a long while since I've seen a good race. I assume you will still support your passengers?"

"Of course," Leathers said with a smile.

"What does that mean?" Brooke asked.

"Most boats take few passengers when they race, but our good captain still makes his regular stops, albeit a little quicker. And he still wins the race," Travis explained.

"Don't believe in tossing passengers off just to lighten the boat," Leathers told him, then tipped his hat and bid them good day.

Playing a card game was a good diversion for Brooke, especially since she found herself winning many of the hands. She also liked the fact that occasionally Travis would have a good hand, but hers would be just a little better. Nothing like good competition. As her winning grew, his scowl became fiercer.

An hour and a half later, after Travis had finally won a respectable hand, he announced to the table, "Gentlemen, I believe that we've had enough for today. Are you ready to go, my dear?"

Brooke smiled, knowing that Travis's reasons for quitting had more to do with her winning than his boredom. "Of course," she said, gathering her money. "Thank you, gentlemen, for allowing me to play with you," she said graciously, then took her husband's arm.

Once outside on the promenade, they strolled down the deck. It was now late in the day, and the *Natchez* was just docking at Baton Rouge where a horde of people stood on the dock.

Brooke and Travis kept their place by the rail so they could watch as the roustabouts unloaded cargo and new passengers were taken aboard.

"How did you learn to play poker so well?" Travis finally asked. Evidently he'd been thinking about the game since they'd left the salon.

"I told you, I played in England. When I was in boarding school, we would sneak into a back room and play cards." She peered around at him. "You're not upset because I took a few hands from you, are you?"

"Of course not," Travis protested. "But I usually win."

Brooke looked at her husband, dressed in a dark blue coat and buff-skinned breeches, then searched his ruggedly handsome face trying to see how he really felt. "You're sulking," she told him.

"I am not."

Yes, he was, and Brooke knew it. Whenever Travis was around, the air seemed to vibrate with his presence. She leaned over and kissed him on the cheek. "I'm sorry I bested you at cards."

Travis realized he sounded childish. "Is that your best apology?"

She gave him a surprised look.

"Come now, I'm sure you can do better than that," he teased.

He couldn't miss the gleam in Brooke's eyes as she stepped into his arms. She slowly slid her hands up the front of his shirt, her fingers sliding into the nape of his hair.

"So you'd like a better apology," she whispered, waiting for his nod of agreement. "How's this?" she asked, kissing him first on the chin and then moving to his mouth, where she placed another soft kiss.

Travis groaned and tightened his hold on her, parting her lips so he could taste her mouth. He really didn't give a damn that they were in public. Where this woman was concerned, passion exploded every time he touched her. He moved his mouth urgently over hers.

"Must be love," a woman passenger said as she passed them.

Somewhere a bell rang thrice, reminding Travis what he wanted to do to his wife couldn't be done out here on the deck, so he forced himself to pull away.

"You're not going to believe this," Brooke said in a husky voice as she laid her head on his shoulder. "But your kisses are so wonderful that I thought I heard bells."

Travis chuckled. "What you heard, my love, was Captain Leathers warning the passengers to find their accommodations and for the visitors to go ashore. It's time to shove off. Turn around and watch, and then we'll go to our room," he whispered in her ear.

Brooke turned in his arms, which he kept snuggly around her. She felt bubbly inside when he held her, and the feeling was addictive. From the moment they had married, Travis had changed so much that Brooke wondered if he might truly feel something for her.

The levee was a crush of waving hats and handkerchiefs. Hands and arms waved at the two boats, cheering them on. Someone on shore fired a volley of gunfire, and the *Natchez* and the *Annie Johnston* sounded their own whistles.

The smokestacks gushed fat, thunder-dark clouds of smoke. A roustabout on the wharf chopped the mooring line. With a deafening rattle of machinery, the *Natchez* backed away from the wharf. Her paddle wheels swirled and bit into the brown water, but the *Annie Johnston* had beaten them away.

"We're behind," Brooke protested.

"Leathers will catch them, my dear."

It was completely dark now, but once they pulled out into the river, there were dozens of bonfires on the levees where crowds had gathered in various places to watch the two boats race. "Catch her," they screamed and waved their arms.

"I can't believe people are out in the dark to watch these boats," Brooke commented.

"Racing is a big thing along the Mississippi, and some people wager a great deal of money on the race," Travis explained. "Hopefully, we will have caught the *Annie Johnston* by morning. Are you hungry?"

Brooke turned in his arms and answered him honestly, "I'm hungry for you." The smoldering flame she saw in his eyes warmed her.

Travis buried his lips in the hollow of her throat, then swept her up in his arms. "Well, we don't want you hungry," he murmured hotly, capturing her mouth in a quick kiss.

After they had made passionate love, they lay locked together in each other's arms for a few minutes until their breathing returned to normal. After a while, Travis moved to the side, but he still held Brooke next to him, her head cradled upon his shoulder.

"How are you enjoying the trip so far?" he asked.

"It has been lovely. Thank you for taking the time to make this trip. I thought we would be married and then go right back to the plantation and work," Brooke said.

Travis's laugh was low, throaty. "That was my original plan. Not sure when I changed my mind."

Brooke smiled to herself. Just maybe Travis wasn't as unaffected by the marriage as he'd planned. "I still find it hard to believe that we are married." She drew in a leisurely breath. "If someone had told me a month ago that I'd be married to a man I'd yet to meet. . . . Well, I would have wondered how much they'd had to drink."

"I can see your point." Travis laughed, too. "It means I'm in bed with the wrong person." Brooke tilted her head up to see his face and then he continued, "You were second choice."

"Thank you very much," Brooke said with a frown. She jabbed his chest with her finger. "Are you sorry?"

Travis glanced down at her upturned face and gave her a warm smile, a sensual expression playing across his features.

"No, I'm not sorry," he told her. "As a matter of fact, I'm enjoying myself." He traced the curve of her jaw with his finger. "I can't remember the last time I've said that."

She reached up and kissed him, then settled back into her cozy spot. She knew Travis was kinder than he wanted anyone to know, and she liked that. She also liked his company. When he wasn't around her, she felt an extraordinary void. She wanted to have more than sex with him. She wanted to know all about him. "Have you always lived in New Orleans?"

"Pretty much."

He didn't seem bothered by her question so she pressed on. "Tell me something about your childhood."

His left brow rose a fraction. "Now, why would you want to hear something so boring?"

"Because you're my husband, and I *should* know something about you."

He eyed her with a calculated expression, but then he surprised her and began to talk. "My childhood wasn't pleasant—no more than yours." He ran his finger up and down her arm as he spoke. "My mother disgraced her family. As you've seen, my family isn't forgiving. We were always kept on the outside. Since Mother couldn't support us, my grandfather was obligated to let us live with him, but he did it begrudgingly. Mother was an outcast of Creole society. As she always told me, 'who wants a woman with a bastard son?'"

Brooke gasped. "That was an awful thing to tell a child."

"But it was the truth," Travis pointed out. "We lived on an allowance from my grandfather, and I wore hand-me-down clothes from my cousins. Then out of the blue, the duke came back to see me."

"Is that the first time you saw Jackson?" Brooke asked, but added, "At least, you got the chance to meet your father. I had never got the chance to meet mine."

"Yes, it was. Jackson settled money on my mother so she would allow me to return to England with him. I didn't want to go. I didn't want any part of the man, but they both insisted it was best for me. So at thirteen I went to study in England.

"The older I got, the more rebellious I became." Travis smiled slightly as he remembered. "By the time I was seventeen, I'd become a problem. I was hitting the cups, gambling away my allowance. Jackson finally washed his hands of me and sent me home. That's when he gave me Moss Grove, the fallen down plantation, to run. He told me he wasn't sure I could do the job, but he'd give me a chance to see if I would become a man of my own."

"And you made a success of the plantation," she said with a smile. "You showed him."

"Jackson never got to see what I'd accomplished," Travis said, and Brooke could clearly hear the regret in his voice. "But I did provide Mother with a home. I figured I owed her that much, since I had been the source of her problem over the years. I wanted to get away from my grandfather."

"Why?" Brooke leaned up and looked at Travis. "You didn't ask to be born. Your mother should have taken the blame. She knew Jackson was already married when she met him."

Travis nodded. "Still, I felt I always had to prove myself. Because of me, she never had the nice things she could have. I had to prove both to my grandfather and father that I could be successful on my own."

Brooke placed her hands on the sides of his face. "You don't have to prove anything to me, Travis Montgomery. Believe it or not, I like you just the way you are."

Travis felt his chest tighten. He'd never felt quite like this before. "Come here, my love," he whispered as he pulled Brooke up to him.

He brushed his lips against her temple, then he kissed her cheeks before finding her soft mouth, her lips parting easily beneath his. When his tongue touched hers, a jolt slammed through him. He'd never desired a woman as much as he did this woman, his wife. But then, Travis reminded himself that it was good to lust after your own wife. *His wife.* He still couldn't believe he'd actually married her. He deepened his kiss, thrusting his tongue into her mouth over and over again.

She moaned with pleasure. Travis loved the needy sounds she made while he stroked her hair, and he felt strangely betrayed by his own body. The exquisite feeling of her in his arms, the taste of her lips clinging to his was deliciously unbearable.

Slowly he slid his hand, trailing his fingers down her throat to her breast where he fondled one globe, its pink nipple tightening at his touch.

This was so different from the other times, Brooke realized. Travis was being very gentle and considerate, and his tenderness made her even hotter. His mouth slid down her neck then lower to her chest until his lips teased her nipples erect with tantalizing possessiveness. The pleasure was pure and explosive, causing her to gasp in sweet agony.

Travis couldn't believe the passion this woman had for him, nor how ravenous he was for her. They had already made love, yet he wanted her again. He couldn't seem to get enough. Brooke just might be the death of him . . . but what a way to go.

His hand moved down to the soft triangle between her legs where he found the special place that made her moan with pleasure. His fingers probed between her legs, sliding in and out until she was slick, wet and ready.

"I want you now, Travis," she whispered, running her hands over his back.

His body flamed at her softly spoken words. He

eased into her with deliberate slowness, and she whimpered and arched her hips, driving him crazy. No matter what it cost him, he wanted to hold back and give her pleasure. He began to move rhythmically within her, loving the way she felt beneath him, the way she smiled.

Ah, hell, he swore silently. Much against his better judgment, he loved the woman. He had fallen into her spell whether he wanted to or not.

That truth had been dredged from a place beyond logic and reason, but he didn't care. Somehow, love had sneaked up on him when he wasn't paying attention.

"You feel so good, my love. I could make love to you all night," he told her as he plunged into her. She answered by arching to meet his thrust.

Travis felt as though he were riding a wave in the ocean—building and building, higher and higher until he reached the pinnacle, then he crested into oblivion until he crashed down on shore, shuddering with his release.

Glancing down at Brooke, he saw the love and contentment in her eyes. Tomorrow at dinner he'd tell her he didn't want their marriage to be a business deal. He wanted Brooke for the rest of his life.

But tonight, he wanted to enjoy this joyous contentment he'd found in her arms. He rolled to his side, enfolded Brooke next to him, and slept like he'd never slept before.

Chapter 15

The *Natchez* had made a swift run the night before. Word had gone out that they would dock for a very short time in Memphis to unload cargo and pick up a few passengers. However, the *Annie Johnston* was not doing its regular run. Nevertheless, the *Natchez* had already begun to catch her. Captain Leathers believed that a captain should keep his normal operations and then race.

Brooke hurried to the railing to watch the morning's docking activity as she waited for Travis to return. Today he'd opened his gold case to find it empty. Needing some cigars, he had left the ship, heading for one of the stores that fronted the shore. He promised Brooke he'd return well before the boat was ready to shove off.

Brooke had actually experienced a twinge of loss as she watched him leave the ship. She realized it was silly. After last night, she knew he was coming right back, but she felt nervous when Travis wasn't near her. She'd finally found that mysterious thing called love, and she felt like shouting to everyone that she was normal after all.

Hoping that the fresh air would help her piece her thoughts together, she pondered her new feelings. This was uncharted territory for Brooke, and she didn't know how to deal with it. She'd always felt so sure and confident before.

Could love be a miserable uncertainty?

Travis hadn't told her that he loved her, but Brooke had felt it in the way he held her and looked at her. It was wonderful. In the past, whenever she found happiness, something always seemed to come along to take it away. She wondered what it would be this time.

Brooke watched Captain Leathers from where she stood on the hurricane deck. He was snapping orders to his crew. George Devol, one of the gamblers Travis had played cards with, strode over to speak with the captain. It appeared Devol was carrying a stovepipe hat full of banknotes and silver coins.

"Captain," Devol said to get the man's attention. "There is a poor widow lady down there with six children. She told me she had tried to board the *Annie Johnston*. When Captain Blake found out she had no money, well sir, he kicked her and her children off his boat. So, I've passed this hat among the passengers and officers, and I think we have enough to buy the family passage."

Captain Leathers waved aside the hat. "Give the money to the woman. She needs it more than I do. I'll instruct one of the crew to find a room for her," he spat. "Sounds like something Captain Blake would do."

Brooke smiled. She had thought the captain was a good man. Now she had the proof. Brooke turned her attention back to the wharf to see if Travis was on his way back. She didn't see him, only the passengers waiting to board. They would take on fourteen passengers beside the widow and her children, as well as loading cargo.

Captain Leathers was very efficient in loading cargo and passengers quickly. By now, everyone knew that they were in a race, so they cooperated by boarding quickly. However, there was an older woman and a young lady, accompanied by their maids, who seemed to be arguing with a crew member about their luggage. Evidently, the crew must have satisfied the woman because she eventually nodded, and several men rushed down to lug all of the bags aboard, which was so much more than what the normal passenger carried.

Brooke spotted Travis out of the corner of her eye as he walked briskly down the wharf toward the boat. Travis made the turn and started up the gangplank. As he hurried by the passengers, a woman squealed and threw herself into his arms. Not only that, but the hussy kissed him—full on the lips—which Brooke didn't care for at all. The woman had some nerve.

Brooke watched as Travis tried to disengage the young woman's arms from around his neck. Then the older woman moved over and kissed Travis on the cheek. That was when Brooke realized this had to be Travis's mother and Hesione. *Of all the rotten luck*, Brooke thought. She had wanted to have a little time with Travis before they returned home and had to untangle the ugly mess made by him marrying someone else. She'd expected to have at least another month before Hesione and Travis's mother returned.

Evidently, that wasn't to be. Brooke sighed. She wouldn't have to wait any longer to meet them.

The trio marched up the gangplank, Hesione's arm linked with Travis's. His mother was beside him, happily chatting away.

Once they were aboard, Brooke heard Travis introduce them to Captain Leathers, who was his usual gracious self.

Captain Leathers excused himself so that he could greet the other boarding passengers and get the boat moving. He was now only an hour behind the *Annie Johnston.*

"Cast off the lines," the captain barked his order to a roustabout.

Travis glanced around until he spotted Brooke. When he saw her, he motioned her to come to him.

Brooke straightened her rich brown skirt and started his way. Before she reached him, he disengaged himself from Hesione and strode over to Brooke.

"I think you know who they are," Travis nodded toward his mother. "Are you ready?"

Brooke took a deep breath before nodding. Travis grasped her elbow and quickly closed the distance between them and his mother.

"Mother," Travis said to gain her attention.

Brooke noticed that his mother was small with a medium complexion and dark brown hair, but she didn't have Travis's eyes. Her eyes were green and cold, though she wore a smile at the moment.

"A lot has happened since you've been away. I'd like you to meet Brooke Montgomery, my wife. This is my mother, Margaret deLobel."

Travis's mother started to nod, but stopped as her son's words apparently sunk in. Hesione, a puzzled look on her face, stood before them dumbfounded. "What did you just say?" Margaret asked as though she hadn't quite understood him.

"We were married three days ago," he replied confidently. Then he looked at his former fiancée. "I'm sorry, Hesione."

"How could you!" Hesione screamed. Tears of rage ran down her lovely face. "What about me?"

"Have you lost your mind?" Margaret asked her son. "You know that we were shopping for Hesione's trousseau. Did you forget that you already had a fiancée?"

"No, Mother, I didn't forget, but a few things have changed."

"Look how upset you've made Hesione." Margaret put an arm around the sobbing girl. "There has to be some mistake," Margaret insisted as she swayed as if to faint. Travis had to reach out and steady her. She glared at Brooke, utter contempt on her face. "After all, this woman is English."

"Perhaps I should take you to your room," Travis suggested, looking around at the curious passersby. "You'll feel better once you're rested."

"Is there something wrong with being English?" Brooke finally found her voice after watching the spectacle in front of her.

"You are not Creole!" Margaret snapped, her eyes filled with loathing.

Brooke sighed, wondering how many times she'd heard that statement. "Well, we cannot all be so fortunate as to be Creole. I assure you I do come from a good bloodline, however."

"Now you are insulting me with your sharp tongue," Margaret spat, not looking quite as sick as she had a moment ago, Brooke noticed. She must have been using a ploy she'd developed over the years to control Travis. Apparently, he had finally learned to ignore it.

Margaret turned to her son. "I'd like to see you alone."

"If you don't mind," Travis glanced at Brooke, "I'm going to escort Hesione and Mother to their rooms. I'll see you back in our room."

Brooke nodded as she watched Travis grasp the woman's elbow. What choice did she have? His mother wasn't taking the news well at all, not that Brooke had expected she would. However, she hadn't expected the women to make such a scene, especially in public.

Perhaps the Creoles didn't have the manners of the English, Brooke smiled.

She really didn't want to go to her room where she'd have nothing to do but worry about the situation, so she turned to watch the last passenger board.

"Oh, my God," Brooke said under her breath. Could her day get much worse? She watched as a man strode up the ramp. Not just any man, but the Earl of Whatsbury.

A man who could identify Brooke and her past.

Quickly, she turned away from the rail and started

for her room. What was she going to do? The boat wasn't that big. It would be impossible to avoid him. Thank God she had never slept with the Earl, but she'd attended several parties that he had attended.

She remembered Whatsbury at one of the soirees where he'd been very much in his cups. He had propositioned her, telling Brooke he'd treat her like a queen. She'd been so repulsed by his behavior that she'd cut him off, telling him he didn't have enough money to afford her.

Whatsbury had gotten so angry he'd grabbed her arm, gripping it painfully. Thankfully, the duke she was keeping company with at the time stepped in and rescued her, making Whatsbury apologize. He never bothered her after that.

Now she would have to face him again. Would he have forgotten her? She could only hope.

As soon as Travis delivered the hysterical Hesione to her room and his mother to hers, he tried to excuse himself. He had no desire to be around either of them, but he knew he wouldn't get away from his mother so easily.

"How could you have married a stranger?" Margaret rounded on him, her face a mask of fury.

"My father died."

Margaret stopped short and gasped, her hand coming to her mouth. "How do you know?"

Travis folded his arms and leaned against the door. "His solicitor, Mr. Jeffries, came to see me."

"Did your father leave you anything?"

Travis nodded. "Yes, he did. He left me half of Moss Grove."

His mother gave him a questioning look. "Half?"

"That's correct. The other half was left to Brooke."

"Well, I never!" Margaret protested, and then she began to pace. "Jackson told me himself that you were the only child he had. Who was this woman to Jackson? And why did you marry her?"

"There was a stipulation that if I married Brooke, Jackson's money would go toward the plantation. The sugarcane crop was ruined by a storm, leaving me virtually penniless. I had no choice."

"I see now. You did it for the money," Margaret concluded, the wheels spinning in her head. "But if you had married Hesione, you would have had money, too," she pointed out. "This other woman isn't one of us." Margaret stopped pacing and faced her son. "You know that by marrying Hesione we would have finally received my father's approval. I can well imagine what he thinks with you marrying that little tramp."

"Do not call my wife names," Travis warned.

"She means nothing to you," Margaret stated as if she knew with certainty. Then she began pacing again. "And she won't be your wife for long. You can have the marriage annulled and then you can marry Hesione."

"I don't want an annulment," Travis told her in a terse voice. "And I most definitely don't want to marry Hesione any longer. I do not love Hesione, so I see no reason to undo what I have done. She can find somebody else.

"Mother, you might as well get used to the fact that I don't give a damn whether Grandfather approves of me or my wife. The only people I need to please are myself and Brooke. This marriage started out as a business arrangement, but it has become more than that now."

Margaret whirled around. "You fool. You love her, don't you?"

"Mother, do not push me on this," Travis warned. "Yes, I do love Brooke. I don't expect you to feel the same, but I expect you to accept her. If you cannot do that, I will make arrangements for you to live elsewhere."

"I cannot believe you are speaking to me like this. Don't you love me?"

"Yes, Mother, I love you," Travis said patiently. "I've tried to provide you with a good life. However, I intend to live my own life and be happy. Hopefully I will give you many grandchildren with Brooke, but I won't have constant bickering in my house, so if you cannot be civil to the woman that I have chosen, then you can find someone else to take care of you."

Margaret swayed. "I think I'm going to faint."

He steered her toward the bed, then let her go. "I suggest you get some smelling salts," Travis said. Then he left her alone. He'd seen this routine before.

As soon as Travis left, Margaret straightened. Her son didn't know what was good for him, and she did. Hesione was Travis's intended and Margaret intended for him to have her. Whether he wanted her or not.

When the sound of Travis's footsteps had faded away, Margaret made her way out of her stateroom to see to Hesione.

Margaret knocked on the door. Not waiting for an answer, she stepped inside. "Are you all right, dear?"

Hesione's eyes were red and puffy from crying. "Yes," she said, wiping her eyes. "But your son has shamed me. How will I hold up my head when we get home?"

"I don't know what is the matter with him. It's obvious that he doesn't realize what he has done. He's probably been bewitched by the girl," Margaret said as she turned back the bed for Hesione. "It's clear that I will have to fix this situation."

"But what can you do?" Hesione sniffed. "He's married," she wailed. "And not to me."

Margaret patted Hesione's hand. "I know, dear. But we'll do something to undo this. I just have to think about it for awhile." Margaret was certain that Travis had been blindsided by that woman, and given a little time he'd come to regret the marriage and want out. Or at least she hoped. Hesione would have been the way to finally please her father, but Travis had ruined that. She'd have to find a way to undo the damage her son and that woman had done.

Margaret hurried back to her room. She'd have to tread carefully around her son. He definitely had a mind of his own and could be very stubborn when he wanted to be.

She'd have to think of a way to make him want the same thing she did.

When Travis returned to his room he found Brooke pacing. "I suppose our peace and quiet has come to an end," Travis remarked dryly. "I had no idea that we would encounter them on our wedding trip. Then again, I guess this was bound to happen sooner or later."

"I would have preferred later," Brooke said. "Much, much later." She gave him a small smile. Then she placed her hands on her hips. "She was none to happy to see me, but then again, I can understand the shock. I'm sure it will be a long while before she even considers the idea of liking me."

"If ever," Travis said with a slight chuckle.

"You have a point there." Brooke couldn't help giggling. "I can see a lot of your grandfather in her."

"Yes, you can," he said with a nod. "We're having dinner at the Captain's table tonight, so mother shouldn't make a scene. I'm going to the salon to play some cards again this afternoon. We must appear as if nothing were out of the ordinary, especially after the scene a few minutes ago."

"Grand," Brooke said with a sarcastic frown. She wondered if she could convince him to stay with her in the cabin. Not only did she have to deal with a disgruntled mother-in-law, but she also had to worry about the earl. He was someone who could bring her past to the light of day.

Brooke took great care dressing for dinner. She swept her hair up into a glorious heap on the crown of her head, then pinched her cheeks. She wore a dark blue gown that was cut low and worn off the shoulders.

She had just finished dressing when Travis returned. He'd dressed earlier, then taken a stroll around the deck while she finished getting ready. This was one of the times when she wished she had brought her maid with her. At least she'd have another woman to talk to. Of course, now she had Travis's mother, but Brooke doubted that the woman would ever want to chat with her.

When Travis opened the door, he stopped in the doorway. Every time he saw his wife, she appeared more beautiful than the last time. Just the sight of her made his blood run hot.

Brooke waited for him to say something. "Is something wrong?"

"My God, you are beautiful," Travis said, coming out of his trance.

Seeing desire in his eyes, Brooke smiled. "Thank you, kind sir. Are you ready to go to dinner?"

"After seeing you, I'd be happy to go hungry," he murmured, taking Brooke in his arms and kissing her soundly.

"Since I've gone to the trouble to get dressed . . ." Brooke said with an amused smile on her lips. "However, I am more than willing to forgo dinner," she said but didn't add that it would save her a lot of worry about running into the earl.

"We must have dinner first, then afterwards . . ." Travis gave her a wicked smile. "Besides, Mother and the captain are probably already there. We cannot leave them waiting."

"I guess not," Brooke said. She just lost her appetite.

The dining room hummed with conversation when Brooke and Travis arrived. They entered and waited for the maitre d' to take them to their places. The dining room was the finest on the river. Black and red carpet adorned the floor. Round tables draped with white linen and red velvet covered chairs that were scattered around. Each table would seat six.

Finally the maitre d' came to seat them at the Captain's table, where Margaret and Hesione waited.

Brooke groaned inwardly.

"Mother. Hesione." Travis greeted them.

"I hope you had a pleasant afternoon," Margaret said, the comment directed only toward Travis.

"As a matter of fact, I did," Travis replied as he pulled the chair out for Brooke. "I played poker with an old school chum from England, and he played as lousy as he ever did."

Brooke's stomach twisted. She could only hope his chum was not Whatsbury.

"Anyone I know, dear?" Margaret asked.

"I don't believe so," Travis replied, then addressed the captain. "How is the race going?"

"If Blake beats me to St. Louis, you have my permission to hang me from the crosstrees," Leathers stated grimly.

"That's a bit drastic, captain," Brooke said with a wry smile. "I assume we are ahead."

Leathers laughed. "Not exactly, but there is still hope."

Travis and the captain continued to talk about the race as dinner was served. It consisted of catfish, roasted red potatoes, and Praline Chicken topped with pecan sauce.

Too bad their dinner company couldn't be as pleasant as the food, Brooke thought.

The women were unusually quiet throughout dinner, and that was fine with Brooke. She could endure all the hateful looks from Hesione, but Brooke didn't know whether she could keep a civil tongue and be nice if they were nasty, so maybe quiet was better for all.

"We'll be in St. Louis tomorrow if the fog is not too bad," Leathers said. "I believe that is where you wanted to go, Mrs. deLobel."

Margaret replaced her coffee cup. "It was where I wanted to go originally, but since seeing my son our plans have changed. Hesione and I will continue on back to New Orleans."

"That can be arranged," Captain Leathers said. "I know you are anxious to get to know your new daughter-in-law. Now, if you'll excuse me, I need to visit the other tables so they do not feel neglected." He stood. "Be sure and enjoy the bread pudding. It's the best on the Mississippi."

Brooke leaned over to Travis, "I bet it's not as good as Prosper's."

"Prosper's is the best," Margaret stated.

"I definitely agree," Brooke said with a smile. She didn't receive one in return.

"Just how long have you been at Moss Grove?" Margaret asked, bluntly.

"I came toward the end of September."

"And none of your family accompanied you?"

Brooke felt as though she were being interrogated. "I have no family. I was accompanied by Mr. Jeffries."

"He was Jackson's solicitor," Travis interjected.

"I well know who Mr. Jeffries is." Margaret pushed back her chair. Travis leapt up to assist her as she turned to Brooke. "That is highly unusual," Margaret said, her voice haughty. "You didn't even have a lady's maid with you?"

"I was accompanied by several friends," Brooke said. "It seemed pointless to disrupt some poor woman's life when I knew I'd have other servants at Moss Grove," she tried to keep her voice pleasant.

"And who is your maid?"

"Millie Anne," Brooke supplied. "She's wonderful."

"Millie Anne works in the fields."

Brooke looked at the old bat, her patience wearing thin. However, she forced a smile. "Not any more. She has become a wonderful companion for me."

"Come, Hesione," Margaret snapped. "It's time for us to turn in. Travis, accompany us to our rooms."

"Yes, Mother." He took her arm, but turned to Brooke. "I'll be right back, my dear," Travis told her, giving her a smile not intended for his mother or her companion.

Brooke decided that Hesione must be a timid little mouse. She looked as if she'd like to hide behind Travis's mother. It probably was a good thing that the girl hadn't married Travis. He would have chewed her up in the first week.

Brooke was just finishing her coffee when she heard a crisp English accent from behind her.

"Bloody hell, I can't believe my eyes," Whatsbury said as he invited himself over to Brooke's table. "It is a small world, I dare say. I see you have decided to try America."

Brooke didn't answer him.

"What's wrong? The men in Europe didn't have enough money for you?"

She glared at the earl, who once again had had too much to drink. "Do I know you, sir?" Brooke finally asked, hoping he'd think he'd made a mistake.

"Don't play coy with me, Brooke Hammond. I couldn't ever forget a face like yours."

Brooke stood. The only thing she could do was play dumb. "Excuse me, sir." She made her way across the room to where Travis had just stepped back inside.

"I see you've met Whatsbury," Travis said. "He's a bit odd."

"Yes, he is," Brooke agreed. "I have a headache. I'm going to our room to lie down."

"Certainly. I'll walk with you. I just need to collect some money from Whatsbury first." Travis placed his hand on her arm.

"It's just a short walk. I'll be fine," Brooke told him.

"If you insist. I'll see Whatsbury then join you shortly."

As Brooke made her way down the walkway, vagrant puffs of fog were lingering in the air. It was an eerie feeling that sent chills up her arms.

She couldn't face the earl on Travis's arm and take the chance that he would publicly humiliate her. Maybe he wouldn't make the connection between her and Travis unless he saw her talking to him. She hoped the earl kept his mouth shut about her past, but she knew that was very unlikely.

So she'd go to her room, change her clothes, and await her fate.

* * *

Travis strolled over to where Whatsbury stood in a corner looking very much like a peacock. The man had always been full of himself, even back in England.

Whatsbury turned toward Travis. "Damned if your luck hasn't change, old boy."

"If you are talking about cards," Travis said, "You'll recall I use to beat your rather soundly back at school."

"No. I'm talking about Brooke Hammond, old man," Whatsbury said with a wicked grin. "I was most surprised when I saw her here, even though she pretended she didn't know me. No two women could look like that. She was all the rage in England. The finest circles, you know the routine, old chap."

"You know my wife?" Travis asked.

"Your wife!" Whatsbury laughed. "Surely you jest."

"Why do you say that?" Travis asked, trying to hold his temper and not placed his fist right in the middle of his old friend's face.

"You don't know?"

"My patience is wearing thin," Travis warned.

"She's a courtesan, old man."

Travis grabbed Whatsbury by the shirtfront. He stared down at him with cold contempt. "I demand satisfaction for that slur."

"Wait a minute. Wait a minute," Whatsbury said holding up his hands in defense. "I'm telling you I tried for her myself, and she turned me down flat. I'm only telling you what she evidently did not. If you don't believe me, ask her." Whatsbury said and Travis let him go. "Then you'll see there isn't any reason to fight over this. Sorry, old chap, I thought you knew."

Travis could only see a red haze as he left the dining room. Had he been played for a fool? Had Brooke been his father's whore and she'd somehow convinced him to give her a portion of the plantation?

Travis shattered inside. God help her if that were true!

Chapter 16

The cabin door flew open.

Brooke's head snapped up.

Travis stood in the doorway, glaring at her as if she were the enemy. A muscle twitched in his jaw, and his blue eyes were so cold and distant she actually shivered. Travis's glance seemed to accuse her without him having to say a word.

Brooke held her breath. Her pulse began to throb erratically as her panic built and welled in her throat.

He knew.

As the tension between them increased with frightening intensity, Travis finally entered the room and shut the door behind him. However, he didn't come toward her. Instead he went and stood behind one of the two chairs, his hand clenching the back.

A wave of apprehension swept through Brooke.

"Would you like to tell me," he paused and took a calming breath to calm the menacing fury in his eyes, "exactly what you were to my father?" Travis didn't let her answer before he shot her another question. "Were you his whore?" There was a bitter edge of cynicism in his voice.

"No. I was not," Brooke told him. "How could you think such a thing?"

His contemptuous eyes raked over her. "How?" Travis gripped the chair until his knuckles turned white. Brooke knew he struggled to control his temper. "How?" he repeated. "Whatsbury just congratulated me for succeeding in getting you as my courtesan. Seems he never managed to get you for himself," Travis grated out.

Travis made everything sound so ugly, Brooke thought, but he wasn't finished yet. . . .

"I challenged him to a duel for the insult," he continued. "Whatsbury merely laughed and told me to ask you if I didn't believe him. It seems you were all the rage in England," Travis sneered. "Can you imagine how foolish I felt telling him you were my wife?"

Brooke knew her heart was breaking. "I know how awful this sounds," she whispered, her stomach twisting into a huge knot as an odd kind of chill enveloped her. "And you deserve answers," she paused. "But are you prepared to listen? Really listen? Or will you stand in judgement of me before you know the entire story?"

Travis's face clouded with uneasiness and she was certain that he already thought her guilty and really didn't want to hear the facts. But then, as he usually did, he surprised her by saying, "I've always considered myself a fair man."

Brooke motioned to the chair. "Would you like to sit down?"

"No," he snapped, a muscle twitching in his cheek.

Brooke took a deep breath. She knew what he must be thinking. It irritated her that he hadn't bothered to give her the benefit of the doubt. At least until he heard her out.

She sat in the middle of the bed, her back ramrod straight. She needed to remain calm. Brooke would not cower in front of him, or any man. She might not be proud of her past, but at the same time there'd been little else she could do. She'd had to survive.

But that was in the past.

"I believe you know that I was raised in a girl's school," Brooke began, her outward calm belying her inner turmoil.

His lips twisted with amusement. "That wasn't a lie?"

"Travis"—Brooke took a calming breath—"I have never lied to you. I might not have told you everything about my life, but I've never lied to you," she said, daring him to say more.

Instead he nodded for her to go on.

"If you remember the stormy night we lost the sugarcane, I told you then my mother was killed, but what I didn't tell you was that three days after the funeral, my father, the Duke of Winterland, cut off my funds. I was tossed out on the street with the clothes I was wearing and nothing more. I was frightened and hungry. I had no family . . . no one to turn to. And most of all, I had no money." She clutched her hands to keep from shaking; the mere thought of that time terrified her, even after so many years had passed.

"Can you imagine what that was like, Travis?" Brooke looked at him, holding his gaze. "You say your life has been hard, but your experience was nothing compared to mine. You've always had a family, even if they were difficult. And you have had your mother near you. So don't try to tell me that you know what I've been though," Brooke said, daring him to say anything to the contrary.

To his credit, Travis remained quiet.

"After three days on the streets," Brooke continued, "three days with no food and sleeping in alleys and dodging lechers, I remembered my mother had told me if anything happened to her, and I was in trouble, to look up her friend, Fanny Sinclair. I dug down deep in my reticule and thankfully found the woman's address.

"Fanny was gracious, and she took me in with open arms. She told me she owed my mother a great deal. At first, I didn't know Fanny was a courtesan, but later I figured it out. And then she told me my mother had been a courtesan, too.

"Fanny never encouraged me to go into the business. However, I couldn't continue living off of her. I had no other way of making a living, so I asked her to teach me how to use the one thing I had, my beauty, to make a living. I knew I didn't want to be poor or live with another family as a servant, depending on them for my room and food.

"I didn't want to be a courtesan, Travis. You'll have to believe me, but I knew what it was like to be hungry and to have no money. I didn't want to be a common whore, so I chose only old, wealthy men, men who enjoyed lavishing money and jewels on me. Only a few of them were even capable of having relations. Most just wanted to go around town with a beautiful woman on their arm, so their peers would be jealous."

"How could you do that?" Travis rasped.

"When you need money, you'll do just about anything. I learned to turn off my emotions. I became numb, only going through the motions until the job was done. Then I met Jackson, and he offered to get me out of the business. He was like a father to me. He never made those kinds of demands of me. If he went to the opera, I would accompany him, but *never* did I sleep with your father," Brooke said. "I'm sure there were those who thought I was Jackson's mistress, given my past, but there was nothing I could do about that.

"That was three years ago. Then your cousins Jocelyn and Shannon came to live with us, and they became sisters to me."

"Why did they move in?"

"They both have their reasons, but I don't want to go into them. It's not my story to tell. Jocelyn and I were good friends in school, so I already knew her." Brooke thought of her friends, wishing she could see them now. "If you should ever get to meet them, you would like them."

Travis's left eyebrow rose a fraction. "And my father just took them in?"

"I know you never got to see that side of your father, but he was a caring man, and he loved the girls."

"I suppose it was just me that he couldn't love," Travis said sarcastically.

"That isn't true. I believe Jackson did love you, though he didn't show it well. When he got sick he wanted to be sure he could leave us enough to get by on. Shannon and Jocelyn wanted to come to America, and Jackson thought that would be a good idea. It would be a way for me to leave the past behind and to start a new life." *Or so I'd thought,* she said to herself, pausing. She gave a half-hearted laugh. "He never said anything about the plantation until he was dying, and he most certainly didn't say anything about you."

Travis's brow arched in ironic amusement. "I have no doubt of that."

Brooke ignored his sarcasm. "I didn't know any of the details until I arrived at Moss Grove. However, your father did say one thing before he died that didn't make any sense to me then, but it does now."

Travis folded his arms. "So, are you going to tell me?"

"Jackson told me he was trying to right a wrong." She watched Travis's brow rise in question, so she explained. "I believe he knew that he had not done right by you, and he wanted to make up for it. Somehow, Jackson sensed we were very much alike. I have no doubt he sent me to you," Brooke finished in a whisper.

She was more shaken than she cared to admit. She felt achy and exhausted now that she'd poured everything out. There wasn't anything else she could do or say. What happened next was up to Travis.

Travis had so many emotions swirling around in

his head and heart that he felt like he'd been in a fist fight. Strange and disquieting thoughts raced through his mind. "Well, I don't know whether to thank Jackson or slug him, if he were still alive."

"When I first met you, slugging Jackson did cross my mind, too," Brooke admitted, smiling.

Travis chuckled and pushed himself away from the chair. Somehow, his anger had been washed away, and all he could see now was a beautiful, scared creature sitting in the middle of the bed, her golden hair cascading around her.

Brooke was right. He couldn't possibly know what it was like to be thrown out into the street with no hope. His heart actually ached for her. And he had believed that his childhood had been bad.

Just thinking about all the things that could have happened to Brooke gave him chills.

When Travis reached the bed, and Brooke, he wasn't sure what to do or how he felt, so he acted on instinct. He sat on the edge of the bed and removed his boots. Then he climbed onto the bed. Brooke still sat in the middle of the bed like a frighten animal. She turned and watched him warily, but she didn't move.

Travis propped the pillows behind him and leaned back against them. He was still unsure what to say. He didn't have the correct words to describe what he felt for Brooke, so he'd have to show her. Finally, he opened his arms to her, and she came to him without hesitation.

Travis gathered Brooke into his arms. Without a word, she turned her face into his chest and wept. He had a feeling that it had been a very long time since Brooke had cried. She had probably had to be strong for so long that it had built inside her. Most women would have cried through the telling of the story, but Brooke never flinched.

She never begged for his forgiveness because there was nothing to forgive. She had done what she had to, never blaming anyone for her fate. He was proud of her, he thought as he stroked her hair and let her cry. Sometimes crying cleansed the soul.

Neither of them said anything. Words were not necessary. This was a night of healing.

A little later, when she'd fallen asleep in an exhausted slumber, Travis whispered, "I love you."

The next morning Brooke was emotionally spent when she woke up in Travis's arms. She gazed up at him, admiring his firm jawline and handsome face. There was nothing boyish about Travis. He was all man, and she loved him more than she'd ever thought she could. Even after last night's unpleasantness, she felt safe when she was in his arms.

Last night Travis had surprised her. He had not criticized her. He'd simply offered her comfort as if he truly understood. Did he? It was most unusual for a man.

Travis's eyes opened. Once the sleep cleared, he looked at her with tenderness. She could also see desire smoldering in his blue eyes, making them appear very dark this morning. Was he purposely letting her see how he felt? It would help if he told her he loved her, but that he hadn't done.

"Did you sleep well?" he asked in a raspy voice.

Brooke nodded. "And you?"

He gave her a slow smile. "I always sleep well when you're in my arms."

Tenderness swept over Brooke. She reached up to touch his face. His jaw was rough with stubble since he'd neither shaved nor gotten undressed from the night before. He turned his head and kissed her hand.

"I love you, Travis," Brooke said, "But I can understand if you no longer want me as your wife."

Travis pulled her up to him and kissed her with a tenderness that Brooke knew she'd never be able to forget. His mouth came down on hers with fierce hunger, and Brooke twined her arms around his neck. She parted her lips, and Travis groaned, clasping her tighter, as if he'd never get enough of her.

Finally, he tore his mouth away and whispered, "I want you, darling, now and always."

Brooke's heart gave a wild leap. She felt happier than she could ever remember. They didn't make love. Instead, Travis shaved and dressed in clean clothes while Brooke took care of her own toilet. He went ahead, telling her that he'd meet her in the dining room.

When Brooke was finally ready, she left the cabin. The fog was so thick that moving about the boat was difficult. Still, Brooke tried to make her way through the white mist. Every once in awhile a body just seemed to jump out at her, though the other person was merely walking down the walkway. She made herself smile and tried not to be so jumpy. There was no reason to be that way. It was just a little fog. It couldn't hurt her. But still, Brooke had the oddest feeling.

Brooke heard a commotion coming out of the clinging fog, and since she couldn't tell exactly where it was coming from, she decided to stop at the rail until whatever it was had passed.

Up above her, Captain Leathers was swearing at the pilot to watch out and make sure they didn't hit anything.

Certain that the commotion was over, Brooke turned and bumped into Travis's mother, who must have been standing behind her. "I'm sorry," Brooke said. "I didn't see you."

"I don't wonder. It's impossible to see anything this morning," Margaret snapped. "Where is Travis?"

"He went on ahead of me. I think he's already in the dining room."

Margaret put her hands on her hips. "I hope you don't plan on making any changes at Moss Grove," she said abruptly. "We like it the way it is. We don't need anyone from the outside interfering."

"I rather like Moss Grove myself," Brooke told her. Brooke realized that Margaret was trying to establish who would be mistress of Moss Grove, and she did what she could to mollify her. If the woman had been the least bit cordial, Brooke would never interfere, but she wasn't about to let the irritating woman have the upper hand.

"Moss Grove isn't your home, young woman," Margaret snapped. "So don't get used to living there," she warned Brooke. "Travis told me exactly why he married you. It's a pity he had to stoop so low. At least after a year he'll be free to marry his rightful fiancée once he divorces you."

This woman was vicious. "He told you that?" Brooke asked, unsure of what to believe.

Margaret laughed. "Of course he did. You don't really think that he loves you, do you? My son told me he did what was necessary to save the plantation, which has always come first with him."

Brooke folded her arms. "I hate to tell you this, Mrs. deLobel, but I'm half owner of Moss Grove. So I can do pretty much as I please with my half," Brooke told her, entertaining a lovely dream of tossing the woman out. "If you insist on causing trouble," Brooke said, because she could see that was the woman's intention, "I'm sure other arrangements can be made for you."

Margaret stepped closer to her, poking one sharp finger toward her face. "Now you listen to me," she hissed through clenched teeth. "You will not talk to me like that. I'm going right now to find Travis. He won't appreciate how you have treated his mother."

Brooke watched as the woman stormed off into the fog. The old harridan. As Margaret hurried off, Brooke turned to the rail, trying to gather her wits before she had to face that battleaxe again over breakfast.

Could Travis really be playing her for a fool? Brooke really didn't think so. She believed that Travis loved her, though he'd never said as much. If only all this weren't so new to her, she might know what to do. She breathed in a deep sigh. What if Travis was just a very good actor?

Brooke decided she had better go on and find

her way to the dining room. At least there she'd have the comfort of seeing Travis. Perhaps if she could see him, she could sense what he was truly feeling.

Suddenly, without warning, something hard slammed into Brooke's back, knocking her over the rail. So shocked at what had happened she could barely scream as she flailed about, trying to find a handhold. Her dress caught on something, and for just a moment she thought she'd been saved. But her salvation was short lived.

The deadly sound of ripping fabric told Brooke that her luck had not held. The dress tore and she plummeted toward the dark water below.

Brooke screamed as she flailed wildly through the air, hoping to grab anything to stop her plunge. Why wasn't anybody there to help her?

Oh God, she thought, she was going into the water. This was the end.

Would anybody save her?

Chapter 17

Travis wondered what was keeping his wife. How long did it take her to get ready?

For the third time in the last five minutes, he glanced at the door. No Brooke, and to make matters worse, his mother had decided to make her appearance and was striding toward the table. At least she was alone.

"The fog is terrible this morning," Margaret said as Travis held out a chair for her.

"Yes, it is," he replied. "Captain Leathers isn't happy about the fog. It makes his job just that much harder," Travis explained as he moved back to his seat. "You didn't happen to see Brooke?"

Margaret unfolded the linen napkin and placed it across her lap. "Seeing anybody in this murky mess would be difficult. However, I did see her talking with a gentleman as I made my way here. I asked her if she'd like to walk with me to breakfast, but she declined my invitation." Margaret managed to shrug and say offhandedly, "The woman definitely needs better manners, and if you ask me, she was standing much too close to the man with whom she was speaking."

Margaret looked around. "I would have thought that she'd join us by now. Does she make a habit of being late?" she asked with an eyebrow raised to indicate her disapproval.

"Brooke isn't late, Mother. I was early," Travis told her without bothering to hide his irritation. He stood up. He couldn't imagine who Brooke could be talking to. She didn't know that many people in America. "I'm going to see what has delayed her."

"As you wish, son," Margaret said as she reached for her café au lait. Then she added, "Perhaps you should inquire after Hesione. I couldn't persuade her to come to breakfast, even though she was already dressed."

Travis didn't bother to answer as he went in search of his wife. Once outside, he noticed that the shores of the river had been so blurred by the lingering fog that they were almost invisible.

He hadn't gone more than five feet when he came across Captain Leathers. Could Leathers have been the one Brooke had been speaking with?

With long, purposeful strides, Travis covered the distance to the captain. "Have you seen my wife this morning, captain?"

"No," Leathers said, rubbing his chin. "Of course, I could have walked right past her and might never have seen her. You can't see anybody unless you're on them. This thick fog is a damnable mess," the captain grumbled. "The only good thing is that *Annie Johnston* has to travel through this fog as well."

Travis pulled out his gold case and offered a cigar to the captain. "Looks like you could use a good smoke."

"Thanks."

"Have you ever seen it this bad before?" Travis asked him.

"Once or twice," he said, shrugging. "Most of the time the sun comes up and burns the fog away. I've seen it happen, and rather quickly, too," Leathers said, stroking his red beard. "Let's hope it does so today."

"Have you already eaten breakfast?" Leathers asked, abruptly changing the subject.

"Not yet," Travis replied, shaking his head. "I was waiting for my wife. It appears I will have to go and find out what is taking her so long."

The captain placed a hand on Travis's shoulder. "Listen, son. From my experience with women, when it comes to dressing, they never move quickly." Leathers chuckled. "You're young. You still have much to learn."

The captain looked searchingly out into the fog. "I'm going to send out a yawl and some oarsmen with poles to sound out the river. The river is low and it would be disaster if we hit any of those sandbars." He turned quickly. "I'll see you back in the dining room."

Slowed by the clinging clouds, Travis hurried on to his cabin. He pushed open the cabin door to find the room empty. *Strange*, he thought as he glanced around the stateroom. Could he have somehow passed Brooke in the fog? Not likely, he concluded, but she might have walked the other way around. He would go that way just to make sure.

Travis strode down the fog-filled walkway, nodding curtly to the passengers he stumbled upon in his haste. He found no sign of his wife.

Maybe she hadn't gone back to the room. His mother had mentioned that she'd seen Brooke talking to a gentleman. Travis didn't know whether to believe his mother or not, but she had no reason to lie.

Could Brooke have bumped into Whatsbury? And if she had talked to him, why hadn't she come to breakfast? She hadn't seemed to care for the man when they'd met last night, so why would she take the time to speak with him now? Nothing made sense. Had he been blind where she was concerned? Travis had thought that she truly loved him. What he'd found about her past was now causing him to have doubts that he'd rather not have.

Could Brooke still be a courtesan at heart, using him to get what she wanted? Mainly the plantation.

He would find out.

Jealously drove Travis to act rashly. It didn't take him long to find Whatsbury's cabin. He stood outside preparing to knock when he heard the sound of a woman's laughter coming from behind the door. His blood froze and then he saw red. Brooke!

His courtesan wife had obviously reverted to her old tricks. He started to leave, but his anger propelled him. He slammed his fist against the door.

A moment later, Whatsbury, dressed in a silk robe, a smug expression on his face, answered the door. "Travis, old boy. Rather early for you to come calling."

Travis shoved past Whatsbury and discovered a

young woman with brown hair clutching a sheet up to her chin. Not his wife!

He didn't know whether to be happy or sad about what he'd found. At least it wasn't Brooke's laughter he had heard. But on the other hand, he still didn't know where his wife was.

The boat wasn't that big. Where in the world could she be?

Travis nodded curtly to the woman, who had the grace to blush as Travis quickly turned away. He felt like a fool, murmuring, "I beg your pardon."

Whatsbury leaned against the door, his arms folded across his chest as he barred the way. "What the devil is this about, Montgomery?"

"Just a mistake." Travis gave an impatient shrug. "Have you been out of your room this morning?"

"With what I have in that bed?" The earl chuckled, cutting his gaze toward the bed. "Not on your life. Why?"

"Nothing," Travis mumbled. "Just a mistake." Travis left as quickly as he could, feeling very foolish for letting jealously rule his head.

Although happy that he hadn't found his wife with Whatsbury, he was still becoming more worried about Brooke's whereabouts by the minute.

Where in the hell could she have gone?

Travis's search of the entire boat proved fruitless. The only recourse he had was to consult Captain Leathers. It was not reassuring to have the captain appear quite concerned about Brooke's apparent disappearance.

Leathers released a few men to help Travis look

for Brooke, but the rest were needed to keep the ship from hitting anything during the fog.

By eleven o'clock, the sun had finally burned the fog away, but Brooke was still nowhere to be found. Travis was beside himself with fear.

At noon, one of the ship's personnel came and got both Travis and Captain Leathers.

"I believe I've found something, cap'n. You'd best come and look."

A wave of apprehension swept through Travis, but he told himself his fears were premature as he and the captain followed the crewman.

He took them around to the railing on the port side, then pointed over the rail. "Look there."

Travis and the captain peered over the side. Fear, stark and vivid, hit Travis full force. A piece of blue fabric caught tight on a sliver of wood flapped in the wind.

Captain Leathers straightened, his expression grim. In a strained voice, he asked the question Travis was already expecting. "What was your wife wearing this morning?"

Travis opened his mouth to speak but nothing came out. He closed his eyes, his heart aching with pain. After a moment he managed to get out, "A blue gown."

"Good God," Leathers roared. He shook his head in disbelief. "She has gone overboard. Man overboard!" Leathers bellowed, then turned and waved at the pilothouse. "Stop the engines!"

"What can we do?" Travis asked. He felt completely helpless. His mind, congested with doubts and fears, wanted to do something. Anything. But what?

"We will go back a short way and look for her. I'll send out some skiffs," Leathers said. He placed a hand on Travis's shoulder. "We'll find her, son. We'll find her."

By six that night, a crewman in one of the boats found a torn blue dress, but no sign of Brooke.

Travis stood looking at the wet garment at his feet. He felt as if his life had been sucked from him. Just when he had finally found the woman he wanted, she had been snatched from him. All that was left was an aching, empty hole in his chest where his heart had been.

"We cannot continue to search with darkness upon us. Your wife must have drowned." The captain rested his hand on Travis's shoulder in a fruitless attempt to offer comfort. "I'm sorry," Leathers said.

His grief overwhelming, Travis shook him away.

Leathers left Travis alone in his thoughts, muttering as he walked away, "But what I don't understand is how she went overboard."

Margaret, with Hesione in tow, arrived curious to see what was going on. "Perhaps she jumped," Margaret suggested when she'd heard the explanation.

Travis swung around. "My wife did not jump."

Margaret wasn't put off by his sharp tone. "How do you know that, son? After all, you have only known the woman a few weeks. Perhaps she couldn't fathom the thought of running a plantation."

"Mother," Travis warned, a muscle beginning to twitch in his jaw. "Brooke was afraid of nothing. She was not afraid of running the plantation, and she did not jump! She might have slipped on the wet decks, somebody could have shoved her, but she did not jump! And I never want to hear you say that again!"

"I know you are upset, son," Margaret soothed. "But in time . . ." She stopped when she saw a warning in his eyes.

Travis left his mother and went to find the captain. Drawing in a ragged breath, he said, "Captain, I know this has cost you the race."

"Not to worry." The captain threw up his hand. "No race is as important as a human life. There will be other races. I'm just sorry that we were not able to find your wife. She was a very beautiful woman, and we all liked her very much."

"I will pack our things," Travis said, "and take a skiff to shore so you can continue on with the trip." He raked his hand through his hair as he tried to think. He felt numb all over. "Will you see that our things are delivered back to Moss Grove?"

"Consider it done," Leathers said with a handshake. Then he left Travis alone to grieve.

Travis hadn't seen his mother and Hesione walked up behind him, so when he turned to leave he bumped into them.

"You are leaving the boat?" Hesione asked.

"Yes. Maybe I will find something before I return to Moss Grove," Travis said, turning his back and walking away.

"Well, I never!" Hesione said to Margaret. "He hasn't given us one thought. Can't he see he's better off without that woman? She ruined everything."

Margaret slipped her arm around the girl. "He'll

come around. Soon he will forget all about her. You just need to be patient, my dear, and everything will turn out as it should have done to begin with."

Driven by the scant hope that Brooke might still be alive, Travis spent the next month searching for some sign that she had made it to shore. All he found were dead ends.

Finally, as a last desperate measure, he commissioned an artist make several sketches with Brooke's likeness. He had flyers offering a substantial reward posted in shops, the telegraph offices, and post offices up and down the river.

Travis knew it was doubtful that he would hear anything, but he was not ready to face the idea that that the woman he loved was dead, and he would never see her again.

He could still picture her in his arms the last time he held her.

She never begged for forgiveness because there was nothing to forgive. She had done what she had to, never blaming anyone for her fate. He was proud of her, he thought as he stroked her hair and let her cry.

Neither of them had said anything. This was a night of healing.

A little later, when she'd fallen asleep in exhausted slumber, Travis whispered, "I love you."

Now he had lost her.

After having exhausted all his resourses, and with a sad heart, Travis returned to Moss Grove.

* * *

Brooke could feel herself trying to float out of the comfortable mist she'd been drifting in. She opened her eyes and wondered where she was. Nothing looked familiar. She tried to sit up, but she was so weak she couldn't hold herself up, and the movement made her head hurt horribly. She fell back on the bed, groaning from sheer exhaustion.

"I t'ought you gonna sleep forever, de way you were goin'," a woman said, her voice coming from across the room. A moment later, wearing a concerned smile, she appeared next to the bed and looked down at Brooke. "What pretty eyes they are."

Brooke blinked several times. She tried to say something, but her throat was so dry the words wouldn't come out.

"Ah, you poor little t'ing, let me get you some water," the nice woman said.

She came back a moment later with a cup. The woman helped Brooke to sit up, then held the cup to her lips. The cool liquid soothed her parched throat.

"Thank you," Brooke said. "Why do I feel like a limp rag?"

The woman placed the cup on a small, brown table beside the bed. Brooke looked into her warm brown eyes. The stranger was a heavyset woman, perhaps middle-aged, with gray-streaked hair and a kind face. She smoked a corncob pipe.

"'Cause you been pretty sick. Here, let me," she said, placing her pipe in a tray. "I put a few pillows behind you so dat you can sit fo' awhile. Then you be mo' bettah."

Once Brooke was situated and comfortable, the woman offered her a piece of dry toast and a cup of water. If she didn't move her head much, at least the pain was bearable.

"W—what happened to me?" she asked.

"Dat's a question we hope you tell us de answer to."

"Us?"

"Me and my two boys. It was 'em who fished you out o' de river. You was real lucky dat they be fishin' near by when you hit de water."

"Water?" Brooke frowned. "Why was I in the water?"

"We t'ink somebody t'rew you off de big boat, chere."

Brooke felt the panic build inside her. The thought of water made her very uneasy. "But why?"

"I'd say somebody was tryin' to kill you, no."

Brooke gasped.

"You remember not'ing at all, den?"

Brooke shook her head. "Nothing."

"What's you name?"

"It's—it's . . . I don't know," Brooke whispered. She felt the screams of frustration at the back of her mind as she groped for something, anything about who she was. She stared at the kind lady beside her, wondering if she was supposed to know this woman.

Evidently, the woman sensed her confusion and panic, because she reached over and touched her arm.

"I don't even know who you are," she admitted.

"That be 'cause we never been introduced. My name is Penny Locoul. Take your hand an' feel de back o' your head," Penny said gently.

Brooke did as she was told. "It's tender."

"I bet it is, chere. It's probably de reason you can't remember anyt'ing. Don't you worry none. You mem'ry will come back as soon as you mo' bettah. You can stay wit' us 'til it does."

"Are you sure?"

"To be sure. We not ones to turn somebody away 'cause they down and out." Penny shrugged. "'Sides, where you go? Me and my boys is river folks up from Nawlins.

"You on our houseboat right now. We jus' left St. Louis, headin' back home. Mebbe by de time we home, you will have remembered where your home is, chere. You don' talk like folks from 'round here," Penny said as she shoved out of the chair.

"You mus' be starvin'. I'm goin' to start fixin' dinner. De boys should bring home a mess of fish. You can join us at de table if'n you feel like and I'll get somet'ing fo' dat empty belly."

She knew she'd heard Penny's accent before, but she just couldn't place it as she fell asleep. She slept for an hour, having worn herself out from just a few minutes of talking.

Voices woke her. Brooke opened her eyes to discover that the boys had returned home. Since the family apparently all lived in the same room, she could observe the young men as they cleaned the fish for their mother.

Étienne was the younger, maybe seventeen, she guessed. His sandy blond hair and blue eyes contrasted with his skin, burned brown from many days outdoors. Paul was not only older but taller by a foot. His hair was darker, but they shared the same color eyes, and they both spoke with an accent that she was certain she'd heard before.

By the time dinner was ready, Brooke was famished. The aroma of warm food filled the small cabin, and her mouth watered in anticipation. She tried to get up, but she quickly realized that her legs were not strong enough to hold her.

"Wait jus' a minute, yes," Étienne said. "You much too weak, chere. Come on, Paul. Let's give her a hand."

"I don't know why I can't stand," Brooke said as the young men helped her to the table. She could take steps, but with difficulty. Her legs felt much too heavy.

"Problee 'cause you been in bed fo' so long," Penny told her. "Once you get your strength back, you be runnin' 'round like ever'bod', yes."

Brooke took her first bite of fish. She chewed carefully, savoring each bite and thinking she'd never tasted anything so good. The fish was nicely flavored and succulent, and most of all, it warmed her. She was so hungry that she didn't talk at all. She just listened to everyone else talking while she ate her fill.

Étienne glanced at her. "You don' like to talk, no?"

It was an effort to jerk her attention away from the plate, but she finally won the battle and placed her fork down. "I guess I have been concentrating too much on the food. How rude of me."

"After only eatin' broth, I bet dat fish tastes real good," Rita commented.

"Yes, it does. Did you catch these in the Mississippi?" she asked the boys.

"Nope," Paul spoke up. "Found a brook wit' good fresh water instead of de muddy Mississippi."

Brooke froze as she lifted her cup. She stared at Paul.

"What's wrong?" Paul asked.

"That's my name."

"What?" Étienne chuckled. "Fish?"

Brooke laughed, too. It made her head hurt, so she wished she hadn't. "No, not fish. My name is Brooke."

Penny reached for the gray metal pitcher of water and refilled everyone's cup. "Dat's a good start. Mebee when you can tell us you surname, we can find your home, yes?"

Paul poured a small puddle of blackstrap molasses onto his plate, then ripped a biscuit apart. As he sopped up the molasses, he said, "Well, one thin' we do know is you married, yes."

Brooke frowned. "How do you know that?"

"Leesten to you," he said, like she had asked something silly. He smiled. "'Cause you have on weddin' rings. I've seen dat kind in Nawlins before. So the way I figure, dat's where you from." He scratched his head. "Only problem is, you don' talk like nobody down dere."

Glancing down at her left hand, Brooke saw not only her gold wedding ring, but also a twinkling red ruby. Surely she should remember receiving something so beautiful. Why couldn't she remember? Her husband must truly love her to have given her something so valuable. Could it be possible that she might not *want* to remember anything?

"Can you tell me what you saw when you found me?" Brooke asked the boys.

"Didn't see nothin'," Paul told her quickly. "Fog was so thick it remin' me o' dis here molasses. We's lucky we was not run over by de paddleboat, to tell you de trut', but you was lucky we were so close."

"We heard you rip a blood curdlin' scream, and den we hear de splash," Étienne told her. "We know somet'in' is wrong *tout suite.* By de time we get to you, you done managed to get out o' your frock and you's splashin' in de water like a drowned puppy."

"You sure was," Paul agreed. "And it was darn lucky dat you hadn't passed out. You didn't do dat 'til we pull you in de skiff." He shrugged. "We t'ought about chasin' de boat, but we was afraid somebody tryin' to kill you. We surely did not want to put you back in dat danger."

"Thank you," Brooke told both of the boys. "I'm sure I would have been dead if it hadn't been for both of you."

"Only t'anks we need is fo' you to get mo' bettah," Paul told her. "I bet your family is real worried about you."

"Perhaps they are," Brooke said softly, then thoughtfully glancing down at her hand, "or maybe it was one of them who intended to kill me."

She glanced up with tears in her eyes, but the boys didn't say anything.

Who would want to kill her? She needed her memory back, straight away. Brooke shivered involuntarily and hugged herself to fend off the chill. She had to know what was what before they found her and tried again.

Chapter 18

Travis was going through the motions of living.

At night he'd sit in his study, feet propped up, a drink in his hand, thinking of Brooke, trying to forget her touch, yet having a difficult time of it.

Instead of forgetting, he remembered how Brooke felt when she'd melted in his arms. And her rare golden eyes . . . how could any man forget those eyes? They haunted him day and night.

Travis had wanted her from the moment he'd helped her mount Gray Mist, and she had told him that they were more alike than he knew.

Brooke had been right. They were very much alike . . . bastard children who had to learn how to survive in a world that looked down on them. He sipped his drink, welcoming the numbing of his senses.

How could she have become so much a part of his life in such a short time? When he came in at night, he still expected to hear her voice or to see her glaring at him as she always had when they argued.

One morning he finally realized why he couldn't forget her. Even though it had only been a short time, he'd truly been happy with Brooke—maybe for the first time in his life. She had filled an empty place inside him that he hadn't known he had.

Travis slugged down the rest of his Scotch. Anything to dull the ache. Every night it took a little more liquor to ease the pain.

How could Brooke have jumped overboard? It wasn't possible. How could she have left him? Especially after the night before when he'd felt they had bridged a gap in their relationship. What a fool he'd been. From the moment Brooke had entered his life, he'd quarreled with her, resenting her, and not once had he realized that she was the first person he looked for when he entered a room.

Now she was gone.

The rail was a little lower in the place where they found the tattered scrap of material, so it was quite conceivable that Brooke had tripped and fallen over, but even that was hard to believe. She was such a graceful and sure-footed woman.

Why hadn't he stayed with her?

Had I done so, perhaps none of this would have happened, Travis thought ruefully. Had his impatience cost him the one thing he'd finally realized he couldn't live without?

Since their return, his mother had been understanding and sympathetic. She'd even told him that she was sorry that he'd lost his wife. And then she had made the mistake of trying to remove Brooke's clothes from her room as if she'd never been there.

That's when Travis knew that his mother had been

putting on a show for him. He realized then he'd never be able to make his mother understand how he felt. He was just coming to terms with it himself.

Lately, his mother had begun to mention Hesione. She'd casually worked her name into conversation, and Travis really didn't want to hear it. He didn't want to forget his beautiful, young wife. He wasn't ready to move on. His mother might as well learn that she wasn't going to push him into anything. He was not going to allow her to make him feel guilty. He had nothing to be guilty for.

Brooke had been right. None of his mother's problems had been his fault.

Everyone and everything irritated Travis of late. Especially the person who had been trying to kill him. He wanted to find out who the son of a bitch was before he got lucky and put a bullet in him.

Twice when he'd been riding around the plantation, someone had taken shots at him. The first time, he'd brushed it off as a stray shot from hunters, but now he wasn't so sure.

On top of that, a fire had been set in the sugar mill, burning half the millhouse. Workers were rebuilding so it would be ready by the next harvest, but it was a slow process. At least rebuilding kept him busy and his mind off Brooke.

Mr. Jeffries was being difficult. He had stopped all the paperwork transferring everything to Travis and Brooke. Travis remembered their conversation well. . . .

"I'm sorry, sir," Jeffries had told Travis.

"Sorry doesn't help one damn bit," Travis grated out

from behind his desk. "Not only have I lost my wife, but I still have a plantation to run!"

The unflappable Mr. Jeffries looked at Travis and said, "There is no reason to raise your voice. I understand completely what you must be going through, but we have no proof of Miss Brooke's death." Jeffries folded his hands on his lap as if he were thinking, then he said, "I can tell you that Miss Brooke would not have taken her own life. She's been through very difficult times, and she is a survivor."

"Well, I sure as hell didn't push her," Travis retorted sharply.

"I would hope not," Jeffries said. "But others might look at the way the two of you used to argue and think differently."

"You son of a bitch." Travis pointed his finger at the man. "Don't you ever say that again."

"As you wish," the solicitor said. "But until her death is confirmed, we will have to proceed with caution.

Mr. Jeffries hadn't accused Travis again. The man was paying some of the bills to keep the plantation operating. Since there had been no body found and, therefore, no proof of death, Jeffries couldn't turn over Moss Grove to Travis. They would have to wait until a body washed up on shore or a good amount of time had passed. No matter how much the man had protested, Jeffries sometimes seemed to look at Travis as if he'd pushed Brooke overboard himself.

At first Travis had been furious that the solicitor didn't believe him about Brooke. Why would he make up something like that? Then he remembered all the disagreements he and Brooke had had. Finally, he began to see how Jeffries could have doubts. Travis himself would have had his doubt, too. Given his and Brooke's past

In retrospect, his life with Brooke seemed like a dream. Now there were moments when he wondered if he was living in a nightmare and might eventually wake up. Travis grabbed the decanter on the table and poured another drink, part of it sloshing out onto the table. He downed that glass, too.

Brooke had been in his life one minute and gone the next. He would never have imagined how much it hurt. He'd have to put everything behind him in order to move on. For now, he just functioned.

He'd forgotten that Christmas was fast approaching, and he had no desire to attend the party his mother was planning. However, his mother was insistent, and he was certain he'd have to die to keep from being there.

There were moments when he knew that the option would be preferable to continuing this barren and empty life.

He felt no joy. Why celebrate?

Work was what Travis needed. It was what he understood. He could tamp down his memories when he was hard at work.

With plenty of rest and good food, Brooke finally regained her strength. She had lost all concept of time while she'd been recuperating her memory. The best she could do was concentrate on the things she understood.

She occupied her time helping Rita, but no matter how much Brooke did to stay busy, she couldn't shake the feeling of sadness that lingered. It was as though something very important was missing from her life.

She had hoped that her memory would have returned by now, but little had. Brooke only saw glimpses every now and then of people she didn't recognize, nor remember.

One morning, Étienne announced that they were nearing New Orleans. With the dishes done and little else to do, Brooke decided to walk outside to the small porch. She wrapped a wool blanket around her to keep warm and watched as they drifted past the large mansions facing the river.

They were all so pretty and elegant, and Brooke wondered who lived there. As she stood on the small deck, she imagined the occupants and their lives. Brooke had been so lost in thought that she didn't notice when Paul joined her.

The next mansion the boat floated past was much larger than the others, Brooke noticed. The regal house sat back from the river's edge among a large group of live oak trees. "How beautiful," she murmured, pulling the blanket tighter around her. She glanced at Paul and nodded toward the house. "Do you know the name of that one?"

Paul leaned against the rail. "Well now . . . that's de largest plantation in Nawlins. It's call Moss Grove."

"Such a pretty name. Moss . . ." Brooke stopped. There was something familiar about the name. She repeated it. "Moss Grove." The name kept running through her mind again and again. She grabbed her head and shut her eyes. "Moss Grove."

"What de matter wit' you, chere?" Paul asked. He looked at her, concern in his eyes.

Brooke merely repeated the name of the plantation over and over.

"Jus' you set you'se'f dere," Paul told her. He helped Brooke to a barrel so she could sit down, still holding her head, shaking it as if demons had taken her over.

Brooke couldn't let go of her head because it hurt like hell. She squeezed her eyes tight while images formed in her memory and began to flash through her mind: a plantation, a promise, a business partner, and a carriage with a man and a woman riding up to the front of Moss Grove. A man on a white horse . . . her husband.

Travis!

Penny rushed out and put an arm around Brooke. "What's de matter? You not feelin' well, chere?"

Finally, Brooke was able to open her eyes. Unbidden tears spilled down her cheek. She looked up at the woman. A crooked smile brightened her face. "I'm a little dizzy," she whispered, awestruck. "But I remember everything. I own that plantation we just sailed past. I'm half owner of Moss Grove."

"Ooowe. You are rich, no?" Paul said, clapping his hands. "So what you doin' in de river, chere?"

Brooke managed a strained laugh. "Not exactly rich. My name is Brooke Hammo—no! Wait! I had just been married, which is the reason I was on the *Natchez*. It was my wedding trip. My name is Brooke Montgomery." She looked up at them, grinning with triumph.

"Sweetie, you were on yer honeymoon and you fell overboard?" Penny asked. "What you were doin'?"

Everyone hurried inside where it was warmer so they could talk.

"I didn't fall, Penny. I was pushed," Brooke said, and then she told them all about her life—at least, the parts she wanted them to know.

"What you gonna do now?" Penny asked.

"When we get to New Orleans, I'll send word to Mr. Jeffries—he's my solicitor—to meet me. I must speak with him first, and then I'll go from there." Brooke wanted so much to go home, to throw herself into Travis's arms, but she knew she had to proceed with caution. She would always remember Travis telling her he was a good actor.

What kind of reception would she get when she got there? Brooke asked herself that along with a dozen more questions.

Everyone must surely think that she was dead. But did they care? Had what she and Travis shared been real? Or had he merely been acting? And had he already moved on with his life?

The biggest questions of all was, did he push her?

By late afternoon, they had docked by the levee in New Orleans. Brooke sent Paul with a message. It was to be given to Mr. Jeffries only. No one else was to receive the note, she warned him. At the moment, she wasn't sure whom, beside Mr. Jeffries, she could trust.

Mr. Jeffries met Paul in the foyer. The man took the note, opened it and quickly scanned the contents. Jeffries glanced up at Paul and, for a moment, did nothing. Finally, tension mounting, he said, "Wait here."

Jeffries found Travis in his study. "If you'll excuse me, sir. I have an invitation to dine in town tonight with a friend. I shall be back later." Jeffries thought this would be the best excuse to get out of the house without raising suspicion.

Travis smiled a knowing smile. "I hope you enjoy yourself."

"Good night, sir," Jeffries said, not bothering to comment on the look that suggested he was meeting a woman. If he'd known just who Jeffries was meeting, Travis would have shot straight out of the chair and demanded to see her himself. Deep down, Jeffries truly believed that Travis loved the girl.

Jeffries had no idea what to think as he rode with Paul to the houseboat. Where had Brooke been all this time? And if she had gone overboard, how had she survived?

When they reached the small houseboat—if one could call it a house—Jeffries saw Brooke waiting on the deck. He smiled broadly. She really was alive and, it appeared, well.

Brooke carefully stepped up onto the wharf, then ran the rest of the way to him, throwing herself into his arms. "I'm so glad to see you."

"I say, not nearly as happy as I am that you are alive, my dear," he said, stepping back he took in her ragged clothes. "I never believed that you were dead, though many people insisted that you were. We'll get you a nice room in the city, and then you can tell me all about what happened."

"Did Travis miss me?" Brooke asked.

Mr. Jeffries nodded. "I believe he did." Brooke's heart soared.

There was nothing to pack, so Brooke told her friends good-bye and thanked them for all their help. As happy as she was to be resuming her old life, she knew she would miss her new, caring friends.

Mr. Jeffries handed Rita a bag of coins. She tried to refuse, but Brooke insisted that they could use the money to improve their boat, then she made them promise to stop and visit her at Moss Grove.

Once Brooke had obtained a room at Le Méridien, one of the nicest hotels in New Orleans, she sat down and told Mr. Jeffries everything that had happened. She held nothing back.

"You sound as if you love Travis," Jeffries observed.

"I do," Brooke said softly. "Or I did. I don't want to believe he was the one who pushed me overboard," she said, and with her very next breath asked, "How is he?"

"What makes you suspect that he was the one to push you?"

"I don't want to think that Travis did," Brooke said quickly. "However, I was hit so hard that it would have taken someone with a great deal of strength. Who else would have wanted me dead? And he would get full title to Moss Grove," she added softly.

"Travis has been a different man since you have been gone, my dear. He has done nothing but work since his return. I see sadness in him that I have not seen before, but he doesn't talk much. I never quite know what he is thinking."

"Yes, I've learned that Travis is a very private

person, but I do believe he cares. Just before I went into the water, I had been talking to Travis's mother. I can't imagine her pushing me either. She doesn't seem strong enough.

"But someone doesn't want me around. What do you think I should do?"

Mr. Jeffries stroked his chin as he thought. "First," he finally said, "we must get you some decent clothes."

Brooke looked down at the ragged, borrowed dress. It was one of Rita's, and had been taken in for Brooke. "I didn't have a lot to choose from. You can have Millie Anne bring me something to wear."

"Splendid idea. Mrs. deLobel is having a Christmas party tomorrow. After all, it is several days before Christmas."

"Really?" Brooke said, a little surprised. "I guess I've lost track of time."

"We'll never know who is trying to kill you if you remain in hiding. My suggestion is that you resume your rightful place at Moss Grove. I'm sure it will be a shock to everyone, especially the one who wishes you dead. Perhaps, it will draw him out."

Brooke's mind whirled with a crazy mixture of hope and fear. "I like that idea. I can just imagine the expressions on everyone's faces when I walk in— especially the culprit." She felt momentary panic as her mind jumped onto the fact that whomever was trying to get rid of her might try again.

She got up and went to the night stand to pour herself a glass of water. "Would you care for something to drink?"

"No, thank you."

"You do realize that getting a home of my own has proven to be a lot harder than I had originally expected," Brooke said.

Mr. Jeffries smiled. "But it has been well worth it. Has it not?"

Brooke smiled grimly. "I'll let you know once I see Travis."

Millie Anne couldn't believe that Brooke was alive. It was just too good to be true, but sure enough when Mr. Jeffries opened the door, there she stood. "We done t'ought you was dead, Miz Brooke."

Brooke hugged Millie. "I thought so, too. But when I woke up, I found that a kind family had rescued me." Brooke stood back. "Did you have any trouble getting my clothes out of the house?"

"No, ma'am, though I had to get Mammy to help me," Millie Anne said as she shook out the red velvet gown she'd brought. "But don' worry, Mammy won't say nothin'. You see, after ever'bod' came home, Miz Margaret said I wasn't needed no more, and she sent me back to de fields."

Brooke was pulling her undergarments out of the satchel, but she looked up. "Why does that not surprise me? Margaret could have been the one who pushed me. Perhaps she has more strength than I imagined."

"Lordy," the girl gasped. "You was pushed?"

Brooke sat down on the bed. "I'm afraid so, but I don't know who did it."

"Well, Miz Margaret is mean enough. Dat's fo'

sure," Millie Anne said then slapped a hand over her mouth. "I shouldn't be sayin' such."

Brooke laughed. "You're only speaking the truth."

Someone knocked on the door, interrupting them.

Brooke answered the door to find several maids with buckets of hot water. She pointed them over to the small alcove where a tin hip tub had been placed for bathing.

Once it was quiet again, Brooke undressed and slipped into the steamy water. It had been much too long since she'd been able to experience this luxury, and it felt wonderful. Her baths aboard the houseboat had consisted of a small tin bowl which Penny called a bird bath.

"Here, let me wash your hair," Millie Anne insisted as she took the sponge from Brooke.

Brooke held her head back while Millie squeezed the sponge over her hair until it was thoroughly wet. "Finish telling me what has occurred while I was gone," Brooke said.

"Well, Miz Margaret told Mammy to clean out you room. So Mammy went t' Master Travis and told him what she'd said."

Millie Anne stopped talking as she soaped Brooke's hair.

"And?" Brooke urged.

Millie Anne giggled. "He told his mother dat nothin' would be touched in dat room 'til he said so. Dey was into a big argument. Mammy said dat you could hear him shoutin' clean out in de kitchen."

Brooke's heart swelled at the notion of her husband taking up for her. Perhaps he did love her after all.

"Well, it's nice to know that Travis stood up to her," Brooke said, gasping as water tumbled over her head and down her face.

"Master Travis has always stood his ground except where Miz Hesione is concerned."

Brooke's happiness plummeted at the mention of the other woman. Had Travis gone back to Hesione? Brooke couldn't bring herself to think about it right now, much less ask. She would know when she saw him. Perhaps she'd imagined their time together as something it wasn't.

Millie held up a towel so Brooke could step out, then wrapped the towel around her.

"What are you goin' t' do now dat you home, Miz Brooke?"

"I'm going to a party," Brooke said with a smile. "I want you to sweep my hair up in a fabulous 'do. I'm going to dress in that red velvet gown over there, and then I'm going to a Christmas party to greet the guest I didn't invite."

"Lordy," Millie Anne said. "You is goin' to cause a ruckus. I wish I could see all dere faces when you walk in. Yes, ma'am. Brooke Hammond back from de dead. Dat is goin' to be a sight to see." Millie giggled.

"You mean Brooke Montgomery," Brooke reminded her.

Once her toilet was complete, Brooke was more than eager to go home. Millie Anne packed what few things she'd brought while Brooke made preparations to leave the hotel.

Mr. Jeffries had hired a coach for her, so it was

waiting by the time she was ready to leave. She settled back into the seat, wondering what would happen tonight. Mr. Jeffries had gone ahead to the party and wouldn't tell anyone that he'd seen her. That way he would be able to gauge everyone's reactions upon seeing Brooke's return from the dead.

"You nervous, Miz Brooke?"

"Yes, I am," she admitted. "I've been dead for over a month, so I'm not sure how I'm supposed to act." She was glad that she invited Millie Anne to ride inside with her. It gave Brooke some much needed company.

Millie Anne giggled. "Well, one t'ing is sure, you don' look dead. You look real pretty."

"Thank you," Brooke said. She'd chosen this gown because it had been made especially for her when she was trying to grab the attention of a Russian prince.

The fabric was soft velvet and the color was vermillion, which flattered her skin and added color to her face.

The full skirt emphasized her tiny waist. The shoulder seams drooped downward, showing off her creamy white skin. The bodice was cut low and came to a vee in the front, where a cluster of small diamonds had been sewn into the shape of a large diamond. The cut of the gown made Brooke's neck look long and graceful.

Brooke didn't know exactly what would happen tonight, but she wanted to look her best.

Finally, the coach pulled up in from of her home. She drew in a long, calming breath. Now it was time to get some answers.

* * *

Margaret was pleased with the way the house had been decorated for Christmas. There had been far too many sad faces around this house. She thought that everyone needed to get over the fact that Brooke was not returning, especially Travis.

Margaret scanned the room for her son. She spotted him in a small group, but she could tell by his stance that he really wasn't paying attention to any of them. He seemed to be ignoring Hesione, who stood next to him. Margaret shook her head.

She made her way over to her son. The musicians had just begun a waltz. "The music is so lovely, son," Margaret said. "Why don't you invite Hesione to dance, so our guests can see us enjoying the holiday season?"

Travis stared uncomprehendingly at her a long moment, but then Hesione touched his arm, and he seemed to understand what was expected. He took the girl into his arms and they stepped out onto the dance floor.

"Don't they make a lovely couple?" Margaret commented to Julia Ross, who was standing next to her.

"Yes, they do, my dear," Julia agreed. "Do you think they will renew their engagement now that . . . well, you know."

"I hope so," Margaret said, nodding. "Of course, Travis will have to allow the proper mourning time to pass, but then I'm sure he'll come around."

* * *

Thomas, Moss Grove's butler, answered the door. He took one look at Brooke and jumped back, his eyes wide as he said in a cracked voice, "You's dead."

After Brooke assured Thomas that she wasn't a ghost, she handed him her cloak, then made her way to the ballroom. Brooke paused at the entrance to the hall so she could take in the beautiful decorations all around her. Margaret had outdone herself. The house was beautiful.

Speaking of her mother-in-law, Brooke spotted her across the room. She looked very happy—that wasn't a good sign. When Brooke saw where the woman had trained her gaze, she knew why.

Travis was holding Hesione in his arms. Brooke's stomach twisted. And Hesione was beautiful, with her dark hair and complexion.

How could he? Brooke fumed. Then she reminded herself they were only dancing.

She had to admit that Travis looked splendid in his magnificent, black evening clothes. Would he be happy to see her? Or had he already turned his attention back to Hesione?

Taking a deep breath, Brooke stepped into the room, hearing a collective gasp as the guests and relatives recognized her. When a frail, elderly woman fainted, a hush slid over the crowd. The music stopped, one instrument at a time as the musicians realized that something was wrong.

Brooke held her head high and tilted her chin up. Her heart thumped wildly as she waited for her husband to see her.

When the last musician halted, Travis jerked

around to see what had caused the interruption. He followed the staring eyes of his guests until he focused on what they had seen.

No. It couldn't be, he thought. *I've made my peace with this.* Surely, it was Brooke's ghost come to haunt him and keep him away from Hesione. Certain that she would disappear as quickly as she had appeared, Travis stared at her in disbelief.

If anything, the image grew stronger. Could it be? Was she truly here?

Brooke easily recognized the longing in Travis's eyes for what she hoped was real surprise.

He dropped his arms from Hesione and started for Brooke. He took several steps and stopped for a moment as if he still wasn't sure she was there. Her heart soared precariously. The ache she saw deep in his eyes made her want to cry.

Brooke wanted to go to him, to run to him, but she needed to be certain he still wanted her. She stood her ground and watched as the sea of people parted to let Travis through.

Travis's gazed remained riveted on her as he made his way toward her. Her pride demanded that she didn't look away, but her emotion was so strong that her heart beat madly and she didn't want to allow anyone to see her vulnerability.

What if Travis was unhappy to see her?

Brooke couldn't breathe nor could she move. She had missed this man more than words could say. She had found something special and perfect about him almost from the very beginning, even when they argued.

Finally, Travis was there, standing in front of her.

A delightful shiver of wanting ran through her. She loved him. And she could see clearly in his eyes that he felt the same.

Still, doubts nagged at her. What would she do if it was Travis who had tried to kill her?

Chapter 19

Travis's legs felt as if they were made of lead as he made his way toward Brooke.

Could his mind be playing tricks on him?

Brooke was dead. Everyone told him she was, so how could she be here?

He fully expected to reach her side only to find that she'd never been there at all. Even so, he did not allow that idea to stop him as he pushed his way through the crowd. He didn't see his aunts or cousins. All he saw was Brooke.

My God she was stunning and provocative in that bright red dress. Except for being a little pale, she appeared fine—certainly not dead.

So, if she wasn't dead, and was here, alive and well, where had she been all this time?

And why had she put him through this living hell?

By the time Travis reached her, his thoughts were in a confused whirlwind, swirling with too many unanswered questions. Brooke lifted her eyes to meet his, and he saw love. God help him, his heart soared. Suddenly, all his unanswered questions didn't matter much.

Travis wrapped his arms around his wife and held her to him. The feel of her in his arms was exquisite, wonderful. Nothing could compare with how he felt at this moment.

Brooke was alive!

Travis had to keep telling himself that he wasn't dreaming, and that she was actually alive and here in his arms. He wasn't sure how everything had happened, and he didn't really care. All that mattered was Brooke.

When the guests started murmuring again, or maybe Travis finally remembered that they were in the ballroom, he found his voice. "Let's go somewhere we can be alone and talk," he whispered into Brooke's ear.

Brooke nodded and tried to hold back the tears that threatened to overflow. Yes, Travis had opened his arms to her, but she had expected more. A kiss, a simple "I missed you, my love, would have been nice, and the words, "I love you," even better. How did he truly feel about her return?

Keeping a hand on her waist, Travis released her from his embrace and turned toward the crowd. "Please, enjoy the party, and excuse us for a moment," he said to the gathered guests. Then he motioned for the music to begin again. As they ensemble's playing resumed, so did the whispers of the guests.

Before they could make their exit, someone called excitedly, "Brooke, Brooke!"

She turned to see Eliza running toward her. The young girl flung her arms around Brooke in a big hug. "I'm so glad you're alive. Welcome home," she said, grinning ear to ear.

"It is nice to see you, too, Eliza. You're looking very pretty, I might add." Brooke smiled at the child while, at the same time, trying not to show how anxious she was to talk to Travis. "We'll catch up later, I promise," she told her. "I must have a moment to speak with my husband."

Eliza nodded before leaving them.

Finally, Brooke and Travis were out of the crowded ballroom. They strode, hand in hand, down the carpeted marble hallway, straight to Travis's study. He held the door for Brooke, and she swept past him and in to the room.

Once the door was closed, she turned to face Travis. For an awkward moment, they just stood, silently staring at each other. Neither of them able to find the correct words. Did he wish that she'd never returned? Brooke wondered as the moments stretched farther and farther apart.

Finally, Travis broke the silence by saying, "I—I thought you were dead," he said, his voice breaking.

Brooke saw the heart-rending tenderness of his gaze, and she wanted to go to him, to throw herself into his arms and pretend the last month and a half had not occurred. But it had.

What happened to the levelheaded young woman she used to be? The one who threw caution to the wind and could walk away from any situation?

Now all she wanted was Travis.

Brooke fought hard against the tears that threatened to fall. Instead of weeping, she answered him. "It's a miracle that I'm alive."

Travis took a deep breath and ran a shaky hand through his hair. She could see he was struggling with himself. "I want to hold you," he said tenderly, and Brooke felt the old familiar butterflies in her stomach . . . the ones only Travis could produce. But she sensed something strange in him, as well.

"I've missed you so much and—" He held up his hand. She could see he was fighting her because he didn't trust her. "At the same time, I see you are well, and I wonder why you have put me thought this hell."

At those casually tossed out words, something in Brooke snapped. Travis thought she'd left him. Of all the nerve! "Put *you* through?" Brooke repeated, her irritation growing. "Put *you* through?" she repeated, still unable to believe what she was hearing. "Wait just a minute! You think I've been gone on purpose?"

"At first, I thought you might have jumped, but I see that wasn't the case. What else should I think?" he told her. As he stared at her, his jaw tightened. "I just want to know how you managed to disappear and why?"

The only good thing coming out of this conversation was Brooke now knew that Travis hadn't pushed her. No one could act this stupid. Yet his accusatory gaze was riveted on her and that only added fuel to the fire building in her.

"You might try saying 'I was worried about you, darling,'" she said in a sugar-sweet voice, then added, "Not tell me that I've put *you* through hell." Brooke's voice grew louder. "What in the hell do you think I've been through?"

Travis lashed back. "What am I supposed to

think? Not one word from you, then you show up dressed like a queen." He swept a hand toward her. "Do I have to remind you that you confessed to be a courtesan the night before you left me? For all I know you could have taken up your old profession."

Seething, Brooke took a step closer and slapped Travis hard across the face. Unfortunately, that didn't quite satisfy her, so she drew back to hit him again. This time, however, he caught her arm.

Travis jerked her up against him and she felt the strength in every inch of his muscular body, rigid with anger.

"I wouldn't do that if I were you," he warned.

"Damn you," Brooke hissed. "And to think . . ." she never finished her sentence. She could feel Travis's uneven breathing on her cheek as he held her close, but he didn't attempt to kiss her. Instead he asked her in a strange sounding voice, "Why did you come back?"

She shoved him and he let her go. All she could think was that she wanted to hurt him like he was hurting her now, so she said the first thing that came to her mind, "For Moss Grove, of course."

Something in Travis snapped. A ragged sigh escaped from him as he faced the truth. Yesterday he'd given anything to have her back, and now he seemed to be doing his best to drive her away. What was the matter with him? Was he doing it on purpose?

She was so radiantly beautiful and so damn headstrong that a man would have to be mad to want to live with her. From the moment she had hurtled into his life he knew Brooke could only be a handful of trouble. She needed someone who could match wits with her. And he was that man. "Is that the only reason?" he asked.

Travis watched Brooke struggle with her emotions and then in a voice raw with emotion she said, "There was one more reason."

Travis took a step closer and whispered, "And that would be?"

"You. I came back for you," she admitted.

He reached for her and she took the few steps into his arms. His demanding lips caressed hers. It had been much too long since he held her. He kissed her until she melted in his arms and he knew she was surrendering to him.

What was it about this one woman? She turned his life upside down, and made passion explode within him with nothing more than a look. Yet no matter what she'd done, he could not let her go.

"I've missed you," he whispered achingly. "More than I ever thought possible."

Brooke's heart swelled at the tenderness she heard in his voice. Perhaps, at long last, she had found happiness. "Are you ready to listen?"

Drawing back slightly, Travis nodded.

Brooke really didn't want to step out of his arms, but she needed to so that she could think clearly while she told him what had really happened to her. "Let's sit down, and I'll tell you everything. The first part being that I was pushed off the boat," she told him then watched his features carefully. To her great relief, she saw genuine surprise.

Travis sat back against the corner of the sofa. "You didn't trip and fall?" he asked.

"No. I had just spoken to your mother or, you

might say, argued with her. When she left, I turned around to get my wits about me and that's when someone shoved me over."

"That's hard to believe."

"Travis," Brooke said sharply. "Do you think I'd make something like that up?"

"Well, no. But my mother said you were talking to a man. Who was it? Maybe he was the one. If so, he'll soon be a dead man."

Brooke took a deep breath. How low would that woman stoop? "To put it very bluntly—your mother is a liar."

"So it would seem," Travis agreed. "Why would she so blatantly lie?"

"Because she doesn't want me for a daughter-in-law."

"So you think that she pushed you? I know my mother can be difficult, but—"

"I have no idea who did it," Brooke told him, but didn't add that she had once thought Travis had been the one. "I only know I ended up in the water."

"And?"

"I managed to get out of my dress so it wouldn't drag me under and cause me to drown. However, when I went over the rail, I must have hit my head. The next thing I remember I was waking up with the river people who'd fished me out of the water. I had no memory when I woke up."

"Do you know how far-fetched that sounds?" Travis asked.

Brooke stiffened. Here she was trying to be truthful and tell him everything, and he sat there doubting her. "I assure you that it's true," she snapped.

Travis pushed himself up off the couch. "I need a drink. Would you like one?"

"Well, at least you've learned some manners," she commented wryly, referring to their very first encounter.

He was irritating her by being quiet. Brooke knew that what she'd told him was hard to believe, and she could probably show him the knot on her head as proof. But if they were going to have any kind of marriage, he was going to have to learn how to trust her. He was going to have to take her word for what had happened.

"So, tell me, what have you been doing? Rejoicing that you no longer had a wife?" When she only received stony silence in answer, she got up and strolled over to where he stood.

"I noticed who was in your arms when I entered the ballroom," she said, trailing a hand lightly down his arm. "I must say, you didn't waste much time."

Travis flinched. He said nothing in his defense, just handed her a glass of Scotch, which she immediately drank down. The liquor felt good as it warmed her cold body.

"It's better if you drink it slowly."

Brooke gave him a small wistful smile. "Yes, but not when you need immediate results."

Travis took a swallow of his drink and smiled. His wife was jealous of Hesione, so she must really care for him, but he decided to test her further. "You were supposed to be dead, my dear, so I assumed I could dance with whom I pleased."

Brooke's eyes widened for a moment, then she drew back and slapped him again hard on the face.

Travis wouldn't let most women get away with that, but he was purposely goading her. "You are beginning to make that a habit, my dear."

"You could have at least let my body get cold before you replaced me!"

Travis jerked Brooke toward him, molding her body to his. His steady gaze bore into her defiant eyes. They were pure gold when she was angry.

"Sweetheart, your body has never been cold, and I'm glad to see you're jealous. Does this mean you love me?"

She slid her hands up his hard chest and wrapped her arms around his neck. He tightened his hands possessively on her back and hips, molding her closer to him. But he didn't kiss her, he quirked a brow and waited for her answer.

"More than you'll ever know," Brooke whispered.

That is what he'd been waiting to hear. "By God, you had better mean every word," he told her in a husky voice. Then he lowered his mouth hungrily to hers.

Finally satisfied, he drew back for a moment. "God, how I've missed you," he whispered and lowered his mouth again until it touched hers. Brooke kissed him back and desire exploded in him as a tenderness that he didn't know he'd possessed blossomed within him. He kissed her long and hard, enjoying the moment he'd never thought he would have again. "Do you have any idea what you do to me?"

"I—I think I have a vague idea," Brooke whispered, feeling the rigid evidence against her stomach. "You don't play fair."

"I told you that from the first time we met."

Chapter 20

They did not return to the party.

Instead, Brooke and Travis left the study. He swept Brooke into his arms and hurried up the stairs. They figured they had spent too much time away from each other and a party was the last place they wanted to be.

"We really are remiss as hosts by not returning to the party," Brooke said as she snuggled up against her husband's broad chest.

"I thought it might be preferable to seek our privacy than for me to remove that lovely gown of yours in the ballroom," he told her, then kicked open the door.

Brooke chuckled softly as they swept into the room. "It has been a long time," she said softly when he set her down.

Travis grabbed her arm before she'd taken two steps into the room and pulled her back into his arms. "Yes, it has, my dear," he groaned, his eyes full of desire. "You feel so damn good. Kiss me," he whispered, trailing his mouth across her cheek until he found Brooke's mouth. His tongue drove into her mouth, possessing her completely. Raising his lips from hers, he gazed into her golden eyes. "I thought I'd never be able to hold you like this again."

"And I wasn't sure you wanted me back," she said kissing his chin.

"Don't want you?" Travis squeezed her so tight she was afraid that he'd cut off her air, but finally he eased up. The shocking pleasure of being held again in Travis's strong arms warmed her more than any fire.

"This last month, thinking that you were dead, has been a living hell. I can't tell you how many bottles of Scotch that I've been through."

"I'm so sorry that you were worried, but I couldn't come home until I remembered where home was," Brooke said with a soft smile. "I'm glad that you didn't replace me with Hesione while I was gone."

Travis laughed richly. "A funny thing happened," he said, pausing to think, "After having you, I have no desire for another woman . . . only you."

"I love you," Brooke said.

With a silent groan, Travis bent his head, his mouth closing over hers with urgent hunger while his tongue plunged into her mouth, withdrew, and then plunged over and over. A shudder racked his body. She was driving him crazy with desire.

He slid his lips along the curve of her neck. It had been much too long. Sweeping Brooke up in his arms again, he carried her to the bed, from which he didn't intend to release her until some time the next day.

Lost in a sea of desire, Brooke knew she'd found heaven as she yielded to his tender kisses. She kissed him with unrestrained ardor. When she lifted her head to trail kisses down to his chest, she felt Travis's muscles harden as he jerked at the unexpected direction her lips were heading.

Tonight she held nothing back.

The next morning Brooke opened her eyes and looked around. Relief flooded her when she realized that last night hadn't been a dream. She was still home, wrapped protectively in Travis's arms.

Brooke didn't feel well this morning, however. She'd felt like this on and off for the last week, figuring it was the anxiety from not knowing what would happen to her.

She didn't go down to breakfast. Instead, she and Millie Anne moved some of her things into Travis's room, their room.

They had nearly finished when Travis came back up. Leaning in the doorway he said, "I'm going to the mill this morning. I see you've kept busy."

"Yes, I have," Brooke said with a happy smile. "Your room may never be the same again."

"So I see," Travis commented dryly, shoving away from the door.

Brooke held up the drapes. "Do you mind if I take down these dark drapes and have something a bit lighter hung in here?"

"My love," Travis said, coming up behind her and gathering her into her arms. "You can do anything you please." His mouth slanted over hers and he kissed her with fierce tenderness. As always, Brooke melted against him.

It was amazing how wonderful Travis made her feel. He'd managed to turn a cold-hearted woman into anything he wanted her to be. Of course, Brooke would never tell him that, she thought. Drawing back, she looked up at Travis. "I'll see you tonight."

Since he still hadn't let her go, Travis leaned down and kissed her on the end of her nose. "You can count on it. By the way, I asked Mammy to bring you something to eat. I don't like you not eating. You're too thin as it is."

"Thank you," Brooke said with a smile. Travis's loving concern touched her. "I just felt a little queasy this morning. It was probably too much excitement.

"I know it might seem soon, but I also wanted to get my things moved into yours so the servants wouldn't gossip about my room being the furthest away from yours. I believe those were your instructions the first day I arrived."

"Ah," Travis said with a grin, "I remember that day well. And I was wise to keep you at arm's length, because you were much too tempting even then."

"So that is the reason you were so hard to get along with," Brooke teased. "And all the time I thought it was because you didn't like me."

"Well there was that, too." Travis chuckled, then he grew serious. "Listen, I'll talk to my mother. I don't want to think that she pushed you. Nevertheless, if she cannot get along with you, I'll make arrangement for her to live elsewhere."

A lump formed in Brooke's throat when she realized that he would actually do that for her. But the woman was still his mother, no matter what. "I don't want to come between you and your mother. She really has never given me a chance, so perhaps now that she knows I'm here to stay, she might change."

Travis kissed her briefly before letting her go. "I'll leave it to you then, because you are here to stay."

"I love you," Brooke said.

"I love you, too," Travis said with a smile, and then he was gone.

Millie Anne sighed. "Dat's so beautiful. I never seen Master Travis look at anyone else de way he looks at you."

Brooke blushed. "We've come a long way." She stepped over to the window and fingered the heavy velvet drapes. "This room will look much more inviting with these gone, so you can pull them down."

"I broug't you somet'in' nice fo' dat empty tummy," Mammy said as she swept in without knocking on the door. "And I trus' you've not forgot how good Prosper's cookin' is, yes?" She set the tray down.

Brooke felt like her mother had swept into the room. She went to Mammy and hugged the big woman to her. Brooke couldn't talk for the tears that were threatening to fall.

"What's dis," Mammy said, and Brooke could hear that her voice sounded funny, too. "Tell you de trut', I missed you, too. Now why don' you eat at least a biscuit."

"Oh, Mammy," Brooke said with a smile. "I think I missed you most of all." She lifted the cloth from a bowl and removed a big fluffy biscuit. "I am a bit hungry now, but this morning I just felt queasy every time I thought about eating. I suppose my stomach will settle down now that I'm back at home."

Mammy raised her brow as she peered at Brooke.

"You do look pale, yes. I suppose you've not been takin' care o' you'se'f."

Brooke sat down and invited Mammy to do the same, and then she told her everything that had happened since the last time she'd seen her. Of course, Brooke gobbled down three biscuits, talking with her mouth full as she ate hungrily.

Mammy had an odd look on her face by the time Brooke finished the story.

"What are you thinking?"

"Fo' someone who wasn't hungry, you sure devoured dem biscuits. When is de last time yo' had yer monthly?"

The question surprised Brooke and she felt her face flush. "I—I'm not sure." She thought for a moment. "Not since I've been married."

"Lordy, Lordy," Mammy said with a grin. "We's goin' to have a baby, yes."

Brooke opened her mouth then quickly shut it. "I feel so stupid . . . I never even thought about that possibility, but I think you might be correct." Just like Travis had predicted. It worked well with his lie.

"Jus' you keep you'se'f derc and let me get de curtains," Mammy said as she got to her feet. "You got to take care o' you'se'f."

"I don't think I need to worry so soon," Brooke said. "Maybe once I'm further along."

But Mammy would have none of it.

Once the room was straightened, Brooke surveyed the room, pleased with the improvement. Without the heavy curtains, the light poured into the room, taking away the dark uninviting appearance it had before.

That done, Brooke was still full of energy. She decided she needed to seek out Margaret, since the woman didn't seem to be coming to her.

Brooke found Travis's mother in the sunroom located at the rear of the house. Margaret was bent over, working on an embroidering frame. She glanced up, then right back down to her work as Brooke swept into the room and took a seat next to her.

"I see you're back," Margaret said briskly, glancing Brooke's way then back to her sewing.

Brooke took a deep breath. She wasn't going to let this woman get under her skin. "I assume Travis told you what happened?"

"Yes. He told me this morning," Margaret said as she jabbed the needle into the fabric. "You were very lucky to have survived such a fall."

"Yes, I was. It's a good thing that I could swim enough to save myself. And probably even better luck that you were not still standing there, or you might have gone over with me," Brooke said.

Margaret swung around to Brooke. "I never thought about that. I'm sure I would have drowned since I cannot swim."

"Well, you were lucky, then. I'm puzzled, though. Why did you tell Travis that I was speaking to a man, when you know you were the only one with me?"

"Because I wanted you out of our lives," Margaret said bluntly, surprising Brooke by being truthful. "Everything was going along so smoothly until you barreled into our lives. Travis was going to marry someone else—someone of his own kind."

"I am his own kind," Brooke pointed out. "Have you forgotten that Travis is half English? I believe you fell in love with an Englishman yourself. If that is so, then Travis is no different than you."

Margaret stiffened. "That is none of your business." She glanced down at her needlework. "And I'd have hoped that Travis would learn from my mistakes."

"I believe it *is* my business now that I'm family. I knew Jackson very well, and I can tell you he was a lovely man."

"Yes, he was," Margaret said softly. "Tell me, was Jackson still married?"

With that question, Brooke felt that a brick had crumbled from the wall between them. "I never met his wife. I stayed with Jackson and his two nieces. The girls told me that their aunt died."

"And he never came back to me," Margaret said with a faraway look. Then she added. "She was touched."

Brooke looked at her, not understanding.

"She was touched in the head," Margaret explained.

"Mad," Brooke said, "I didn't know."

"It was one of the reasons that Jackson couldn't leave his wife," Margaret added softly. "He couldn't divorce her, nor could he live with her."

Brooke nodded. "He had no children of his marriage, but I'm sure that he loved Travis. Why he didn't spend more time with him I truly cannot say, but I think he regretted it in the end."

Margaret secured her needle in the linen material, then turned to Brooke. "Jackson didn't know about Travis until much later. I sent him a letter, but his wife intercepted the note, and he didn't find it until much later."

"How sad."

"Yes, it was," Margaret said. "As it was, we were always outcast."

"At least you raised a good son despite everything that happened."

Margaret nodded. "He is a good son. It is unfortunate that my father has never really accepted him."

"I've met the man," Brooke said. "He seems unable to bend. That is so very sad, I think."

"He is the head of the family," Margaret told her.

"But that doesn't make him right," Brooke pointed out. "I resent the way he treats Travis. Travis has taken this plantation and built it up from nothing, and with very little help from someone older to guide him. His grandfather should be proud of what he's achieved instead of condescending."

Margaret looked at Brooke with an odd expression. "I think you're correct. I've never thought about it that way."

"I hope you will from now on," Brooke said softly. She felt good about their little talk, and perhaps there was more to Margaret than the side Brooke had seen thus far.

"I've taken enough of your time," Brooke said as she stood. "I just wanted to say I hope that we might become friends later on down the road." She smiled. "Especially since you're going to become a grandmother."

The shocked looked on Margaret's face was priceless. She stood abruptly. "I heard some of my relatives say that you were expecting, but I did not believe it."

"Well, that was a falsehood, told by Travis. He'd hoped that I would be accepted quicker into the family if I were pregnant. However, I was not expecting at that time."

Margaret pulled Brooke into her arms. "I'm still going to have to have time to adjust to you," she said with a smile. "I'll be honest. A grandchild will help."

"Perhaps it will make up for the fact that I'm not Creole."

Margaret smiled. "We cannot all be perfect. Does Travis know?"

"Not yet. I only just realized it myself. I'll tell him tonight."

Later on that day, Brooke sat down and wrote a letter to Jocelyn. Brooke couldn't believe she was going to be a mother, her of all people! She would have expected it of Shannon, but Brooke had never thought of herself as a mother. It was a scary thought. She hoped that she would know how to be a good one.

Brooke had just finished the letter when her bedroom door swung opened, banging loudly against the wall.

"Miz Brooke!" Millie Anne announced as she burst thought the door. "There's been an accident at de sugarhouse. You got to come quick. Master Travis has been trapped!"

Chapter 21

Brooke's heart hammered in her chest as she flew down the stairs. She found Mammy and Margaret already there.

"What happened?"

"Come on," Mammy said, motioning for Brooke to keep moving. "Somet'ing done happen at de mill."

Margaret glanced at Mammy as if the woman would never know her place, but she said nothing. Instead, she told Brooke, "There's been an accident. That is all we know. Mr. Jeffries is already there. He was looking over the improvements to the sugarmill."

A buggy had already been brought around to the front and was waiting, ready to go. In no time, they were pulling up to the mill. At first glance, it looked as if the second story at one end of the sugar shed had caved in. A crowd was gathered around as a group of men were frantically digging away the rubble.

Brooke leapt out of the buggy almost before it

had stopped and dashed toward Mr. Jeffries. "Where is Travis?"

"Under there, I'm afraid." Jeffries pointed to a frightening pile of wood and timbers.

"No!" Margaret screamed. "We must hurry."

Looking at the pile of rubble made Brooke feel numb, but she knew she had to keep her wits about her. Especially now that Margaret was sobbing uncontrollably.

"What about a doctor?" Brooke asked.

"He's been sent for," Jeffries answered. "In the meantime, we must get him and the others out before it's too late."

Brooke, Margaret, and Mammy stood by, watching helplessly. Finally, after an hour of digging and painstakingly moving the rubble one stick, one board at a time, they pulled out two men, one of whom was dead. Now there were two more men to find, and one of those was Travis.

Panic seized Brooke. "Can you see him?" she called, but no one answered. She started toward the workers with the intention of helping, but Mammy intercepted her.

"Where you goin'?" Mammy said. "Dey are doin' all dey can, and you wouldn't want to get in de way, you hear."

"But Travis might be—" She couldn't even say the words. What would she do if Travis was dead? She'd never planned to have him in her life in the first place, but now that she did, she didn't want to live without him.

"There he is," a worker called out.

Brooke hurried around Mammy, frantic to get to

her husband. He wasn't moving, but someone said he was still breathing. The rescuers carried him over to a clear area and placed Travis on the cold ground.

Margaret, finally recovering her wits, rushed to get some blankets from the buggy. Brooke knelt down beside her husband and reached for his hand. It was cold, but she could feel his heart beating beneath his chilled skin. There was blood everywhere from cuts, and she needed to stanch it. She tore strips from her petticoats and tried to clean his face. She needed to find where he was bleeding from in order to stop the flow of fresh blood.

Travis was deathly pale. "Oh, my God," Brooke murmured over and over again. All she could do was shake her head. He'd lost so much blood. "Open your eyes, darling," Brooke murmured. When nothing happened she spoke more forcefully. "Don't you die on me." She well remembered how sweetness never seemed to work with her husband.

A buggy came barreling down the road, and Doctor Smart wasted little time getting out before the horses had barely been drawn to a halt. He strode over to where they were. "Get out of the way so I can see my patient," he ordered.

"You have to do something," Brooke implored.

"Just give me some room, and I'll do what I can. I don't need you hovering over me and getting in my way."

Brooke stood back and bumped into Ben, one of the men she recognized from previous visits to the mill. "How did this happen?"

"Master Travis said he thought that someone had been messing with the timbers," Ben said. "It appeared that the support beams had been cut," he went on. "Master Travis said he knew who was responsible."

"So someone meant for this to happen?" Brooke said more to herself than to anyone.

She stood back while the doctor examined Travis. While she waited, impatiently wringing her hands, Mr. Jeffries came to stand beside her.

"Do you have any idea who would like to see harm come to Travis?" he asked.

"Travis could have any number of enemies, I suppose, but the only one I can think of is Hesione's father. After he was shown to be a coward at the duel, Jeremy said Travis could have trouble from him."

"I see."

Doctor Smart stood up and shook his head. Brooke's heart was hammering with fear. "What's the matter, doctor?"

"He's lost a lot of blood. I've got the bleeding stopped but there is nothing else I can do," Doctor Smart looked at Brooke and Margaret. "Best take him home and wait. It's in God's hands now."

Tears spilled down Brooke's face, but she managed to nod in agreement.

Mammy put an arm around Brooke in a comforting embrace. "Don' you worry, Miz Brooke. I ain't goin' to let not'ing happen to dat boy, you hear." Mammy told her.

Brooke nodded numbly. She wanted to believe Mammy, but Travis's face was much too pale. Even to her unskilled eyes, he appeared near death. She watched, feeling helpless as the men lifted him into the carriage.

Flinching at every bump and jostle, Brooke cradled Travis's head as they drove home. Margaret was very quiet, and that was all right with Brooke. Her mother-in-law was the least of her worries now.

They took Travis to his room where his clothes were stripped from him and he was placed into his bed. Brooke had a chair placed beside the bed, and she took up her vigil all through the long night.

Mammy kept checking on her to make sure she was eating, but Brooke refused to move. Nor did she let anyone else take her place. She was so afraid that Travis would die, and she wouldn't be with him.

Margaret tried to help, but she cried inconsolably every time she looked at her son. She finally had made herself so sick from worrying that she took to her bed.

For the next two days, Brooke talked to Travis constantly, trying to get some kind of response from him. She begged him to get well. She pleaded, she demanded, she forced him to drink broth, though little of it went down.

And she prayed.

The days passed slowly until it was Christmas Day. The house was too quiet, and no one felt any Christmas cheer. Doctor Smart told them if Travis finally woke up, then he'd survive. But the waiting was difficult. They wouldn't know anything for a few days.

It was the middle of the night when Brooke awoke with a start. Had she heard something? When she looked at Travis, his coloring appeared better but his eyes were still closed.

"Please don't leave me," Brooke begged. "I might

not have wanted you in the beginning, but sometimes we don't know what we want until we think we might lose it." Her voice broke as the tears she'd been trying hard to hold back began to slide down her face. "I don't want to lose you, Travis. Please don't give up. I still don't know enough about Moss Grove. I need you to teach me.

"And I can see your smile, that is, if your eyes were open, so please open your eyes. You always told me I'd never be able to run a plantation. All right, I'm admitting that *perhaps* you were correct. And if you would just look at me, I would give you permission to gloat as much as you wish. I know how much Moss Grove means to you. It means more to you than anything else—you've always told me so."

"Not more than anything," Travis murmured, his voice faint. He moved his fingers within her hand. At first Brooke thought she had imagined the movement, but suddenly his fingers moved again, closing over hers.

Brooke looked intently at Travis, willing him to wake. And finally he opened his eyes. They were a bit hazy, they looked warm, not the clear blue she was used to seeing, but he was alive and that was all that mattered.

She jumped to her feet. "You don't know how wonderful it is to see looking at me. How do you feel?"

"Awful," he rasped. "Water."

Brooke poured water from a pitcher by the bedside with trembling fingers. She held the glass to his lips, and he took several sips of the cooling, reviving liquid. When he'd finished, she sat the glass back on the stand and returned her attention to him. She wanted to throw herself into his arms, but she was afraid she'd hurt him.

"What else can I get you?" she asked.

"A gun," Travis said in a deep ragged voice.

"A what?" Brooke asked. She couldn't have possible heard him correctly. "You must be delirious. You've been unconscious for three days. Why would you want a gun?"

Travis winced in pain as he attempted to move. "I'm going to shoot that son of a bitch like I should have the first time."

"George D'Aquin?" Hesione's father was the only one Brooke could think of. "Why?"

"Because he is the one who's been trying to kill me. This time, one of my men saw him and they caught his foreman, who confessed. He was also the one who pushed you from the boat," Travis said. He tried to sit up. The effort was too great. He sank back to the pillows with a wrenching groan. "Damn. I think my entire body aches."

Brooke knew by the set of Travis's jaw that her headstrong husband was going to be hard to get along with. Then she remembered the last time he'd been shot. She'd had to leave his care to Mammy because he'd been absolutely impossible.

But now she was his wife, and Brooke was going to take care of him if it killed both of them. And she wasn't taking any nonsense from him, either.

"I guess you would feel terrible. After all, a building fell on you. You're very lucky that you survived. Two of the men who were with you did not."

"Which two?"

Brooke thought for a moment. "John and Jeff, I believe I heard someone say."

"Help me sit up," Travis ordered.

"A please might be nice," Brooke informed him.

"All right, please," he grumbled.

Brooke smiled as she placed several pillows behind his back. *It's like trying to tame a wild animal,* she thought as she struggled to get Travis up and in place. And to think a moment ago she'd been praying for his recovery.

"Thank you," Travis said then gawked at her a long moment. "You look like hell, my dear."

Brooke raised an eyebrow. "Thank you so much for the compliment."

Travis reached for her hand. "You're always beautiful to me, but you do look tired. I see dark circles under your eyes."

"I guess so," she snapped. "I've been sitting in this chair for three days, wondering if you would live or die. Unfortunately you lived. And what are the first words out of your mouth? An insult."

Travis chuckled. "I know you don't mean that."

"Don't I?" she replied. Brooke tried to jerk her hand from his. "You haven't said anything nice to me since you woke up. I'm beginning to think I prefer you the other way."

Travis ignored her. "You said I'd been out for three days?"

She nodded.

"In that case, how about Merry Christmas, darling," he said.

Travis had such a boyish look about him, much like a bad child who knew he'd been bad but was trying to charm his way out of a punishment. The look melted Brooke's heart. "Merry Christmas to you, too."

"I don't have any mistletoe," he said with a grin. "So I guess I can't kiss you."

"I don't need mistletoe," she told him, leaning over the bed. "The only thing I need is you."

"In that case, my dear, you should be exceptionally happy for the rest of your life because you definitely have me now and always."

"And you'll always have us, too," Brooke said as she kissed him.

Travis pulled her up on the bed with him and gazed questioningly into her eyes. "Us?"

Brooke presented him with an enormous smile. "It seems your plan worked better than you expected."

"What are you talking about?"

"You're going to be a father, Travis Montgomery," Brooke told him.

Many expressions filtered across Travis's face, but the last one was the best. Brooke finally saw true love in Travis's eyes and she knew that she had found something she never through she would ever have.

Brooke had truly found happiness in a man's arms.